MW01247661

Praise for *Namaste Mart Confidential* and Andrew Miller

"*Namaste Mart Confidential* heralds the arrival of a distinctive new voice in crime fiction. It's a wild tale of wannabe private dicks, twisted religious nuts, psychopathic Armenian gangsters and crazed celebrity-chasers. And those are just the likeable characters! Andrew Miller is a talent to watch." –Steven Powell, author of *Love Me Fierce in Danger, The Life of James Ellroy*

"*Namaste Mart Confidential* zips through the seamy sides of LA with panache and entertaining PI heroes—and a cool ending that I've never seen before in a missing-person novel. From godforsaken religious cults to aging Hollywood stars to thistle milk drinkers, this has everything you might want in a Hollywood crime yarn." –Matt Witten, bestselling author of *Killer Story*

"Andrew Miller's debut novel evokes the boozy spirit and black humor of James Crumley and early Joe Lansdale but stands apart because of Miller's distinct, winning voice and attitude. It's 2013: In their day jobs as grocery clerks, Adam Minor and Richie Walsh brush shoulders with midlist movie stars and *Sopranos'* supporting players. But the duo also prowl the streets of L.A. as parttime private detectives. Their latest missing person's case ranges the duo against religious cliques, a particular thinly disguised Armenian reality TV star, and brutal mobsters who are angling to kidnap her. I can't wait to see what Andrew Miller's sophomore novel brings."
–Craig McDonald, Edgar & Anthony Awards Finalist

"'Samurai '81' by Andrew Miller is one of the best concepts I've run across this year—you've got a young LAPD detective being mentored by an older, but not that-jaded detective. Not just in how to be a better homicide detective, but in being a Japanese-American detective in the early '80s. Then you throw in modern-day samurai—with the swords and everything. Who puts these things together? And how isn't this a series already?"
–H.C. Newton, *The Irresponsible Reader*

"In Andrew Miller's 'Samurai '81', a modern business rivalry between Japanese electronics manufacturers culminates in a murder with an old-fashioned weapon—a samurai sword. Los Angeles Police Department detectives Junichiro Genji and the young detective Akira, our narrator, know who the killer is. It's a former LAPD detective and they travel to Hawaii to track him down. Along the way, Akira learns about a brotherhood of Japanese law enforcement professionals and discovers the strengths and limits of tradition. Miller's weaving of culture and plot makes this story a highly enjoyable read."
–Vicki Weisfeld, *Crime Fiction Lover*

"Andrew Miller's *Lady Tomahawk* caps off the narrative grind-house with a buffed-out heroine who lives up to her name and turns on its ear the notion of the innocent girl who comes to Hollywood with stars in her eyes. Film and fashion references streaming throughout this section herald the coming decade of, up until then, unparalleled greed. The behind-the-scenes view glimpsed here of rampant hypocrisy might seem over-the-top in tamer times, but these are not tame times. Like in Gore Vidal's novel, *Hollywood*, about how American power and influence migrated west with the rise of cinema to make La-la Land a twin capitol, here that concept is sexed-up, debauched and left ship-wrecked in bloody sheets while the perps shower and go to church." –Nevada McPherson, author of *Poser*

Editor: Krysta Winsheimer of Muse Retrospect
Cover design: Scotch Rutherford

ISBN: 979-8-9869930-8-9
Run Amok Crime, 2024
First Edition

Printed in the USA

NAMASTE MART CONFIDENTIAL

by

ANDREW MILLER

TO

Mely Corado

1991-2018

The son stood outside the house in the mud in his huaraches and tilted his umbrella against the rain as it swept in from the sea. He held a fresh scroll of papyrus and a goose feather quill pen against his chest.

This was a gated compound in a secluded stretch of Quintana Roo, miles from resorts and accessible only by a single and winding dirt road guarded by soldiers of the Mexican military who were paid off by his father.

The wooden door squealed open. The son wiped his feet and looked to the corner where the father sat. His freshly shaven face was glossed a muted white from the light shining through a high window, and a damp green towel rested around his neck. On the ledge was a bowl of lather, upon which a straight razor with a mother-of-pearl handle lay.

"'Tis imperative for you to take another bride." The son had not yet unrolled the papyrus. Whatever this was, it was not to be recorded. "By 2090, if our people populate at the crucial rate we have established, our political power will be enough to terminate this dark era. You are now a man, and I grow old. When I am gone, you must learn to realize our Heavenly Father's will. My fortune will mean nothing if this divine process is not understood."

"I want to learn."

From the ledge, the father picked up the open razor by the blade and held it out. "Lack of commitment is a violation. My latest is not committed. She spreads the poison of dissent."

The son grasped the gleaming handle, wiped the remaining lather onto the side of his pant leg, and nodded.

Out in the mud, he walked through the many rows of aqua and lemon-yellow houses, now also carrying a bundle of rope. A tortoiseshell cat shielding itself from the rain hissed his way. A soldier posted under an awning in front of the house he sought raised a hand in a welcoming gesture.

The father's thirty-eighth wife painted her toenails alone on the living room davenport. She was sweet and tender on the surface. She was fourteen. He walked to the basement door and opened it. The stairs descended into the black.

"Come down here with me," he said.

ONE

OUR BOSS CHRISTY, an old-school surfer from Malibu, recited notes sent to her by corporate in Azusa. "Because of the upcoming legal and financial implications of the recent Affordable Care Act legislation, Namaste Mart is reviewing whether our company-provided health care benefits will remain intact." She changed to a more casual tone, "They're saying that because of Obamacare cuts could be on the horizon, and they don't want us to be surprised. The truth? I don't know what this means."

Southern California was in a years-long drought and rain wasn't expected until November, a lifetime off. Most of my deodorant had already wasted away in the heat. I crossed my arms and sent my hands into my armpits, hoping to guard against the smell. The previous night's booze in my pores wasn't helping.

This was the Namaste Mart at Santa Monica and Gardner, one of three locations in West Hollywood. Every crew member at our location was here at this meeting, except one front-end manager and a few other crew members running the registers.

My good friend Richie Walsh, standing beside me, was hungover too. Richie is a wild man with a legendary temper, but if he hasn't lost it, he always seems cool and composed, and he sails through hangovers far smoother than I do. People are always saying we don't seem like friends.

FOUR YEARS AGO, I packed my life into my silver '03 Camry and left Ohio for L.A. I had seven hundred dollars in the bank and a part-time job at the Eagle Rock Goalmart waiting for me. In my rearview was a girl I loved who would never love me back.

For my first month in town, I slept on the couch of an Ohio friend named Seung Moon who had already scored big in Hollywood by milking his friendship with a privileged kid he'd met in college who had contacts in the Industry.

As kids, Seung and I used to make VHS movies together. We

loved imitating crime movies, mainly Scorsese or Tarantino. If my mother caught me taking powdered sugar from her kitchen, she knew we were using it for a *Goodfellas*-like scene involving gangsters snorting blow. "None of my babies aren't making it to heaven with me," she would say, and put the sugar back in the cupboard. "I don't know why you and Seung can't ever make Christian movies."

My plan in L.A. was to become a famous writer-director. I took a room in a huge old Victorian house in Angeleno Heights with a middle-aged artist and practicing witch who regularly cast spells on other tenants in the building who were mostly large, working-class Latino families. The witch was always pissed about them making too much noise in their units. If I ever ran into any of them, I explained how I didn't agree with bruja blanca. She was just my roommate for now until my Hollywood success arrived.

On top of my gig at Goalmart, I did freelance production jobs, usually as the guy who hauled Seung's apple box around while he filmed trade college commercials for daytime TV. I also did PA gigs on all sorts of forgettable movies.

Time went by. Nothing life-changing took root and Goalmart kept refusing to give me enough hours to stay afloat, even with the great deal on rent I was getting from the witch. So, I put in an application at Namaste Mart.

After getting hired, my vision for my future career changed. Fuck the movies. Fuck the Hollywood phonies and their endless networking. I wouldn't join their club if invited. I was meant for a purer path. I would become a literary man. I would write crime novels instead.

I developed a strict writing regimen, churning out at least three to five thousand words a week on a short crime story or novel. So far, I hadn't been published.

I moved out of the witch's room and into a guesthouse behind a family on North La Fayette in Silver Lake. I shared the rent with an aging, asexual hipster named Milo who usually left me alone and paid rent on time.

FELIX SAID TO Christy, "Why would this Obama shit mean we lose health care? I mean... What the fuck? I thought that fool was down."

Felix was an active O.G. Hollywood gangbanger. Richie and I were both friends with him. Earlier that year we'd gone to his twenty-seventh birthday party. His six kids and all their mothers were present. We were the only two white people in attendance.

Another crew member named Flaco, who at twenty-four was a retired gangbanger turned family man, raised his hand. "Yeah, what's up with that?" he said.

Many of my coworkers resemble real-life Homies figurines.

THE NIGHT BEFORE, I'd gone out drinking with James LaSalle in Echo Park. After a few beers, I lost track of him and found myself drunkenly talking to a beautiful girl named Parker. Parker was pretty and had a big, beautiful butt. I was in love.

This morning, awake with a hangover, I had memories of sending Parker a message on Facebook, possibly when I got home the night before. Were they real?

How had I even gotten home? I don't have a car, just a bike. The Short Stop was two miles from my pad on La Fayette. Did I find James and get a ride home? Did I walk all that way down Sunset in the middle of the night? Did I just dream about sending Parker a message?

I opened Facebook on my desktop and clicked on the MESSAGES icon. There it was in the SENT column.

I couldn't even remember how I'd met Parker. I was drunk somewhere. We had the Facebook friendship. I cruised her page often but didn't have her number. I had wanted it for a while. Before, I'd been too insecure to ask.

I clicked on the message and read what I wrote:

I don't know why you chose to dance with that hipster pussy in the suspenders and granny glasses. How stupid did he look? Anyway, I've been really lonely lately, female-wise, and I just wanted to tell you that you looked HOT and I was wondering if I could call you sometime? What's your #??

Shit.

She hadn't responded yet.

I fell back into my Ikea futon. I considered calling out from work. Jesus, I was such an asshole. Why couldn't I get it together?

My life was falling apart. There were highs, but the lows like this morning were too much for me to handle. They came often.

My cousin Mary back in Ohio, the only family member I got along with, had killed herself eleven years earlier. Mary had a husband and three kids, and one night, when she was tanked on too much Kroger Chardonnay, she walked to her garage, turned on her minivan, and sucked monoxide. When she checked out, Mary was only four years older than I was now. On the day of her funeral, I contemplated the despair she must have felt and promised myself I would never check out like her, no matter how bad life got.

Kenny, my older brother, fell apart often.

Falling apart for me wasn't suicide. It meant returning to Ohio, to my family and the arms of Jesus, with my tail between my legs. This could never happen.

I returned to my desk, unfriended Parker and blocked her, hoping she understood I would never bother her again. In the kitchen, I made myself a stiff Bloody Mary with Namaste Mart vodka and mix from the Circle H by my house. I took a long shower, then rode the 704 to work.

"LOOK, OBAMACARE IS still new," Christy said, flicking the sheet. She didn't want to be blamed for this. "They're still evaluating what degree of rehaul is needed, but yes, benefits could be cut."

Yes, there was the permissive workplace atmosphere Namaste Mart fostered, but so many of us justified staying for the pay and health benefits.

"Thanks, *Stephan*," Richie blurted in a loud and cartoonishly sarcastic voice. He gave Stephan, a crew member across the room from him, a wave.

Stephan was the only black crew member in the room.

My mouth hung open.

The staff at this Namaste Mart was predominantly Latino, then white, then Asian. There were only three black employees. One was a former Nigerian bodybuilder named Abeo, who on top of working here had his own personal training business. Another was a retired porn star named Shanice. Then there was Stephan here, a goonish sack of protein powder who regularly claimed his hands were registered as lethal weapons.

The room was silent.

As you can probably tell, I don't like Stephan. He's lazy, rude, aggressive, and openly disrespectful to women, especially his wife Maria, who also works at this location. The guy's an asshole. But of course, him being an asshole has nothing to do with his skin color. I wouldn't even have the balls to joke about it.

All eyes were on him.

Stephan smiled.

Stephan was an asshole, but he knew when something was funny. And besides, this was 2013. People could still make jokes.

A crew-wide laughter ensued. Christy covered her face with the sheet. We heard her suppressed chuckle and saw the paper shake. Richie turned and saw me laughing.

"It's all good, shawty," Stephan said to Richie. "My president's a brother, ya heard? Don't even trip 'cause it's all good!"

NAMASTE MART IS a hippie-themed grocery store first conceived in the '70s by a San Diego grocer named Fred Nikolopoulos. The top store executive's official title is Swami, so technically we're all supposed to call her Swami Christy. All positions here have a Hindu name, but none of us ever actually use them unless some big shot from corporate is visiting. For uniforms, us clerks, called Novices, wear long-sleeved hippie shirts covered in colorful tie-dyed patterns. It's all quite stupid, but plays well with our customers, whose desire to be fashionably spiritual makes them treat us with an absurd reverence.

At first, I couldn't believe how well Namaste Mart treated its workers. Everyone got full health insurance, even part-timers. Raises came twice a year and ranged from thirty-five to seventy-five cent increases. Many crew members were capped out, which meant they made twenty-five an hour or more at a grocery store. But the good times couldn't last forever.

Out on the sales floor, an Indian song with a solid tabla beat played over the store speakers. I went behind the demo station and opened the cabinet above the sink. It was full of cooking supplies and vitamins. I grabbed the milk thistle.

Since many Namaste Mart crew members are often hungover, including the managers and Christy, a bottle of milk thistle was always marked off and left for community use. I swallowed two and chased them with a demo coffee.

Richie walked over. He never used the community milk thistle and thought I was getting conned by some hippie superstition.

"Why keep this job if not for the health insurance?" I asked him.

"Even if they take it away, there's still plenty of great tail coming in and we're getting paid to talk to them. You never know who will come in here. Don't worry so much."

Richie watched an attractive Latina pick up one of the little paper cups full of jicama sticks we were giving out as free samples. She tasted one, promptly made a grossed-out face, and chucked the rest in the trash.

RICHIE WAS BORN and raised in Queens, New York. He was a rowdy kid. His mother, Maureen, raised him alone and did her best to keep him out of trouble. After high school, he enlisted in the Navy. While on a ship somewhere near Jordan, Maureen got sick, and Richie wasn't permitted to visit her and say goodbye before she passed, or attend her funeral.

He did stints in the brig. He became a customer at every

brothel worth a damn at all the Middle Eastern cities where his ship docked. He went AWOL repeatedly. He was dishonorably discharged. Back in Queens, he took a job as a plumber. He drank too much, got in fights, and did more time in civilian jail.

Despite the troubles of his youth and all his anger, he looks on the bright side of life. He loves kids, animals, and making people laugh. One day, he quit plumbing and drove west to pursue his lifelong dream of being a stand-up comedian. His family and friends thought he'd lost his mind. He enrolled in improv classes at UCB and attended open mics all around town, honing his act. He saw success. He began performing regularly at the Comedy Store, right on the Strip.

Time passed. Making a living at comedy was hard. So, he applied at Namaste Mart.

In Richie's eyes, Namaste Mart fostered a relaxed workplace culture and no one was taking proper advantage of all the leniency. So, while he was supposed to be working, he focused on testing out his many comedy routines. He would play pranks on customers, usually the boorish old Russians who came in and aggravated us with their incessant rude outbursts. Our store is located in a section of West Hollywood referred to as Little Odessa and is often called "The Russian Store."

He would do funny and sometimes credible Russian accents. Many of the Russians didn't have a good enough handle on English to complain to the managers. He would slip products into their carts when they weren't looking, hoping they wouldn't notice by the time they made it to the register to pay. Every worker in the store, even Christy, knew Richie was a comedian and because his routines so often killed, no one cared if he phoned in a weak work performance now and then. He made our shitty customer service jobs feel bearable.

FOR MY LAST hour, I was on register.

As usual, I took my anger out on our customers in the form of cryptic and condescending insults. My precise word choices were always a point of pride. They were all unwise to have picked my register.

I found myself ringing up groceries for the actor Charles Martin Smith, who I recognized from his appearances in all sorts of classic movies like *American Graffiti* and *The Untouchables*. His 1973 appearance in the Western *Pat Garrett and Billy the Kid*, directed by Sam Peckinpah, was a favorite. Smith was only in one scene of that movie, but he'd been directed by Peckinpah, a cinematic god and rebellious, alcoholic outlaw. I worshiped guys like Peckinpah.

"I recognize you," I said, scanning his bags of frozen chicken. "From *Pat Garrett and Billy the Kid*."

"That was me. Yes. Long time ago."

"That was a good movie."

He bagged his own groceries. "Thanks."

"So you knew Sam Peckinpah?"

He seemed surprised. "Sure."

"What was he like?"

I continued to scan. A bouquet of white dahlias was in his cart. He was buying flowers for someone. "Sam," he said, "... was an angry man."

He gave me a polite nod and left.

I was an angry man. Why was I so angry? Who cared if things didn't work out with one random girl? I would find a good one someday. Richie got drunk and did far more embarrassing things than me all the time and he never dwelled on his mistakes.

I drank from the water bottle I kept under the register. The rest of my last hour was smooth sailing.

RICHIE AND I clocked out. Both of us had 11-7 shifts that day. In the bathroom, I changed into my *Chinatown* T-shirt. It had an extreme close-up of Jack Nicholson's face with the big bandage over his nose.

Out in the parking lot, we met up with our coworker Damien Goldman, who waited in his silver 2010 Challenger. Damien was off today. I got in the passenger seat beside him. Richie, now in a Yankees shirt, got in the back.

"What's up, brotha?" Richie said.

"'Sup." Damien wore his three-hundred-and-fifty-dollar Porsche Carrera shades.

Damien's mother, a famous actress from '80s action movies turned owner of an upscale L.A. lingerie chain, was looking for a private investigator, and Damien had gotten us an interview. You see, on top of working at a grocery store, Richie and I have second jobs operating an unlicensed PI business.

TWO

THE HEADLINE IN the *Times* read GROCERY CLERKS SAVE KIDNAPPED TEENAGER. The story was all over social media. We did TV interviews. "Richie Walsh and Adam Minor aren't just Namaste Mart employees. They're also heroes..." We made a segment of *Good Morning America*, where we were interviewed via satellite by Dan Harris.

For weeks, I was recognized on the street while walking to Circle H to buy a six-pack or jogging at Echo Park Lake. People I'd barely known back in Ohio shared the story. *I used to work with Adam Minor!* I'd been through something notorious, seen firsthand horror most could only imagine, and lived to tell the tale. My Christian family became more interested in me than they had been in years because I'd been on TV.

They ran a staged photograph of Richie and me doing a cart run. We hauled twenty-three carts at once. Any grocery clerk will tell you twenty-three is an absurd amount for one haul. In the picture, Richie's making this ridiculous face. Everyone on our crew knew he was doing an impression of Vladimir, one of our rude, old Russian regulars. We all laughed when we saw the paper actually printed it.

IT WAS AN ordinary day, a year before.

I walked off the sales floor for my ten-minute break. From my locker, I took my copy of *Harlot's Ghost*, Norman Mailer's fourteen-hundred-page novel about the CIA, and sat with it in the chair in the corner of the break room. I was halfway through.

A crew member named Judy was on her lunch, eating stir-fry from a Tupperware container. Mariela, also on lunch, sat across from her.

Judy said in a voice gone hoarse from years of smoking, "Every day when I look out the window, I say to myself, there's something off going on across the street." Judy always spoke at an insufferably loud level. I tried to concentrate on my reading. "I'm telling you, the guy living there is some sort of creep."

Judy was part-time at Namaste Mart. Mainly, she did register and ran the demo station. I could never tell exactly what her schedule was, but she certainly wasn't showing up for more than two or three shifts a week.

Her skin was leathery and always too tan. She wore her hair feathered and always dyed it blonde. She'd been married and had two sons before she divorced her husband and moved to L.A. to live as a lesbian. Like a lot of people in West Hollywood, her wardrobe and language choices seemed to have been fossilized in amber in the mid-'80s.

Judy leaned in. "Some sort of foul play," she said to Mariela in a theatrical whisper.

I put my bookmark down, thinking this exchange might serve as dialogue to co-opt for my writing. Neither of them noticed me listening.

"*Girl,* whatchu mean foul play?" Mariela asked.

"He's all alone in this big house, this freakazoid. I've talked to him a few times and he pretends to be this goody-two-shoes Christian, you know, Mr. Hallelujah. He's *very* fit. Says he's got a Christian fitness club, which is strange because he always seems like he's got too much energy. There's something off about him. He's got a chip on his shoulder."

"A chip about what?"

"On top of being so focused on fitness, he's also a Christian singer. He pitched Lois and she turned down his idea for an album once. She said he stopped her when she was just trying to take Schnapps for a walk."

Lois was Judy's long-term girlfriend, a successful record executive. I'd met her a few times when she was shopping. Everyone knew Judy lived off Lois. Judy only came in for her job here to maintain a vague appearance of independence, and of course, for Namaste Mart's generous health insurance. If Judy wasn't working, she usually lounged at home while Lois was busy at work. She had a lot of time to look out the windows and watch neighbors.

"Whenever I talk to him," Judy said, "he's always got a story about how he's grateful for the glory of God and how he's doing God's business through song and exercise. He very well might be. But I can see that he's cocky, evil, and I think he hates women..."

I would jot all this down in the leather mini-notebook I kept in my back pocket in case story ideas came to me.

"Every window in the freakazoid's house is blacked out with tin foil. Why? He's the only one I've ever seen coming and going, but he always brings home groceries for more than one person. Why? He shops here all the time. If you look at his cart, you can tell he's not just shopping for himself. Who's he got in there behind his blacked-out windows?"

I knew the world my parents taught me about was bullshit. No all-powerful benevolent being could overlook the way humans hurt each other. At this point, I had been free from my Christian family's influence for five years. I had also openly professed my anti-theism many times to pretty much everyone in my L.A. life and repeatedly on the internet. I knew all sorts of manipulative predators used religion as a shield to protect and justify themselves when they did terrible things.

"What's this guy look like? How old is he?" I asked.

Judy looked my way, surprised I'd been listening. "Tall, thin, bald, white. Maybe thirty." She waited. "Why? Have you seen him in here?"

"I don't know. What's his name?"

"Stan Hammond," she said. "His Christian fitness group is called Ascendency to Majesty, but he calls it A to M. Isn't that a weird name? Like, why that? He sells the young girls who come to his fitness club T-shirts that say I heart A to M."

Felix had just come in. From his locker, he got his box cutter and clipped on his name tag. "Yo, I seen some hyna wearing that shirt by Plummer Park."

"That's one of the places they meet for their exercises," Judy said, nodding.

"I didn't know it meant that. I thought that bitch was saying she was down with ass to mouth, like maybe she did porn or some shit."

AFTER MY SHIFT, I sat at my computer and searched the internet for Stan Hammond. He had four songs on YouTube. I recognized two from the worship services at Wilderness Edge Pentecostal, my childhood church. They were "Our God Is an Awesome God" and "I'm Desperate for You."

Stan was tall, thin, and bald, as Judy described. In each performance, he sang in an operatic, Meat Loaf sort of voice while a guitar player and a drummer backed him. They were in somebody's garage. Stan was a mediocre singer but he disguised his subpar voice with dramatic hand gestures. At the end of each song, he looked into the camera. "I know there's a lot of people hurting out there, but I'm here to say you aren't alone..."

Judy was right. Stan was full of bouncing, uneasy energy and gave off the sense of being controlled by his sexual frustrations. The highest view counts on his videos were in the hundreds. Nothing special. The few comments on the videos were mainly by Christian rubes, all seemingly from rural America.

I found his Facebook page. His congregation appeared to be Adventure Song, the progressive mega church on Hollywood Boulevard, which was attended by Justin Bieber, Kaylee Safarian, and other young celebrities. This was almost a decade before their superstar lead pastor was engulfed in his own sex scandal, which precipitated the church's downfall.

I found pictures of his fitness group, Ascendency to Majesty. Young women, presumably Christians from Stan's congregation, wore those shirts that said I love A to M. In one pic, a woman was doing glute workouts, showing off her butt. They didn't appear to know the other meaning Felix picked up on. Or maybe they did. This was back when you first started seeing Christians like Stan claiming the practice of staying physically fit for their faith. They got people there for the exercise, then surreptitiously slipped the religion in.

If Stan Hammond had a job well-paying enough for him to afford a house in West Hollywood, his Facebook page didn't show what it was. I smelled rich parents.

In one picture, Stan was with a skinny, beautiful blonde girl who held up a finger with an engagement ring on it. Stan's post said: *She said yes!*

At the end of my research, I knew two things. I hated Stan Hammond, a man I'd never met. And whatever he was hiding, I would do my best to expose it.

ONE MORNING LATE the following week, Judy and I were on back-to-back registers at work. Neither of us had customers.

I turned. "Any news about your creepy neighbor?"

"I haven't seen him all week."

"Your story sounded so weird that I looked the guy up."

"Looked him up?" Judy made an amused, huffy laugh. "You're reading too many of those detective novels."

I stayed serious. "In one of his videos he made what he called an 'A to M smoothie.' It was just a regular smoothie and the video was eight minutes long."

Judy seemed confused. I noticed her eyes were red behind her glasses. She'd gotten high before coming in. "Yeah?" She coughed.

"What does Hammond do for a living?"

"I don't know. We think he's got a rich dad."

"He's got a fiancée?"

"Lois heard them fighting in the front driveway. Neither of us have seen her come back since then."

"Since when?"

She thought. "That was at least six months ago. I think they broke up. It was after their fight that he blacked out his windows."

"It is suspicious." A shriveled old Russian woman with a thin but unruly mustache came to my line. In her basket she had a stack of one-pound blocks of baking chocolate, organic sour cream, and a bottle of Stoli. After she was gone, I turned back to Judy. "When he shops here, he's always buying for more than one?"

"Every time. You want to know the weird thing?"

"What's that?"

"The past few months he's always buying our frozen chicken nuggets shaped like dinosaurs, energy bars for kids, and juice packs. He's always buying kids food, but he doesn't have any kids."

WHEN WE WERE alone in the break room, I told Richie the story.

I'd seen many times how angry he could get at the thought of possible injustices. It didn't always matter if the injustices had anything to do with him.

"The way she described this guy," I said, "this failed Christian singer who lives alone and buys food for kids when he doesn't have any kids. There's the name of his fitness group. I've seen stuff like that growing up, you know. But his name is so weird. Why did he choose those words for the name? I think he takes pictures of girls in that shirt, makes them think he's some innocent Christian who doesn't know what those words mean."

"He's probably whacking off to those pictures at home."

"My thoughts exactly. All of this makes me think he's up to something. Why would he have all the windows covered in foil?"

Richie kicked the break-room trash can across the room. It slammed into the recycling bin and sent plastic bottles flying all over the floor. "He's probably got some kid chained up in the basement or something!"

"What can we do, call the cops?"

Richie squinted, disgusted. "What are we going to tell the cops? We don't even know anything concrete. LAPD will probably fart into the phone."

"We can watch the house," I said. "Surveillance."

Richie liked that. He didn't miss a beat. "I can put on my construction hat and my old plumber's outfit and go over there to snoop around, acting like I'm on a job."

He was ready to go right now if it weren't for the remainder of our shifts.

Another idea hit me. "Judy's girlfriend has money. She does well for Sony Records."

"I don't follow."

"What if we play up Judy about checking it out? You're this big, bad veteran war hero and I'm the brains of the operation. What if we make her think like it's her duty and get her lady to pay us to go over there, like we're private detectives?"

WE MET LOIS and Judy in front of their condo on Curson. Richie amped up the charm. Judy, standing a little behind Lois, kept interjecting about how smart I was and how I always read such big books in the break room.

Richie and I came off as childish, unprofessional clowns hunting for a quick buck. Lois did not look happy being obligated to listen to her pothead girlfriend's coworkers.

"I don't know what's going on over there," Lois said. "But I'm not paying anyone to go snooping around at my neighbors'. If there's evidence of a crime, call the police." I was surprised she didn't tell us to go home to our mothers.

I'd legitimized Judy's long-simmering suspicions. She was more convinced than ever about Stan Hammond. But Lois was the breadwinner, so her ruling stuck. Our approach had been foolish. I didn't blame her.

Lois and Judy walked through their front gate, back toward their condo. "Those two don't seem like friends," I heard Lois say.

We returned to Richie's olive-green Bronco up the block. He started the engine.

We sat and watched Hammond's house.

It was a white two-story Spanish house with a stucco exterior. The large windows for the living room and the upstairs balcony had the curtains drawn. All the others were blacked out. There was a front gate with an opening to a sidewalk that led to a blue front door and another opening leading to the garage behind the house.

Many people in my life think I have an irrational bias or even paranoia about religion because of my family. Yes, I sometimes let my anger on the subject get out of control. But Richie never judges me or accuses me of bias. He always just listens. I said, "Lois said 'whatever's going on.' Of all the ways to phrase it, that's how she chose. She doesn't want to be involved but she can't deny that something's off."

That night, we got drunk at the Three of Clubs and tried to pick up girls. Neither of us got lucky, but we kept talking about the house. Money or no money, it didn't matter. The cops wouldn't do anything. We knew action was necessary.

I AWOKE ON Richie's couch. Squinting, I looked to the hallway leading to the kitchen. Richie was dressed in his old plumber's outfit. He drank from a cold half-gallon carton of unpasteurized Namaste Mart apple juice.

Now, I saw how my motivation for instigating this whole "investigation" wasn't really concern about what Hammond was up to, and it wasn't me wanting to prove how the religion of my childhood was evil. Those mattered. What I really wanted was action, a life worth writing about. I needed to be more than a forgettable community college dropout who rang up groceries for a living in Hollywood.

Back on Curson, he parked his Bronco in a good spot just up the block from Hammond's. Lois and Judy's pad was in sight.

Richie put on his construction helmet; the same one he'd worn on Halloween last year at the store when he came as a construction worker. At Namaste Mart, crew members could come to work in their costumes on Halloween.

On the side of the helmet was a sticker. It said NO MOSQUE. Richie wore the helmet during demonstrations at Ground Zero in lower Manhattan. He'd been hoping to get in fistfights with anyone who wanted to erect a place of worship where the towers had been.

He checked himself in the rearview. This helmet didn't jibe with his current plumber's outfit, but it certainly made him look more official from a distance.

"You'll be wheelman." He handed me the keys. "Your phone charged?"

In 2012, I still had a flip phone. Richie often gave me shit for it. "Yes, it is. What're you going to do?" Other than vague plans about "going to the house" and "checking things out," we hadn't discussed what was next.

"I'll go through the gate and go around like I'm there to read the meter." He held out the notepad he used to write his jokes on. A pen was shoved into the metal spiral at the top. "While I'm back there, I'll scope out the points of entry and see if I can make a breach."

"What if he has an alarm system?"

"If I set it off, be ready to drive."

"Shit, man. Are you sure about this?" As soon as this came out, I got embarrassed. This whole thing had been my idea.

Richie gripped a heavy wrench in his tool belt. "If that child-molesting fuck tries anything, I'll brain him right in the temple. Don't worry."

He walked toward the house. I slid into the driver's seat and watched him reach around the gate that led to the front yard, unhook the latch, and open it. He looked at me. I nodded. Then he walked through the yard and along the side of the house, leaving my sight.

EIGHT MINUTES LATER, my phone rang.

"What'd you find?"

"Meet me at the front door. I'll let you in."

"You're *inside*?"

"Take it easy. Move. There's not much time."

I took out my key ring and wrapped my knuckles around the keys in my right hand, like how Liam Neeson taped shards of broken glass between his knuckles to fight a wolf in *The Grey*. Then I went through the gate and up to the front door. When I got close, it opened. Richie stood there, still wearing his helmet.

"This way." He led me up the stairs.

"How'd you get in?" I put my keys back in my pocket.

"The kitchen window wasn't locked. The curtains were part open. I watched him sit at the kitchen table and fill a syringe with something. Then he walked up here. I had to move."

He led me to a bedroom. There, I saw Stan Hammond asleep in his bed. He wore a wife beater but was naked from the waist down. His open-air cock was on full display. A thin film of blood had formed around the edges of his lips. His chest slowly rose and fell.

"You hit him?"

Richie waved his hand. "Yeah."

A teenage girl sat slumped over on the bed, sleeping. She was dressed in a costume of a woman from the Bible, like something a woman playing Mary in a Christmas nativity scene might wear. A strand of drool hung from her chin and ran down to the blanket on the bed beside her, pooling into a wet, widening circle.

Richie pointed at a spent syringe on the bedroom dresser. "He was injecting her. I'm not sure with what. But she won't wake up."

I looked the girl over more closely. Her sleeve was still rolled up, and I saw the red dot where the needle had gone in.

"I've already searched every other room in the house. Unless there's some secret compartment, he doesn't have any kids in here. The only other person besides him is her, and she looks at least sixteen or seventeen."

"He's dressing her like the Virgin Mary," I said.

This stopped Richie cold. He snapped out of it. "She's breathing, but I'm not sure how much of this he gave her. I called 911. They're on their way."

We had no explanation for how we got in. "Should we leave?

Just run?"

Richie showed me a purse. "I found this in another room. There's an ID."

I took out the wallet and saw her license. Her name was Emily Glass and she was seventeen. There was an ID card for Adventure Song church next to her ID. "Maybe there's no little kids, but he was drugging and raping a seventeen-year-old. They go to the same church."

"We can't leave," Richie said. "If we're gone, maybe he wakes up and talks his way out of this somehow. Maybe, after it's all over, he finds a way to hurt this girl again. They might go easy on us when they see what we've uncovered."

I thought it over. He was right. "So what do we say?"

"We can tell the cops we were just driving by, and heard her screaming. I'll say I walked around the side and came in through the window because someone was screaming for help, and it seemed like they were in trouble."

"That's good," I said. "But we'll need more."

OUT OF BREATH, I knocked hard on the front door of Judy's. She answered after a few moments. A whiff of weed smoke came with her.

"Adam? What're you doing here?"

Sirens blared in the distance.

I told her everything as concisely as I could. I was honest about every detail.

Her face went white.

The sirens got louder.

"Can you call Lois and ask her to say that she paid us to investigate?" I said. "Say you two were concerned, that we offered to help, and that you would pay us? We need a good story to tell the cops or we might get in trouble."

Judy made a call. "It's about the freakazoid," she said. She told Lois everything, fast.

The sirens were almost to us.

Judy held out the phone. "She wants to talk to you."

I took it.

"He's got some young girl in there?"

"Her ID says she's seventeen. He's shooting her up with something."

Lois waited. "Tell the cops I hired you." Her tone sent a clear message: someone had hurt Lois at some point. "Say that we were worried. Tell them we offered to pay you."

A sheriff's cruiser turned the corner. An ambulance tore in from the other direction.

THE KIDS FOOD in Hammond's grocery cart was a red herring. Apparently, he just liked eating kids food himself. At our Namaste Mart, we have a guy who, while shopping for baguettes, simulates masturbation with all the different options before he makes his pick. An adult who eats kids food is strange, but I've seen stranger.

Emily Glass had disappeared after youth group at Adventure Song five and a half months prior. Her family had been frantically searching for her ever since. Hammond was questioned by the Sheriff's Department and private investigators. He was cleared by both. I remembered seeing Emily's face appear in news articles on my Facebook timeline.

The sheriff's detectives had suspicions about us. No surprise there. Hammond had no criminal record. He was a good Christian. But after Lois vouched for us, it was clear they weren't going to ask many hard questions. One of Lois's ex-girlfriends was a criminal defense attorney. Jersey born and successful, Susan Romano agreed to represent us pro bono during our dealings with law enforcement on the case.

At the hospital, we met with the Glass family. Emily's father told us the drugs Emily was being given were mainly heroin and fentanyl. She would have a long road to recovery, but she was safe. The family thanked us profusely. This was the first time I'd ever heard of fentanyl.

Emily Glass told the police how, in rare moments of lucidity, she remembered Stan would revert to a childlike personality as he raped her. He talked like an eight-year-old. He sucked his thumb. He would sing Christian songs and jerk off in front of her.

We got bombarded with media requests. An important interview with the *L.A. Times* was scheduled. Christy heard about what happened. She told us she was proud of us and said to take as much time off as we needed.

Lois and Judy stopped by Richie's pad in East Hollywood. "I'm sorry I didn't listen at first," Lois said. She handed me an envelope. "I hope that's enough."

"We're just happy Emily is safe now."

Lois shook her head. "You guys should think about doing this more often. You're both too smart and gallant to just work at a grocery store forever."

The envelope had ten thousand in cash. After they were gone, Richie and I split it down the middle and opened some beers. We decided Lois was right. We'd stumbled into a whole different world, and we were going to stay here for as long as we could.

THE *TIMES* STORY glamorized our heroism but buried the sinister Christianity angle. Hammond's father, Stan Sr., was a rich real-estate developer with friends on the city council. He wouldn't stand for the media making Jesus look bad.

We never got an explanation for the weird outfit Stan was dressing Emily in during her captivity. None of the media outlets mentioned it. Even Stan's childlike persona was buried. All of the reporters we spoke to withheld the anti-theist commentary I sprinkled into the testimony I gave them about our rescue of Emily. They knew it wouldn't play with their audience.

Five thousand bucks in a single whack was a lot for a pair of grocery clerks in 2012. Richie and I both used the money to pay off some debt. I finally bought myself a smartphone.

We also used some of the money to party, of course.

For a stretch, I did well with the ladies. Richie probably got laid twenty times because of all the attention. On top of that, he spent a good amount of money on street hookers. He began doing a routine at his open mics about having an addiction to prostitutes. It killed. His audiences clearly thought it was a made-up act.

Richie pushed for us to buy a gun. "We need protection, just in case."

I agreed. Because of his record, the permit would have to be in my name. I bought a Manurhin MR73 Gendarmerie revolver and made regular trips to the L.A. Gun Club to practice with it on the range. If I ever needed to use it on a case someday, I wanted to be prepared.

Susan liked us and agreed to stay on as our pro bono lawyer. This was a lucky break.

She became a dependable resource to call for advice. As PIs, we had no office. We met clients at their homes or workplaces. Our subsequent cases were more missing girls with worried parents. Usually, we found them quickly. None were as dramatic as Stan Hammond and Emily Glass. The need for the gun never came up. Richie didn't even have to hit anybody.

Our last case was four months ago. Since then, everything had been dry.

THREE

Damien hit a red light at Highland. The lingering heat of the early evening made the boulevard shimmer. His AC blasted. A lane over, four cute cholas in a custom lowrider looked our way. I realized they were scoping out Damien's car.

"Can we go over the job again?" I'd already told Richie most of it, but we'd been drinking and I wasn't sure if he remembered the details.

"This girl who works for my mom disappeared," Damien said. "My mom wants to hire someone to find her."

Joan Goldman, Damien's mother, had appeared in big Hollywood movies like *Looming Night, Fatal Firefight 2,* and *Eradicator 2.* Most memorably, she played the badass Private Joan Lopez in James Chalmer's 1987 sci-fi horror film *Martians.* As Joan aged, many of the better opportunities for roles began to dry up, so she shifted gears by opening her lingerie business, Joan's Bras. Her store's focus was, as the website put it, providing high-end bras for full-figured women, a market she saw as too often disregarded. By then, Joan's Bras had locations in Pasadena, Santa Monica, and East Hollywood.

We were headed to meet her at Damien's childhood home in Beachwood Canyon.

"This girl, you said she works at your mom's lingerie shop?" I asked.

"Yeah."

Richie's eyes lit up. He'd forgotten this detail.

The light turned green. The cholas went south on Highland and disappeared.

"This girl models the lingerie?" Richie said.

"She just works at a store, I think."

"I know I'm speaking against our interests here, but why would your mom hire two mooks like us? She could afford a pro."

I turned back to Richie. "Damien doesn't need to work with all the money she's got, and she's still got him working at a grocery store."

Richie shrugged and nodded.

Damien turned north on Cahuenga. "This girl who went missing has a crazy story. She came from a creepy religious background, like you." Damien knew my backstory, as well as all the weird religious details of the Stan Hammond case that had been withheld by the media. I'd given him the insider details during our shifts in the milk cooler. He looked at Richie. "And after that, before she started working with my mom, she got involved in sex work, which I know is your special area of expertise."

Richie laughed and made a *guilty-as-charged* face.

"She'll fill you in on the details. Trust me, you two will be perfect."

We arrived at the foot of the Hollywood Hills and Damien began to climb his Challenger up the narrow and winding roads toward Beachwood Canyon.

JOAN LIVED IN a cantilevered house on Quebec Drive. We all got out of the car, and I looked down over the fence that ran along the side of the driveway. The sleekly built home had three levels going down the side of the hill to where a large patch of land flattened out at the bottom. A young man was in a pool below, floating on a yellow raft.

Damien said, "This way."

He led us inside and down a hallway. Goldman family pictures hung on the walls. Damien's dad was a tall, dark, and handsome square-jawed, Jewish-looking man. I had not yet learned his name or occupation. In another photo, I saw a kid who I assumed must be Damien's brother standing beside a young Damien.

We passed by a section of pictures dedicated to Joan's movies. There was the actor Bill Maddox, her co-star in both *Looming Night* and *Martians*, smiling beside her. Another showed Joan and James Chalmer, her director on *Martians, Eradicator 2,* and *Hindenburg.*

We were led into an open living room with a windowed wall overlooking the canyon below. On the edge of the couch, wearing glasses and reading a large, old hardback book about gardening, was Joan Goldman in a light-green summer dress.

She was in her early sixties, with long and curling black hair mixed with wisps of gray she didn't try to hide. When she saw us, she put her book down on the coffee table beside a cocktail and her phone, took off her glasses, and stood. "Hey, sweetie."

Richie and I watched as mother and son hugged.

"Mom, this is Adam and Richie."

We all shook hands.

"So... the Grocery Clerk PIs." Joan looked us over. "I heard about the girl you saved last year... What a terrifying story."

"The whole thing was his idea." Richie pointed at me.

"We're just glad she got home safe," I said.

"Me too. Also, I *love* Namaste Mart." Joan then went on for a bit about her favorite Namaste Mart products. We were used to this. "I'm so glad Damien works there."

Richie smiled. "It's the happiest place on earth."

It got quiet. "So..." Joan said.

"Damien gave us the broad details," I said. "Richie and I are good at finding people. But we don't have an investigator's license. If that's not an issue for you, we're ready to hear your story and see if we can help. Anything you choose to tell us is confidential."

Joan looked at Damien. "Your brother's tanning down at the pool. You haven't seen each other in weeks. Go say hello."

Damien walked out to the balcony and down the set of outdoor stairs that led to the lower levels of the house and to the pool below.

"Sit down, please," Joan said.

She returned to where she was when we came in. Richie and I took the couch opposite her. The twilight came in behind her and outlined her curls in gold and orange.

A sable-colored Shetland Sheepdog walked in, heading for the food and water on the floor in the kitchen. Richie sat up fast.

"Who's this?" he said.

"Her name is Cassie," Joan said, thrown off by Richie's enthusiasm.

Richie stood. "Cassie girl! Who's my best friend? Who's my best friend?" he said in a cooing voice.

Cassie stopped in her tracks and stared at Richie. Joan sat still, watching.

"Come here, girl," Richie said. Cassie forgot about her food, ran over toward the couch, and lay on her back at Richie's feet. "That's my best friend," he said, then kneeled down and began to pet her stomach. Cassie wiggled with delight.

"That's amazing," Joan said. "She won't even answer like that to my husband."

"That's 'cause she's my best friend."

Richie sat back down on the couch. Cassie jumped up and sat down between us, resting her head on Richie's leg.

"You were saying?" I said to Joan.

"My employee's name is Shayla Ramsey. She works at my East Hollywood location. When I hired her, she was in recovery for alcohol and drug addiction. Last week... Shayla just vanished without a trace. I need someone to find her and determine if she's safe."

"It helps us to start at the beginning," I said. "When did you first meet Shayla?"

"Years ago, when she walked in and asked for an application. I agreed to interview her that day. They hold NA meetings in the church across the street from my store. Shayla was a regular there. She was open with me about being in recovery and serious about getting her life back on track. I could see her achieving so much if someone gave her a chance." Joan picked up her phone from the coffee table, asked for our numbers, and texted us a picture. It showed Joan and five other young, smiling women inside one of her stores. "She's the blonde on the left."

Shalya had golden-blonde hair, deep-blue eyes, was medium

height, and like all of the other women in the picture was full-figured and had a noticeably large chest. A faded gold necklace with an airplane pendant hung around her neck. It had a broken wing.

"Shayla came from an extreme religious background?" I asked.

"She was raised in a Mormon polygamist town in Utah. It's in the middle of nowhere and called Bear Creek. Growing up, Shayla had *seven* mothers. She never left the compound her entire childhood. Her family married her off to some creepy old man who already had over a dozen wives when she was fifteen. She became determined to break free.

"When she was seventeen, she escaped. Her husband pursued her and she was in danger. To get away from Utah, she had to borrow money from some shady characters who prey on Mormon runaways. She made it to L.A. and started looking for ways to support herself. Bear Creek was all she'd known. Her people didn't worry about education beyond how to please their husbands. So, she resorted to dancing at strip clubs, got into drugs, and then later, when her drug problem got worse, prostitution. For years, she sold herself. She was running with a bad crowd. Her boyfriend was a drug dealer. Somehow, she managed to turn things around and got clean. Shortly after that, she walked into my store. Another one of my employees is an ex-Mormon, though not from a polygamist background. Her name is Jessica. Since Jessica was doing well, I figured Shayla could too."

"How old is Shayla now?" Richie asked.

"Twenty-three. She was a stellar employee and regularly kept me updated about her recovery process. She was doing great. The customers loved her."

"Tell us about her disappearance," I said.

"Last Wednesday, she didn't show up for work. Jessica, who is now a good friend of hers, called her repeatedly but got no response. Jessica went by Shayla's apartment in Silver Lake. It was empty. No word had been left to her landlord and all of her stuff was still in her apartment. With most people, I wouldn't pry, but to just disappear is not like her. She'd left no trace. I tried to get in touch with anyone in her life who might have known what happened, but no one knew anything."

"Could she have just left on her own and not wanted to tell anyone?" Richie asked.

"It's possible, sure. If that's the case, I would still want to know that she's okay."

"Did you call the police?" I asked.

"I filed a missing person report over the weekend. Shayla's family back at Bear Creek wouldn't be any help even if they were reachable. None of her friends know anything. The detective suggested I consider a PI since they aren't in a position to do much."

Joan had a warm and gentle manner, but it was evident she could get hardboiled. Today her home was Beachwood Canyon, but Damien said she was born and raised in East L.A. Her portrayal of Private Lopez was based on many of the hard-ass cholas she knew growing up there in the '70s.

"Did you or any of your employees notice anything strange about Shayla lately?" I asked. "Anything that, in retrospect, might be connected to her disappearance?"

"Yes. According to my other girls, her old boyfriend from before she got clean was back in the picture. He would pick her up when her shift was over. I don't know a lot about the guy, just that he might deal drugs, that his name is Arman and might have been in Armenian Dominance. I never met or even saw him."

Richie had a history with Armenian Dominance, the branch of the Armenian Mafia active in Southern California. "Was Shayla back on drugs?" he asked.

"I don't know. If she was, she was hiding it."

"Did Missing Persons talk to Arman?" I asked.

"The detective got him on the phone. He said Arman stonewalled him and said that any more questions should go through his lawyer."

"Anything else happen?" I asked.

"Yes. There was an incident at the store. Evette, another one of my girls, witnessed it. An old man came by to talk to Shayla when she was on the clock. Evette didn't understand everything the man said, but apparently, he told Shayla he wanted to buy underwear for all of his wives. *Plural.* Shayla never mentioned it to me, but according to Evette, who only told me this after her disappearance, Shayla seemed shaken."

"Could this have been someone from Bear Creek?" I asked. "Someone who finally tracked her down and was trying to return her to her husband?

"It's possible. But if it was, it's hard to imagine Shayla not speaking up about it. She told me so much about how abused women are on polygamist compounds and never wanted that for herself. She's been through horrific stuff."

I looked at Richie. He nodded. I looked back at Joan. "If you want to hire us to find Shayla, we'll take the job."

"What will you need?"

"We have more questions," Richie said. Cassie rolled over halfway and he began to pet her belly again. "Do you know the names of any of the clubs where Shayla worked back when she was a dancer?"

"She may have told me at one point, but I don't remember."

"Who would know?"

I could already tell Richie was looking forward to spending time doing detective work looking for Shayla at any strip club where she *might* be.

"Some of my other employees might. Or Shayla's friends from NA. They still hold meetings across the street from the store."

"And when can we talk to your other employees?" I asked.

"All three of my other girls at that location will be working tomorrow. They're all eager to help. The morning and evening shifts overlap in the middle of the day, so it will work if you come just after lunchtime."

I looked at Richie, then back at Joan. "Richie's off tomorrow, but I work a 1–9 at the store. Can we come by earlier, maybe at eleven?"

"Yes, I'll work it out with the girls."

"Thank you," I said. "We should discuss our fee."

"Go ahead."

Usually, Richie and I decided in advance what would charge based on the client's circumstances. We hadn't this time. I decided to just go for it. "Our rate is one thousand a day. Of course, you'll get regular updates on our progress."

"That's fine," she said.

FOUR

We decided to strategize, over drinks, what our first steps in the investigation would be. We went to Short Stop.

Richie held up his Bud Light. "A grand a day. Hell yeah!"

"She was in *Hindenburg*. I figured she can afford it."

We scanned the red-lit bar. Each night at Short Stop the music was themed. That night was soul night. Ladies reliably came to the Short Stop, mainly for the dance floor and music.

"I have a question," Richie said.

"Yeah?"

"The guy who just ran for president against Obama was a Mormon, right?"

"Mitt Romney, yes. He's one of the most famous ones."

"I've heard of Mormons before. The South Park guys are doing that play. But what are they exactly? Is it all just about having multiple wives?"

"Mormonism was started by this guy Joseph Smith. He was a teenage ex-con from upstate New York in the early 1800s."

"Ex-con? What'd they get him for?"

"Fraud. He got charged and plead guilty. A year or so after his conviction, when everyone in that area was starting new religions, Smith walked out of the woods and told all his neighbors that he got visited by an angel named Moroni."

"Moron-eye?"

The music was loud. Close enough. "Yeah. He claimed the angel gave him some golden plates, and that these magic gold plates had what is now the Book of Mormon on them."

"What's the Book of Mormon?"

"Basically, it's a remix of Christianity with a bunch of stupid shit added in, like how Native Americans are really Jews and that when Jesus returns, he'll come back to Missouri."

Richie laughed. "A guy who believes this shit was almost president?"

"Yeah." I sipped my Negroni. "Anyway, Mormonism took off, Smith got rich, got in trouble a bunch of times, and moved his cult around. They ended up in Illinois, where he started his own city called Nauvoo. When Smith was in his thirties, after he ran for president and lost, he started telling every woman he met that God had told him personally that it was their duty to fuck him. He said God now condoned plural marriage."

Two thick black girls walked by. They were cute. One looked at my *Chinatown* shirt and clearly pegged me as a freak. They went to the dance floor. Smokey Robinson sang "The Love I Saw in You Was Just a Mirage."

"You think a line like that would work on a girl today?" Richie asked.

"Depends on the girl."

"Do Mormons still believe in that? Isn't it illegal?"

"The church leaders at the end of the 1800s, long after Smith was dead, said Mormons wouldn't be polygamists anymore. The majority have been against it since then. But back then, some groups split off, and they went on with polygamy, usually in secret. Many live on compounds. Some live in Utah and other parts of the Southwest. Others are down in Mexico."

"I admit, all of this is weird, but you don't think some Mormons really got to Shayla, do you? These people sound goofy as fuck."

"Hard to say. You have to remember that the Mormons went west to Utah decades before any of the first cowboys." Richie and I are both avid fans of Westerns, and Richie is the only person I've ever known who knows more about the history than me. "I wouldn't underestimate them."

MY PHONE RANG. Out front, my landlord's parrot shrieked. It was bloodcurdling. The fucking thing shrieked every morning at eight. The noise was one of the reasons my and Milo's rent was so low. We planned to throw a big party whenever the bird died.

I struggled to find the phone. It was my big sister Geneva calling from Ohio. "Hello?" I coughed into the line.

"Did I wake you?"

"What do you want?" My hangover was almost as bad as yesterday's.

"Hayden fell on his skateboard last night. He's in the hospital."

Hayden was my nephew, the oldest of Geneva's four children.

"He's in the hospital from falling off his skateboard?"

"He broke his wrist and cut open his knee. Eight stitches."

I spat into my trash can. "He'll be all right."

"I'm sure he'd like to talk to you when he gets out."

"He get the movie I sent?"

Hayden liked dinosaurs, just like I had at his age. *Jurassic Park* had been rereleased in a remastered version earlier that year. I spent years of my childhood wishing I could be Alan Grant. The week before, I'd bought a copy of the updated DVD from the Santa Monica Boulevard Goalmart and mailed it to Hayden back in Columbus.

I wanted to be the cool uncle from Hollywood. I wanted Hayden to run away someday like I did, and find a refuge in the fancy pad in the Hollywood Hills I would one day own from sales of my brilliant and best-selling crime novels.

"I wanted to talk to you about that." She waited. "Greg and I didn't know you were going to send him that movie."

How old was Hayden? I counted on my fingers but lost track. Shit. I should know this. "Is it because the movie's PG-13 and Hayden isn't thirteen yet?" Geneva, and all my family, put the same level of faith into the rulings of the MPAA as they did into Jesus and the Bible.

"We looked up the rating on CommonSenseMedia.com."

"On what?"

"There's too much cursing for a boy Hayden's age."

Who cursed in *Jurassic Park*? I couldn't remember. It must have been Samuel L. Jackson, but the only line of his I could remember was "Hold on to your butts." "Are you serious?"

"We'll let him watch if you wanted to send him another DVD. One that's appropriate."

"If you're worried about that movie, the focus of your concern shouldn't be on the cursing. Your focus should be more on lying to him about the existence of dinosaurs altogether."

"What?"

"How old does the Bible say the world is? What's the most liberal estimate?"

"*Adam*," she said.

"Let's say a hundred thousand. That fair?"

She huffed.

"The last dinosaurs died out sixty-five million years back, sis. This fact is a far more dangerous threat to your plans of indoctrination than how many times Samuel L. Jackson or Jeff Goldblum cuss." I hung up and threw my phone onto my pillow.

I went to the kitchen and made myself another Bloody Mary to get ready for the day. The parrot had stopped shrieking.

As I sipped the drink, my anger over the call wore off. Strangely, I began to feel grateful. Grateful to be free. Grateful for my wacko family, despite everything. Where it mattered, they were good people. They did their best to take care of me and had always been well-intentioned. Good intentions mattered.

My background was not the horror Shayla Ramsey knew. My past could never catch me and drag me back against my will. I would not take my freedom for granted.

We would find her. I would look into her blue eyes. *"Living free is hard, but worth it,"* I would say. *"Humans weren't born to follow. Back when you escaped Bear Creek, you were free. You should stay free. There's nothing for you back home."*

Many important clues we'd discovered in previous cases came from online sleuthing. Richie and I often split up our duties, and investigating online usually falls to me.

I searched for Shayla on Facebook. Her page came right up. It said: *Worked at Joan's*. Her privacy settings didn't allow much. She probably didn't want any of the Mormon freaks from her past finding her.

I had the same privacy settings on my own page.

I SLID OPEN the gate and walked out to Richie's Bronco. He looked hungover but fine.

I wore a white Gucci short-sleeved, button-down dress shirt. It was the most expensive and dressiest piece of clothing I owned, and I always kept it close for when I needed to look presentable on a case. "How'd you do last night?" We hadn't seen each other since the Short Stop. Again, I didn't know how I got home.

"I ran into Fast Eddie." Fast Eddie was a coke dealer Richie knew. "I bought a few grams off of him. When I came back into the bar, I couldn't find you. I was tuned up big time, so I decided to do some investigating and went to Forty Niners." Many of the dancers at Forty Niners were under the protection of Armenian Dominance. "I asked if any of the ladies might know Shayla. I didn't get any helpful answers, but I got a hunch that if we find this Arman fuck, we'll find our girl. I didn't want to look more like a cop than I already do, so I paid for a lap dance and flashed the coke I had to the dancer. She invited me into their depressing back room..."

Richie was laser-focused on Arman. I suspected he might be. He didn't like the Armenian Mafia because they'd already tried to kill him once.

WE WERE IN BETWEEN cases last year.

I worked a closing shift at Namaste Mart. Richie was off, but later he was taking a girl he'd met on Plenty of Fish to Dartmouth and Flower, a hipster bar in East Hollywood. Roberto, our friend and coworker, came along.

Roberto was a strange dude. For Halloween, he came to work dressed as Yolanda Saldívar, the woman who murdered the Mexican pop singer Selena. He wore a conservative blue dress and a Selena Fan Club pin, and did his hair up in a bun. Roberto worked his entire shift in this costume, serving free samples from the demo station.

Richie wanted me to tag along. I wasn't planning on going out. The hipsters at Dartmouth and Flower were insufferable, but hot girls went there. After finishing up a late shift at the store, I rode over on my bike.

For most of the night, we all got drunk and clowned around. Closing time came without me getting any numbers. Richie, the girl, Roberto, and I all walked out to the street.

A tiny old Mexican lady sold bacon-wrapped hot dogs from a cart. Beside her, a huge Armenian guy stood and ate a dog. He was flanked by two smaller friends also eating. All three guys eye fucked Richie's girl as we passed. One whistled.

Richie stopped and turned. He zeroed in on the big guy. "Hey pal, who the fuck are you whistling at?" If there was a speck of fear inside him, I couldn't see it.

The big guy smiled. He probably had four inches and a hundred pounds on Richie. He said, "Don't leave until I give your girl a hot dog, bro."

His buddies both laughed.

Richie began counting out loud. With each number he raised his voice. Roberto stepped back. So did I. The Plenty of Fish girl was clueless. I pulled her back with us. Sometimes, I was drunk enough to step in and help Richie when he got in fights. Other times, I was too scared.

That night I was in the latter category.

On ten, Richie swung. The collision was brutal. The big guy dropped his hot dog. He tapped out still on his feet. His enormous body tipped over slowly, and his head made a fleshy bounce on the concrete between two parked cars.

His two friends tossed their hot dogs and took up defensive positions.

Richie ripped off his jacket and clenched his fists. "Make your move!"

Both looked scared. The big guy on the ground was clearly the shot caller.

The crowd from the bar gathered.

A red Mercedes screeched forward. The driver's side door swung open. An Armenian with slick hair and a purple dress shirt got out. He popped the trunk. He took hold of something. He ran toward Richie, under a street light. The thing in his hand gleamed.

I shouted Richie's name.

It was a knife. Richie didn't see the guy. He shanked Richie three times in the side and stepped back. Richie slowed down and touched his side. He looked at his blood-smeared hand.

The Plenty of Fish girl screamed.

The big guy came to. The Armenian with the knife and the other two helped the big guy up. Drunk hipsters screamed. Everyone saw the knife and the pool of blood growing on Richie's side. The Armenians rushed into the Mercedes.

A hipster mob rushed the Mercedes. They pounded on the windshield. They jiggled door handles. One rabid hipster jumped on the back and kicked hard at the windshield. It spiderwebbed. He kicked harder. It caved in. The Mercedes tore off. The hipster flopped into the street. The car disappeared down Hollywood. Richie clenched his bleeding gut. "I'm fine," he kept repeating. "I'm fine."

The LAPD arrived.

"I got stabbed," Richie told the uniformed officer, still holding his side. The blood had slowed. A hipster wrote down the plates of the Mercedes. Richie read them to the cop. He said nothing about being the one who swung first. "Whenever you guys find it, the back windshield will be missing. The guys in the car will be Armenians."

"Whoa, whoa, whoa," said the cop, visibly offended. "How do you know they were Armenian?"

Richie looked at me, then back at the cop. "How do I know the fuckin' sky's blue?"

Richie wouldn't press charges. We moved on to Roberto's nearby pad on Mariposa and kept drinking. Roberto and I tried to convince Richie he should go to the hospital. Richie cited all the other times he'd been stabbed and turned out fine. He hated hospitals. One wasn't necessary in this instance. He just kept demanding more beers.

Other Namaste Mart crew members stopped by Roberto's. They gawked at Richie's wound. Richie must have recounted the story two dozen times. He took the Plenty of Fish girl up to Roberto's roof and fucked her as the sun rose. "It was pretty romantic," he later said, when describing the scene.

The next afternoon, he showed up for a shift at the store. He still hadn't been to the hospital. He showed his wound to all the crew in the break room. He told the story over and over.

After encouragement from me and many others, Richie asked Christy if he could leave work early to finally get his wound checked out. A doctor took a brief look and scheduled him for minor surgery the following week.

Richie finally went to Hollywood station to file a report on the Armenians. He gave the plates of the Mercedes. He didn't like snitching, but these guys had casually shanked him without even thinking. They were still on the streets, able to do it again.

"Where'd this happen?" the Major Crimes detective said.

Richie gave the address of Dartmouth & Flower.

"Let me guess. Armenians?"

"*Ding, ding, ding.*"

"You probably got six fuckin' carloads of them after you. They're all cousins." The detective left and came back with a six-pack of mug shots.

Richie pointed. "That's him. He was the driver and he stabbed me."

"You sure?"

"Yes."

The detective made notes. "That's a validated member of Armenian Dominance. He's been evading open warrants for months. Watch your back, especially in that neighborhood."

RICHIE WAS READY to ignore the Mormon angle and just blame Shayla's disappearance on Arman because Arman *might* be connected to Armenian Dominance. He knew AD was full of murdering psychos. These days, a particularly ruthless AD gangster called Hollywood Sam was garnering a lot of attention on the streets and in the media. Sam was one of the original cofounders of the gang, back in the '80s. He spent almost two decades in prison, but was out now and making up for lost time. He was accused of fearsome violence and escalating the actions of Armenian Dominance to a far more brutal level. Reporters covered his court dates. Sam craved the spotlight. He gave charismatic and defiant interviews on the steps of the downtown courthouse. He was not the type of guy any sane person would want to piss off.

I knew Richie wouldn't care. He craved payback and had long been wishing for a justified path to get there. Arman might be involved in our current case. Arman might be that path. He told me repeatedly he'd let the whole thing go. He obviously hadn't.

Earlier, I'd searched for any L.A.-based Armenian men named Arman on Facebook. A bunch popped up. Most lived in Glendale. Most looked too old to be dating Shayla.

There was one whose profile was a full body shot of him standing next to a red Firebird. He was in his late twenties. He dressed gaudy and was chained up. He looked cocky.

His privacy setting had limitations too. All I could see in detail were pictures of cars in a sales lot. It looked like it might be somewhere on Brand Boulevard. It was a long shot, but *maybe* this was our Arman.

FIVE

It was a single-floor Melrose storefront. A powder-blue sign over the door read *Joan's Bras* in black cursive script. Inside, there were racks of fancy-looking bras delicately displayed on hangers and many full-figured mannequins dressed in the merchandise. A stack of old pastel-colored *Playboys* sat on a coffee table.

We saw three twenty-something female employees. I recognized each from the picture Joan texted us at her house. They wore tasteful conservative dresses. Their outfits did not disguise their stunning figures.

A short black woman with brown and orange-tinted curls walked up. "Good morning. Is there anything I can help you guys with?"

I told her we had an appointment with Joan.

"Oh." She scanned us over. "Are you the detectives?"

"Yes."

"Who work at Namaste Mart?"

"That's us."

Joan appeared from the back. "You'll have enough time before your shift, Adam?" She looked at her watch. "Damien started at five this morning."

"I should be okay if we get started soon."

Joan's office was at the end of a short hallway. On the side wall, I saw a framed *Los Angeles Magazine* article about the original opening of this location.

"It's best if we speak to each of your employees separately," I said.

"I'll send Jessica first."

JESSICA STEPPED INTO the doorway. She had scarlet-red hair and her oval-shaped face was perfectly symmetrical and her eyes were emerald green.

I was in Joan's high-back swivel chair. "Please, have a seat."

She sat and crossed her shapely legs. A gold anklet on her left leg sparkled. Jessica was the loveliest of the three girls by far. She looked like a young Christina Hendricks in *Mad Men*.

I told her about how we were there to find out what happened to Shayla.

Richie was in the corner. "How did you and Shayla first meet?"

"We were both regulars at an ex-Mormon support group."

"Are you from a polygamist family too?" Richie asked.

"No. Shayla's people are FLDS. Fundamentalists. They're one of the most notorious groups who still try to call themselves Mormon. Almost all regular Mormons are strongly against polygamy and have been for almost a century. I was raised by the regular ones."

"But you still left the church?" I asked.

"Yes."

"What brought on that decision?"

"I'm also the type of woman who asks questions. While most wouldn't admit it, many LDS leaders, even in this day and age, don't approve of women who ask questions. Over time, I realized the church didn't appreciate the way God made me, so I left."

Richie walked around the desk. "When you referred Shayla to Joan, did you know she was a junkie and a hooker?"

"A crass way to put it."

Richie laughed sarcastically. "Excuse me for being crass."

"All that was behind her. She was sober."

"Still, isn't hiring a person like her a risk?" Richie asked. "Unreliable?"

"I believed in Shayla. I knew Joan would too."

Jessica seemed to have her post-church life down strong. I thought about asking for her number. Generally, I avoided pursuing girls with religious baggage since I had more than enough of my own. Jessica had clearly invented some weird, elastic personal religion for herself, which would almost certainly drive me crazy with its stupidity if I ever had to hear about it. But she was *so hot*. It was thrilling just to sit across from her. I imagined her big, glorious butt sitting right on my face.

"So Shayla got hired on here," I said. "What then?"

"Her life got on track. Over time, we both gave up on the ex-Mormon meetings. Neither of us needed them anymore. Sometimes, we would have one-on-one deep-dive discussions about religion. Shayla said she was free of God. She didn't need Him anymore."

Richie looked at me. "You and this Shayla broad would get along."

I ignored him. Sure, I had my opinions. But I wanted Jessica to like me. "Would Shayla ever consider going back to Bear Creek?"

"She would die first."

"Describe Shayla's life in the last few months before she disappeared."

"She would seem upset at random times. Stressed out. Her ex was back in the picture, even though she kept that from me."

"Could you recognize Arman?" Richie asked.

"No. I never saw him, just heard about him."

"Was Arman in the Armenian Mafia?" Richie asked.

"Maybe."

I said, "What about this creepy Mormon that came in?"

"It's just a story Evette brought up after we found out Shayla was missing." Evette was the Latina who we'd be talking to later. "We have all kinds of strange guys come in here. This one was some type of Mormon who was buying lingerie. You can ask her about it, but I doubt it meant anything. Mormons get misunderstood."

"Do you know anyone else in the L.A. Mormon world we could talk to who might know something about Shayla?" I asked.

Jessica hesitated. "No," she said finally.

She was holding something back.

"You sure?" Richie asked. He caught her hesitancy too.

"Yes." She got up, reached into the front pocket of her blouse, and pulled out a business card. "If there's any other help I can be." She leaned forward and handed it to me.

Then she left.

Richie said, "You could totally hit that, Minor-man."

"*Lower your voice.*" I didn't want Joan to hear.

"She knows something more. And she wants to tell just you," Richie said.

I put the card in my pocket. "I know."

ALEXIS WAS THE short black girl with an orange tint to her curls. She walked in, closed the door behind her, and sat.

"Joan told us you changed your schedules around for this, Alexis," Richie said. "Thanks for that. Do you normally work the late shift?"

"Yeah, but my schedule is kind of all over the place now. I work here, plus I go to FIDM, and I have an internship too."

Richie said, "What's FIDM?"

"Fashion school, downtown," I said. "My guess is that curriculum is much harder than most people assume."

"You aren't wrong," Alexis said.

"When did you start working here?" Richie asked.

"A year and eight months ago. I'm from the Bay Area and moved down for school. My mom and Joan are old friends. My mom used to be an actress down here and they would go to a lot of the same auditions together, back in the '80s. My mom never reached Joan's success, though. When I applied, I used my mom as a reference."

Alexis had the eyes of a dedicated dreamer. A motor of bright positivity chugged away inside her, dictating everything she said.

"Did you and Shayla first meet here, at the store?" I asked.

"Yes. You see, I don't drink. I mean, sometimes I do, like I'll have a glass of champagne on New Year's Eve or whatever, but I have goals and try to avoid bad habits. Even though Jessica and Shayla had the ex-Mormon thing to bond over, Jessica likes going out to bars sometimes. Shayla couldn't be around that because of her background, you know?"

"We heard Shalya was on the wagon," Richie said.

"I think one of the main reasons she and I got along was

because she needed a sober buddy. That can be hard to find." Richie would take a month off here and there to dry out, and I would take a week off every now and again, but no drinking ever was unthinkable for me, and probably for Richie too. "Do you think Shayla might be with her ex-boyfriend?"

"We're trying to find that out," I said.

"Why do you ask about the ex?" Richie asked.

"He's a messed-up dude."

"How do you mean?"

"He was abusive. He would hit Shayla."

"Was this piece of shit in the Armenian Mafia?" Richie's face was red with anger.

He scared Alexis a little. "I don't know. But that was the rumor. If I brought it up around Shayla, she always changed the subject. I did see him smack her."

"You actually met Arman?" I asked.

"I saw him twice, met him once."

"Tell us about both. Start at the beginning."

"The first was a while ago, when I had just started working here. Shayla had only been here for a short while before me. They'd been broken up for weeks and she still needed to drop off the last of Arman's things. Shayla didn't want to do this alone, and she didn't want to go by his place, so I told her I would drive her by his work."

"Where did he work?"

"At a used car lot on Brand in Glendale. I drove Shayla over there. At the time we arrived, Arman was off and the lot was closed, but he was still there. Shayla got out of the car to give him the box. They had words, and Arman smacked her. I pulled Shayla away, and we drove off. I kept pushing Shayla to press charges on him for assault, but she said she just wanted to put everything behind her."

"The lot on Brand, would you be able to spot it again?" Richie asked.

"I think so."

I said, "Tell us about the second time you saw Arman."

"It was about a month ago. Shayla and I had a Sunday brunch date at Chipmunk, that trendy new spot in Silver Lake. I was under the impression that it was just going to be the two of us, but Arman showed up. She acted like she'd invited him and told me about it, but she hadn't. It seemed like there was serious drama between them she didn't want me to know about."

"Was Shayla back on drugs?" Richie asked.

"It didn't seem like it, but maybe."

I took out my phone and pulled up the Facebook page of the Arman I'd found earlier. Arman Donabedian. I showed it to Alexis. "That him?"

"Yep. That's him."

I showed the picture to Richie.

"What about this creepy Mormon man who came in here?" I asked.

"Shayla never brought it up to me. This was after that awkward brunch, and I think she was embarrassed that I knew her ex was back in her life, so she pulled away. For the most part, she didn't say much to me about her Mormon background, just that she was never going back."

We both thanked Alexis. She left, and I closed the door behind her.

"You're already onto this Armenian fuck, and you don't tell me?" Richie said.

"I wasn't sure. Until now, it was just a guy named Arman. I also know how you feel about Armenians and I didn't want to bring it up too soon just because I knew you wouldn't like the look of the guy."

"Arman hit Shayla. I don't like anything about him," Richie said. "If Armenian Dominance did something to this girl, then this case is going to get heavy."

"We'll pursue every lead," I said. "Let's see what the last girl has to say."

EVETTE WAS DRESSED in the same business-friendly style as the other two girls, but before she said a word, I could tell she was born and raised in L.A. Evette was a stone-cold chola. It was how they carried themselves. Not really with an added confidence, but more of an accelerated instinct. Native Angeleno cholas processed their surroundings faster.

"I know you?" Richie asked her.

I couldn't tell if Richie really recognized her or was playing some angle.

"I don't think so," Evette said.

"Where're you from?"

"East Los."

"How'd you start working here?" Richie said, like he knew she didn't belong.

There were quite a few attractive cholas who worked at our Namaste Mart, and Richie had slept with at least a quarter of them. This included the ones with boyfriends and husbands. Richie is the chola whisperer.

"I was trying to find a nice place to buy some bras, but most bra stores are shit," she said. "Eventually, my homegirl told me about this spot. I remembered Joan from *Martians.* I first saw that movie a long time ago and let me tell you, I didn't even know that bitch was white. I thought she really was Latina. I thought, if she's got the skills to fool me like that, she's got my respect. I saved up some money, bras are expensive here, then I came in to buy myself one. On that first trip at this location, which was the only location back then, I ran into Joan. We started talking, and she gave me an application on the spot. That was five years ago. By now, I've worked for Joan longer than anyone else in the company."

"Some people get offended Joan played that part in *Martians,*" I said, remembering an article I read online. "They say she did brownface."

"I don't care. Joan did East L.A. homegirls right in that movie. Joan is a down-ass bitch!"

"You ever meet Shayla's boyfriend?" I asked.

"That creepy ass Armo? Yo, that fool's definitely AD."

"How come you say that?"

"I can spot 'em. Always seen 'em around. He fucks with Hollywood Sam. At least that's what I heard."

If Arman really was AD, why stand outside in the hot sun selling cars in Glendale every day? He didn't look anything like the guys who stabbed Richie. "Do you think he's got anything to do with Shayla's disappearance?" I asked.

"I don't know. How would I?"

"What about this old Mormon man that came in?"

"Shayla told me that this weird dude came in the store."

"Weird how?"

"Like one of those creepy old Mormon dudes she and Jessica grew up around."

"What else did she say?"

"That he kept on saying Mormon things. I don't remember. I grew up Catholic, you know? I do remember that she said he was wearing expensive clothes and a cowboy hat and that he said something about how he was a Mormon and he lived in a place where it was okay for him to have more than one wife."

"That's quite a coincidence, this particular guy showing up to speak with Shayla."

"I know, right? It's *weird*."

"What else happened?"

"She said he kept looking around the bras, checking the prices, and asking her what she thought about them. He kept on wanting her to say if she liked the bra or not like he was thinking about buying it for her or something."

"Is that common?" Richie asked. "Guys coming in here for their women?"

"It happens, but it's not that common. More often, men come in and buy gift certificates so their ladies can come back and pick out what they like themselves."

"Did Shayla say what this man's name was?"

"I don't think so."

JOAN PULLED UP the site that led to the security feed and put in the code only she knew. She went through dates, there at her desk.

Evette clarified that the encounter she witnessed happened exactly four days before Shayla disappeared, making it exactly twelve days prior. Joan was fast-forwarding through the black-and-white footage from the camera above the front door, slowing down whenever a new customer came in.

Richie was going along in pursuing this lead, but clearly wasn't buying it. He wanted to chase Arman. To Richie, this whole Mormon thing was a distraction.

"Here." Joan waved us over.

We walked around her desk. She hit play. It was black-and-white digital footage. There was Shayla. Her face was to the camera. She was looking at a taller man. He wore a cowboy hat. His back was to the camera.

Richie huffed. "We can't even see him."

"Relax," Joan said. "He might turn around. He's got to leave."

Shalya and the man talked for a long time. Eventually, he turned to the side. He was old, with white hair and a beard. His hat went low. He pointed at a few different bras. Shayla packaged them in boxes. The man bought them and walked away. He kept his head down. The hat blocked his face. Other than his general age, there wasn't much to go on.

SIX

I LEFT THE MILK cooler and was walking through the frozen aisle to clock out when I noticed Drea de Matteo standing in the aisle. I passed her, letting her browse the frozen fish in peace. A different customer blocked my path. She was white, wrinkled, with dyed blonde hair and shades.

"Why is fish more expensive than chicken?" she asked.

If this had been an old Russian, I could have gotten away with not answering the question. Old Russians would never snitch to a manager if you were rude. They might find your car and slash your tires, but they would never snitch.

This woman, however, I wouldn't be able to blow off so easily. She knew how to find the manager and complain. If the manager wasn't enough, she might know how to go higher up the chain to corporate.

"Oh, you don't know?"

"I was asking you." She slurred her words. She wore a winter jacket and it was at least ninety degrees out. I wouldn't be surprised if she was shoplifting. It was probably something she could easily afford.

"I want fish, but I want the price of frozen fish to be the same as the price of frozen chicken," she said. Here and now, she was taking a stand.

"The difference in prices has to do with the effort put into the retrieval process."

"The what?" she readjusted her shades to keep them over her eyes.

"*The retrieval process.* If you're going to catch fish, there's a whole process."

Most of the time, it didn't matter what you said to customers, not really, as long as you feigned sincerity.

"Such as?"

"Such as what?"

"What's the process for getting fish?"

"Oh, it's a *whole thing*. You've gotta rent out the boat, you've gotta hire a ship's captain, you've gotta get the fishing poles. It has to be good weather and there's gotta be a crew. Only after all that, then you've got the fish. With chicken, you just get in your car and drive over to the farm. *Boom*. That's it."

She was in a fog. "Oh."

People like this woman didn't know how to politely end conversations like this with the help. "Have a good day," I said.

I passed Drea de Matteo again, who picked up a piece of frozen ahi. We made eye contact. She smiled at me and put the tuna in her cart.

RICHIE'S BRONCO TURNED in off Gardner to pick me up.

"I've been investigating all day," he said after I got in. "I went to some of those NA meetings they hold in the church across the street from Joan's, same ones Shayla used to attend. For a long while, I thought I was wasting my time, but then I hit gold. I found this ex-meth-head girl who knew Shayla. Her name's Saabir and she's been on the wagon four years. She and Shayla were friendly. Saabir's Armenian and from Glendale."

"And?"

"Saabir met Arman once. From the neighborhood, she knew who he was, that Arman was in the AD and worked at the New Millennium Honda dealership on Brand. I pulled up the Facebook picture. She confirmed it's the same guy. Said one time Arman came by the church after her and Shayla's NA meeting and they got in a big argument. Saabir said it stuck out to her because she already knew this Arman was mobbed up. This was a while back, before Shayla and Arman broke up the first time."

"Most of this sounds like what we already know."

"Except for the confirmed twenty on Arman's employment."

"You want to go over there?"

"Talking to Arman is our best move."

"All right." I suppressed my reluctance. Dealing with some asshole customer in the frozen aisle suddenly didn't seem like such a pain in the ass. "Let's go to Glendale."

"You got the piece?"

It was in my backpack, encased in a holster and next to a six-pack of Harkening Back Lager I'd bought after clocking out. "I've got it."

RICHIE PULLED INTO the lot of New Millennium Honda. There were rows of cars, most of them used. Weather-beaten signs on poles said *Certified Pre-owned* in a tacky gold font. At the back of the lot, a glassed-in showroom was inside a large two-story building. I saw two young Armenians, both with neck tattoos, sitting in an old Honda. Spotters. This lot wasn't right.

"We'll just be two guys looking to buy a car from Arman," Richie said.

I removed the six-pack and put it on the floor behind me. The gun would stay in my backpack. "Let's be sure to keep this about finding Shayla, and not about your mercurial history with the Armenian American diaspora, all right?"

"*Ohh*! Did I say it was about me and the diaspora? Did I?"

We stepped out of the car, and a female employee approached. She had a dark complexion, long black hair, far-too-long fake lashes, and was soaked in a tacky perfume that smelled like mothballs and fruitcakes. Her name tag said Anoush.

"Can I help you boys?"

"Is Arman working today?" Richie asked.

"He is." Anoush smiled, then made a case for her being the one to help us. She wanted the sale for herself. We insisted on Arman.

Anoush went in, and we waited. Then a man walked out. He had a unibrow and wore an opulent crucifix around his neck. His face matched the Facebook photo.

"You asked for me?"

"Oh my God, it's Arman" Richie said, pretending to be wildly effeminate. Richie was great with impressions and voices. I'd seen him do them at the store and on stage. "We were at the Abbey last week and this... friend of ours said we should buy a car from you. We decided to come this way." Richie looked my way. "Isn't that right, babe?"

I had no idea Richie was going to turn this part of our case into a homophobic skit from an '80s movie, and I couldn't come up with a character, so I decided to just play myself.

"Um, yes."

"Who recommended me?"

"Oh, I can't remember her name," Richie said, then launched into a rambling speech about the Abbey and partying with other gay friends in West Hollywood. Arman, who also wanted a sale, was noticeably uncomfortable and off guard.

"You two have me confused with someone else."

"Oh, you aren't the only Arman that works here at New Millennium Honda?" Richie said. "Because I think we came here for you."

Arman swallowed. "What kind of car were you interested in?"

Richie began another rambling speech about which cars were the sexiest.

I scanned the lot. Through the glass in the showroom, I saw Anoush talking to two other big guys in tracksuits. A box truck was parked behind the building and it was being unloaded.

I focused back on Arman. What did Shayla see in this guy?

"That's quite a crucifix," I said. "Doesn't Jesus get heavy around your neck, hauling him around like that all day?"

"You trying to say something about my cross, bro?"

Richie squealed. "Arman, can you believe my lover here rejects our Lord and Savior Jesus Christ? Isn't that a knee-slapper?" Richie slapped his own knee, back and forth.

Arman looked at me. "You should let Jesus into your heart." He pointed to the clouds, like Jesus was watching us now. "Might bring some happiness into your life."

"You live a happy life, Arman?"

"Life's got ups and downs. Being able to buy yourself one of our cars, like this certified 2006 Mazda, that's called being blessed."

"Are you married?" Richie asked. "Even if it was legal, this little slut Adam won't just pop the question."

"No, I'm not married."

Richie slapped my shoulder. "Now I remember who told us about Arman. It was the cute blonde girl with the really big boobs." Richie held both hands out in front of his chest.

"Right," I said, glad to be getting to the point. "What was her name?"

"Shannon?"

"No, that wasn't it," I said.

"Sandy?"

"Not Sandy."

Richie snapped his fingers. "Shayla."

"That was it."

Arman froze. "So you two don't want to buy a car at all, do you?"

"Fuck selling cars, Arman," I said. "You should become a detective."

Richie stepped forward. "What's with the scared look on your face? You do know a girl named Shayla, don't you?"

"Are you here because of her?"

"Shayla's been hard to find this past week or so." Richie was using his normal voice. "We'd like to see her. Do you know where she is?"

The front door of the showroom opened. The two big guys in tracksuits came out. One waved Arman their way. "I can't help you two," he said. "You should leave. Now."

He walked away fast, toward the big guys.

"That's okay," Richie said, bringing his flamboyant voice back. "We'll see you soon."

"DIDN'T YOU SEE that mook's face? He was guilty."

We were at Chuy's Tacos on Glendale Boulevard, sitting at an outdoor table close to the street. I coated everything in El Yucateco. "If we had handled it how we normally question people, we could have found out more."

"You think he would have given us anything if we just walked up to him at work and asked him, 'Excuse me, Mr. Armo, did you kidnap Shayla? Or kill her?' And besides, you denigrating the cross around his neck was what really pissed him off."

"I'm just saying that now we're burnt. If either of us tries to go anywhere near that place again, those guys will be on high alert and we'll get nothing."

"Still, Arman had a guilty face. Don't tell me you didn't see it."

"Maybe. Until seeing it for myself, I wasn't sure Arman even really was AD. I still don't know for sure. He struck me as too religious to be a real gangster. But that lot looked shady as fuck. Maybe his reaction was about his sensitivity to that."

"Yeah, and maybe not."

"We still need to learn more." I finished my last taco.

"What do we do next? You gonna call up that Jessica broad, find out what she wasn't telling us the first time around?"

"For now, I say we focus on surveilling the dealership, quietly and from a distance. I'll call her when the time is right."

Richie pointed toward Brand, back the way we'd come. "You want to go back now?"

"Not tonight. After work tomorrow, we can come back with our binoculars and sit on the place from a distance. It'd be helpful if we could get ourselves another car, one those guys wouldn't be able to spot."

"This Plenty of Fish broad I've been banging this week drives a nice BMW," Richie said. "She might let us borrow it."

SEVEN

I STARTED ON the half hour today, at eleven thirty. Usually, when you start a shift on the half hour, a manager would tell you to face some section of the store, which means to pull all the product that's been shopped up to the front of the shelves so it all looks full and orderly.

I was facing the cereal when I overheard two women, both on separate shopping trips, talking behind me. Both were pretty blondes in their midtwenties. At first, I pegged them as former showbiz kids. Both had a manic and desperate energy to their voices which inspired me to eavesdrop.

"I'm proud of you for getting out, but I have to ask... Have you been allowed to speak with your family yet?"

"I've tried. But since I dashed, they aren't permitted. I wish I would have known that was the rule before I left. I mean, I'm glad I left..."

"I am too. You *soo* did the right thing, Leslie. You are like, number one girl boss."

"I just didn't know I was going to be cut off from my family."

Dashed. So they were ex-Beyonders.

Beyondism is the famous cult started in the late '50s by the science fiction writer H. Moses Randolph. Rank and file Beyonders, who all wear what look like purple flight-attendant uniforms, are sometimes permitted to leave their church posts throughout Los Angeles for brief shopping trips to various Namaste Mart locations. These two, however, were dressed in plainclothes T-shirts and jeans. Both had dashed. This is the church's official term for leaving without proper authorization.

I listened to them share over their shopping carts about the emotional toll of being separated from their families. If Beyonders have a family member who dashes, those current Beyonders are obligated to cut off the dashed family members entirely.

I wondered if any current members might come in. If so, it was the obligation of current members in good standing to openly harass the ex-members. This was H. Moses Randolph's will, something he'd clarified without ambiguity in the era before the Church of the Beyond received official tax-exempt status from the IRS.

I kept on facing the shelves, moving on to the nuts and dried fruit. A few customers asked me some questions, then at the start of the noon hour, I went to relieve Shanice on register. I began ringing up customers and periodically looked over to see how things were going with the two ladies. They were still chatting. I was happy they got out.

Then two current Beyonders walked in.

Oh shit.

I wanted to help. But what could I do? Jose, the manager currently in charge of the front end, wouldn't have any idea what the fuck I was talking about if I tried to explain my concerns.

Maybe it would be nothing.

I watched closely.

The two ex-Beyonders saw the two current Beyonders. The two ex-Beyonders split apart quickly. They abandoned their carts. They walked in opposite directions, fast.

The little old Russian woman in my line got upset about how slowly I was ringing up her cart full of kefir and organic sour cream. "Work faster!" she shouted, waving her EBT card in my face.

One of the ex-Beyonders, the one named Leslie, stopped Flaco, currently stocking the bananas. They were too far away for me to hear, but I watched them, all while moving on to the stack of chocolate blocks in the back of the old lady's cart. Flaco shook his head. Leslie carefully made her way out the front door without buying anything. I lost track of the two other Beyonders.

My coworker John the Juggler, who had no customers on his register, showed up to help me bag. Before getting hired by Namaste Mart, John had worked as a juggler at the circus. He noticed I was having a hard time, and he wanted to entertain me. So he juggled the produce of all my customers before putting it in the bags for them.

The two current Beyonders came through my lane. Both had their little yellow Post-it notes. When Beyonders are given their short window of freedom to go grocery shopping, they are given a Post-it note of items to buy from a church superior. They may only purchase items on the list. Their transaction concluded and the Beyonders left the store. If they'd been aware of the two dashers, they didn't show it.

THE HOUR PASSED, and I was relieved on register.

I found Flaco.

"'Sup, fool?"

"Remember that white lady who stopped you?"

"By the bananas?"

"Yeah. Her."

"Crazy ass lady."

"What'd she ask?"

"If there was a back door she could sneak out of."

"What'd you say?"

"I told that bitch fuck no."

I went to work in the milk cooler, my section.

I was in the cooler, backfilling the yogurt, when Richie stepped in. He often stepped back to the cooler to bullshit with me or Fabian, the cooler section leader.

"I need you to bring the piece over after work," he said.

"Why?"

"Someone's watching my house. Someone Armenian."

WE STOOD BY the front wall of the store, under the *Eat, Love, Namaste* sign. Richie ashed his cigarette into an empty Gatorade bottle.

"He was in a used Monte Carlo, cruising by over and over and then just watching my place. I even scoped him through my binoculars," Richie said. "He was an Armenian."

"How could you tell?"

"Because I know Armenians." He sounded offended I would doubt his expertise.

"How would the car guys from Glendale know where you live? You think someone was tailing us?"

"Maybe. They had spotters on the lot. They were unloading swag. They have to keep track of who comes and goes."

It wasn't impossible. "Maybe it's unrelated to our case?"

"It's not unrelated, Minor-man."

We heard shouting, then a hard, metallic noise. A homeless guy was using a metal rod to beat the side of a car parked in our lot. Richie ran over and I followed.

This guy, wiry, sunburnt, and obviously high, had been showing up at our parking lot and damaging our customers' cars for months. The LAPD had been called many times but he always skipped before they showed. His clothes weren't as dirty as the average homeless person you saw around West Hollywood. He had a cell phone. I'd seen him charging it at the Baja Fresh on La Brea. The evidence I saw pointed to him being just a lazy asshole who liked damaging random cars whenever he did drugs.

Richie threw his Gatorade bottle at the guy's head. It connected and bounced. The plastic split open. Wet cigarette ash stained the guy's neck and face.

"Stop that shit!"

The guy determined a fight wasn't worth it. He turned to leave.

"Wait!"

He turned back around.

"Put the fucking bar down. Now."

It clanged on the pavement.

"Now *fuck off*. And don't let me see you back here again."

He ran off. Richie looked at me. "Just bring the gun over when I'm off."

I ARRIVED ON my bike at Richie's on Lexington. It was

eleven thirty. I'd come up the back way like Richie asked, up Kingsley. According to Richie, the Armenian was back, as he'd predicted, and he didn't want my arrival to be spotted.

I carried my bike in through his small yard and knocked on the back door. Richie answered the door shirtless. He looked around the darkened street.

"Anybody see you?"

"I don't think so."

"You bring the piece?"

"It's in the bag."

I propped my bike against the wall of his kitchen. I'd wanted to come over earlier, but Richie insisted I not show up until eleven thirty. In the living room, I saw why. Sitting on Richie's broken futon was an enormous black prostitute in a blonde wig. She wore a tight miniskirt made of pink netting. Her bra and panties were plainly visible underneath. She was struggling to put her frayed pink pumps back on her feet.

"Minor-man, this is Paloma." Richie looked at Paloma. "That's my buddy Adam. He writes books. This guy's a fucking literary genius."

"Actually, I haven't started my debut novel yet."

"My nigga, you need to write a book like *The Secret.*" Paloma smelled like bubble gum and ashtrays. "That shit would make *mad bank.*" She looked me over. "You two don't seem like you'd be friends."

"Yeah, we get that a lot."

Richie saw Paloma out the back way.

When he was back, I said, "It's so serious we need the gun but you can still pay for pussy to come over?"

"What do you want from me? Paloma may not be everything in the looks department but she knows what she's doing, *believe me.*" He put his shirt on, then walked to the front window. The blinds were closed, but he peeked out. "We need to make this motherfucker talk."

"What's your plan, just shoot him? Evette said Arman is with

Hollywood Sam."

Richie groaned. "Arman doesn't run with Hollywood Sam. I'm just going to point it at him and scare him so we can find out what he knows. If he sees it in his face, he'll talk."

"There has to be another way."

"What other way?"

I thought. Richie's binoculars sat on the front windowsill, facing Lexington. I pointed at them. "You said you got a good look?"

"Yeah. He's driving a used Monte Carlo."

"You get his plates?"

Richie got his joke notepad and read the plate to me from the most recent page.

I got out my phone and called our coworker Felix.

Felix was the shot caller of Kingsley gang, one of the many Hollywood gangs under the umbrella of La Eme, the all-powerful Mexican Mafia. If the guy parked outside in the Monte Carlo was an AD soldier as Richie suspected, then he was in Kingsley territory.

Felix lived just a few blocks away. His cousin Rocio worked at the DMV and illegally sold DMV info for a price. We'd gone to her before. If Felix brought her the customer, Rocio always went along.

"Yo," Felix said.

"I've got a fresh request."

"Don't trip. I'll hit you back." This meant that he would hang up and call me from a fresh burner. It took less than a minute.

"What'chu need, homie?"

"Can Rocio run a number? It's on an old Monte Carlo."

"This for Damien's Mom? Private Lopez?"

"I can't talk about clients."

"Fool, you two ain't got a license."

Richie started shadowboxing.

I said, "We've still got a code."

"You still paying? 'Cause this shit ain't for free."

"Same as last time?" Last time I'd paid Felix three hundred. On this job, three hundred wasn't too steep and I'd hopefully appease Richie by taking it out of my end.

"Órale, homie."

"You got a pen?"

"Go ahead."

I read him the number.

"Should have this for you by tomorrow."

"Good. This car's watching Richie's house. He thinks it's the Armenians."

"Oh damn." Felix knew the stabbing story. "That fool Richie's about to go wild?"

"He sure as shit wants to. I want him to know who we're up against before he does. You get that info, call me here, right away."

"Word. You work tomorrow?"

"Got another mid. You?"

"I'm in early, but I'll pop out real quick and hit you up on a new burner with whatever Rocio has for me."

"Thanks, man."

I hung up and told Richie.

"I don't like just sitting here and waiting," he said.

"I brought the gun. You had a hooker over. That suggests to me you aren't too worried about an immediate ambush."

"That doesn't mean I know for sure one's not coming."

"So I'll stay and help you if something happens. We'll keep the gun close."

He shrugged. "You want a beer?"

"Sure."

Richie went to the fridge, got two Bud Lights, and brought them back.

We opened them. Richie put in one of his old *Sopranos* DVDs. We started watching.

"I forgot to tell you that Drea de Matteo was in the store."

He sat up. "You're just telling me this now? *When*?"

In 1998, when Richie was thirteen, he'd appeared as an extra on season one of *The Sopranos.* The experience had first gotten him interested in show business.

"When you were off yesterday."

He was amazed. "What was she doing?"

"Shopping for frozen fish."

"Frozen fish... She look good?"

"Yeah. Better than on TV, which is rare. She looked kind of like a flamingo."

"A flamingo? Is that good?"

"Yeah. A flamingo's good."

EIGHT

I WOKE AND put on my glasses. Sunlight poured through the window and it already smelled like morning. Richie was up and lifting free weights. "Our friend still outside?"

He moved on to the pull-up bar in his bedroom doorway. "He left sometime in the night."

"Got any coffee?"

"There's Red Bulls in the fridge."

I cracked open a can. "Joan said our first update about our progress should come tomorrow. So far, we don't have much."

"You should call the redhead."

"I'll see if I can meet up with her sometime later. I'll bet she just didn't feel comfortable enough talking at her work."

"Jessica wants the hard D from the Minor-man. She gets that, she's going to give up whatever we need." Richie moved on to push-up sets.

My phone rang. It was a number my phone didn't recognize.

"Hello?"

"It's me, fool," Felix said.

I grabbed Richie's joke pad and pen. The maroon '88 Monte Carlo was registered to a woman named Janet Markarian, who lived on Vassar in Glendale. I told Felix I would see him later at work, when he would get his money. Then I hung up and told Richie.

"All right, now we're finally getting somewhere. When this motherfucker comes back tonight, we'll jump his ass."

"How does this mean we do that?"

"I thought he was an Armenian and he is one."

"It's a *woman's name.* You live by Little Armenia. L.A.'s got the biggest Armenian population in the country. He could have been waiting for a friend."

"Don't be naïve."

"I'm not, we just need more to go on."

"I waited like you asked. We can't keep stalling."

I put on my backpack, went to the kitchen, and got my bike. "I've got to go home, get ready for work, then stop by the bank to pay Felix."

"If he comes back tonight, we're jumping his ass."

"We'll see," I said.

AT THE LOCKERS, I slipped Felix his three hundred in cash.

"Anytime, fool," he said.

I cursed myself for spending so much on nothing. Then I walked out to the demo station, now being run by Roberto. The free sample items on display today were our frozen vegetable spring egg rolls. As I filled a small paper cup of demo coffee, I saw Roberto pouring fresh figs into a bowl. "New supplier," he said. "How's your guy's case going?"

"Someplace dangerous." Across the store, Richie placed a huge rack of lamb into an old Russian lady's cart when she wasn't looking. This was one of his most reliable go-to gags. He loved watching when it came time to pay at the register to see if they noticed the extra items they hadn't put there. He would howl if they ended up paying for the stuff he planted. "Richie's moving like a freight train, right at the trouble."

"You can't really control a guy like Richie. Sometimes it's best to let him just run wild. At least, that's my philosophy whenever he and I go out and get fucked up." Roberto held up the bowl of figs for me to try. I picked one.

"What's that?" a deep-voiced customer said.

He was a tall, broad-shouldered man with the face of a mastiff. His hair was long, down to his waist. He wore a beard and a suit. I looked down and saw he was wearing cowboy boots. His outfit didn't seem made from some overpriced Echo Park fashion shop. It looked legitimately old. He held a blue shopping basket. It was full of a few dry produce items and some refrigerated steaks. He leaned over the glass, staring at the artichokes.

"They're figs," Roberto said.

"Are figs considered an aphrodisiac?"

Roberto looked at me for help.

"I think I read that in a D.H. Lawrence novel," I said, eating mine.

"And you give this out here for free?"

"No man, it's for product knowledge," Roberto said. "It's only for the crew. I'm about to take it back to the break room right now. But you can totally try one if you want. Here." He held the bowl out for him.

The man pulled back. "The things you encounter in this Gomorrah," he said, and walked to the express lane.

DOMINIQUE HAD PURCHASED two beefsteak tomatoes, and I carried them for her in a green produce bag. As she walked to her car, I kept just behind her, how she liked it.

Dominique was an old-school L.A. celebrity who first came to prominence in the '80s after a series of billboards featuring images of her posing suggestively were put up all across L.A. I remembered seeing them in the backgrounds of movies I'd watched as a kid. She was the first influencer and she would still drive around L.A. in her baby-blue Maserati and hustle for herself. She was a regular customer at our location.

Dominique was old now, in her late sixties, but she still dressed the same way she did in 1984. Her breasts were disturbingly large and covered in dozens of thin blue and red varicose veins. They used to be quite a distraction, but by that point, I usually managed to ignore them.

Sure, Dominique was a pain in the ass. I was annoyed with her at first, like the rest of the crew. But I began to admire how unapologetically herself she was willing to be.

I would always offer to do her carryouts and sometimes, to show her appreciation, she would gift me merch, like a poster she imprinted with a red lipstick kiss or a blue T-shirt with her name on it.

About half the time she came in, Dominique had an intern

with her. Her interns were creepy little mouth breathers who worshipped her unconditionally. The position of assisting Dominique had a high turnover rate. You rarely saw her with the same mouth breather twice. Today she was alone, so she definitely needed a carryout for her two tomatoes.

She opened her Maserati door, took the tomatoes from me, and put them on the passenger seat. While she was inside, she opened her glove box and rifled around. I sighed. It was 6 p.m. and still over 90 degrees. She came out with a flyer, which she handed to me.

It said *Dominique's Art Show*. The address was a bar on Wilcox in Hollywood.

"What's this?"

"I'll be revealing all of my paintings. You should come."

I'd seen a few examples of her paintings online. They were crude, childlike images of Dominique naked, minus all the veins. All those iconic billboards were paid for by her wealthy husband, but he had died recently and she was apparently trying to smoke out a fresh one.

I held up the flyer. "I'll come in the T-shirt you gave me."

She giggled, blew me a kiss, and drove off.

It was my break time. I stood against the wall and took out my phone. I'd been psyching myself up for the past hour while on register. I made the call.

"Mr. Namaste Mart," Jessica said. "Any news?"

"I was hoping we could meet somewhere and talk."

"Oh. What did you have in mind?"

"I'm at my job for a couple more hours. Would you want to meet at a bar? Tonight?"

"How about Dempsey's? Eight?"

"That works." Dempsey's was a bar on Hollywood, just around the corner from the Namaste Mart on Vine. "Jessica?"

"Yes?"

"I do have questions about Shayla, but I also just want to see you."

"I was hoping you would call."

I LOCKED MY bike up a block from the bar. The sidewalk of Hollywood Boulevard was littered with empty neon-colored Buzzballz and a nearby bum was passed out face down on Reese Witherspoon's star. At the front door, I showed the bouncer my ID and ordered a Negroni. The gun was still in my backpack. I found a table on the second floor and texted Jessica my location.

There was a text from Richie. It was eight minutes old.

Open mic tonight. Should be done in an hour. Going after the Armenian then. Strike Team, baby!

Goddamn it, Richie.

Strike Team was a reference to the FX series *The Shield.* The Strike Team was an aggressive anti-gang unit run by Vic Mackey, played by Michael Chiklis. They were dirty, but Richie and I thought they were badasses. They often clashed with the Armenian Mafia.

Jessica arrived in a tight-fitting silk shirt that accentuated her contours. Her hair was down and flowing, and she wore red lipstick. We hugged. She smelled like cinnamon and sandalwood. I offered to buy her a drink but she insisted on getting herself one. I held our seats. She came back with a vodka tonic. I saw stunning women every day in Los Angeles, but Jessica had me by the throat.

"You ever come here with Shayla?"

"Never. I've struggled with mental health issues, but never addiction. I'm lucky in that regard. I've always been able to have a drink or two and just stop." She took a sip. "After you guys left yesterday, I read about that girl you saved last year. What a terrifying story." She leaned forward, pressing her soft chest against my arm. "You don't think some maniac has Shayla, do you?"

"We've got no evidence of that so far... When I asked you at the end of our interview if there was anything else, you said no, but I got a sense there actually was."

"I must have been pretty obvious."

"You can tell me." I touched her hand. "Anything helps."

"Before Shayla disappeared, I overheard a phone call she took."

She let me keep my hand where it was. "At work?"

"Yes. I wasn't trying to eavesdrop. She was talking to Arman."

"You're sure it was him?"

"Shayla was going to meet a man somewhere. He'd invited her to go hiking and Arman didn't want her to go. They argued about it. From her voice, Arman must have been mad."

"Hiking where?"

"Griffith Park. The trail that starts at the Observatory. Shayla liked going to that ledge and putting quarters into the old telescopes."

"What man was she meeting?"

"I don't know. But I'm pretty sure it was someone Mormon."

"Why would Jessica, who would rather die than become a Mormon again, want to go hiking with a Mormon?"

"It was strange. Some customers came in and I never brought it up. Why was she having this private conversation in a place where I could have heard? Did she know I might be listening? Did she want me to hear?"

"So Arman knew where she was meeting this guy... How long was this conversation before Jessica disappeared?"

"The night before."

"Why hold this back from us?" My tone was a little retributive.

She pulled her hand away. "I didn't know what it meant. I still don't. I hoped to talk to you about it alone, away from your friend. He... doesn't seem nice."

"Richie? He's just misunderstood."

"I understand guys like him just fine. With you, I could sense something so familiar."

"I escaped a religion too."

"Yes. I could tell. You know how bad it was... but you have to know it's not all bad. I know you won't judge. You know Mormonism can be a good thing for some people. If that conversation I overheard means something, especially if it really is connected to the LDS, I wanted to tell it to someone I can trust."

I sighed. I could have just agreed and moved on. Most people know stating their positions doesn't always work in their best interests and manage to keep quiet.

When my cousin Mary killed herself, I was already an atheist. But as far as Mary knew, I was just as much of a Christian as my family. Maybe, if I'd spoken up about how I really felt, she would have come to me when she needed help, instead of just being judged and told to go to church, which would have been my family's reaction. Maybe, if I hadn't been too afraid to start drama and just been honest, Mary might have called me. I could have helped. She might still be alive. I promised myself at Mary's funeral to never keep quiet on the subject of God again.

From me, Jessica deserved honesty. I said, "I think the most charitable thing you could say about any modern-day Mormon is that they're being conned."

"What?"

"Joseph Smith was a known forger and fraud. The guy was a grave robber. His whole religion is bullshit and can't be excused by the charitable works of its members. Sure, Mormons may have pulled away from many of his more insane beliefs, but even in its most benign forms, the people who believe it are wasting their lives."

"People are able to practice whatever religion they want and they don't need to be judged by you for it." She already hated me. I could see it in her eyes.

"People are legally free to do that, despite the fact that all sorts of religions directly promote the violations of various laws. They aren't legally free to escape judgment. This is my opinion, and I'm allowed to express it. If you knew about this phone call, you should have told us right away because religious people are capable of all sorts of evil." I stood. There was no need to drag this out any longer. "Thank you for telling me what you did. It's helpful. I've got to get going now."

On my way out, I saw a vacant pretty-boy type notice Jessica was now alone. He made his move. Good luck, dude.

I stepped outside feeling hollow. Before unlocking my bike, I checked my phone. There was a new text from Richie. It was two minutes old:

Open mic canceled. Going home now. Then you know what.

A minute later:

Strike Team, baby!

NINE

I PEDALED TO Richie's and arrived coated in sweat. I'd made great time. I got off my bike and kept low. There was Richie, in the dark. He was crouched behind a parked car on the south side of the street. I craned my neck up and saw the Monte Carlo parked close to where it was the night before. I wasn't too late.

I took off my backpack and removed the MR73. Then I rushed up the sidewalk in a crouch with the gun at my side. I hissed Richie's name. He turned. I pointed toward the nearest alley. He nodded and we both met down there.

"I don't want to hear anything else about holding back," Richie said. "This fuck ain't watching your place, he's watching mine. This ends tonight."

"I hear you."

"The reason I got on his radar is because we took that drive over to Glendale and rattled Arman. I'm going to make him say it."

"I'm not saying you're wrong." I held up the MR73, to remind him I'd brought it to support him. "But what if this really is connected to Hollywood Sam?"

"You ever hear that Hollywood Sam likes to roofie chicks and rape them?"

"I hadn't," I said, surprised by this curveball. "Did you?"

"Maybe it is Sam who's behind this. If it is, how do we know he doesn't have Shayla chained up in some basement right now? You spent three hundred dollars to hear what I already told you for free. We need to move."

I held out the gun for Richie to take from my hand. My heart beat fast. "I don't want to shoot anybody."

"Better for you to keep it," he said, shaking his head. "Give it to me and I'll probably kill the fuck. Just make sure he can see the gun. It's going to scare him. But you need to shoot him, just shoot him in the leg."

I WALKED DOWN the alley and looped around. I kept the gun at my side, moving slowly through the street, toward the back of the Monte Carlo. I could see the back of the Armenian's head as he sat there in the dark.

Richie went inside and put on a hooded sweatshirt. He stood in the shadows up the block. A bat was at his side. I was ready, so I waved to him.

Head low, Richie walked toward the car.

I started from the other direction.

Richie got close. He raised the bat and slammed the tip of it into the driver's side window. A million tiny bits of glass flew.

Richie reached in and grabbed him by his neck. The man pushed open the driver's side door, hitting Richie in his side. Richie's bat rolled away. The man got out of the car. He was heavyset, bald, and wore a goatee. Richie picked up the bat and jabbed it hard into the base of his neck. He screamed. He turned and slammed Richie into the Monte Carlo.

I stepped closer with the gun raised. He and Richie were too tangled up. They fought more. The man wouldn't submit. He looked strong for being so out of shape.

Richie got the bat pressed into his throat and backed the Armenian against the side of his own car. "Why the fuck you watching my house?"

"Fuck you."

Richie kneed him in the balls.

"Talk!"

He coughed. "I said fuck you!"

"Talk!" I said, stepping closer.

He turned my way. He saw the gun and freaked. A rush of adrenaline hit him. He pushed Richie away and ran.

I fired once into the sky. "Freeze, you motherfucker, or the next one's in your back."

He froze. He just stood there, panting.

Richie took the bat and wound up for a hard swing. The Armenian screamed again and fell over, giving up.

"Who the fuck sent you here?" Richie said, shaking the tip of the bat in his face. "Was it Arman? Did Armenian Dominance send you to watch my house?"

"Hit me all you want, I'm not talking." He was sweating, and a rank cloud of his BO wafted our way.

Richie patted him down and found a SIG P365 handgun and a knife. He held the SIG under a street light and pointed at scratch marks on the side where the serial number should be.

A random car drove by. Richie used his bat to direct it around the Armenian, who was still lying there. "Someone probably heard that shot," I said.

A RADIO CAR arrived fast. The officers were named Cortez and Jenkins. I'd never met them before, but I'd seen them around Hollywood.

A neighbor had indeed called in the shot, so they were already patrolling the area when we called it in ourselves. They confiscated my MR73 and said it would be returned to me later, if our story checked out. We told them this:

Richie and I were hanging out after work when we heard a man yelling out in the street. He was claiming affiliation with Armenian Dominance and wanting someone to kill. He looked unstable. He waved a gun around. Richie got his bat. I was licensed to carry and had my firearm on me, so the two of us went out to approach him and, after I fired once into the sky, we disarmed the man and performed a citizen's arrest. The glass of the man's driver's side door was smashed in the altercation.

They cuffed the Armenian and put him in their backseat. He wouldn't talk to them any more than he would talk to us. His license said his name was Narek Yeghoyan. Jenkins noticed the filed-off serial number on Yeghoyan's SIG.

Our story was mostly legit. We suppressed our roles as unlicensed PIs. Some cops, especially the ones who remembered Emily Glass, were sympathetic to us.

So far, they were buying our story. It didn't feel like they were planning on charging us with anything. My adrenaline rush had petered out, and I was starting to crave more.

"We're arresting him for possession of a stolen firearm," Cortez said. "Since you claimed he admitted to having connections to the Armenian Mafia, we were required to update two Major Crimes detectives who wanted to know about anybody from that world getting flagged lately. They want to speak to the two of you at Hollywood station."

"Do we have a choice?" I asked.

"The detectives will consider not poking too many holes in your story if you two come down willingly."

"Poking holes in our story?" Richie said.

"Why you withheld being the Grocery Clerk PIs."

WE WAITED IN an interrogation room. It was small, mostly featureless, and smelled like stale donut-shop coffee. An old security camera with a blinking red dot pointed our way.

A male and female detective entered. The woman was Latina, about forty, had curly black hair, and had a face like a sharpened hatchet. The man was about fifteen years older, doughy all around, and looked Italian.

We debated calling our lawyer, Susan, but decided against it.

"Richie Dubs," the Italian said.

"*Ohh*, Ricky Boy. There he is."

Rick Angelis was the Major Crimes detective who'd taken Richie's statement about the stabbing last year. Outside of his job, Angelis was a big stand-up comedy fan. He questioned Richie about his career and craft and even began coming to Richie's shows at the Comedy Store. A true friendship had emerged between them. He knew about our PI work and advertised his willingness to give us a pass, if it was in his power, as long as we stayed out of trouble. Angelis introduced us to his partner, whose name was Escobar.

"We heard about what happened, Dubs," he said. "You can't get away from the Armenians, can you?"

Richie made a comic shrug. "I'm just... naturally drawn to 'em."

Angelis chuckled. "Are you two working something?"

"We are," I said. "Another missing woman."

"What woman?" Escobar asked.

"We're not required to give up that information," Richie said.

"That's if you're an actual private detective, fuckhead," Escobar said. "You two work at a grocery store and you've already lied to the unis."

Angelis held up his hand, telling Escobar to calm down. "Who is the girl?"

"Shalya Ramsey," I said, and told them all the basic facts we knew about Shayla's Mormon past, her disappearance, and how we came to be hired by Joan.

"And?" Escobar said, her tone full of attitude.

"We learned Shayla's abusive ex-boyfriend, Arman Donabedian, is affiliated with AD," Richie said. "He'd been back in her life recently, so we decided to go talk to him at his work, a car lot in Glendale. He clammed up before we got anything concrete."

"Since then, this fucking Narek guy's been sitting outside my house," Richie said. "We decided to confront him, see who sent him and why."

"Confront with a gun?" Escobar said.

"I had the baseball bat," Richie said. "Minor-man had the gun."

"I've got the permit. I already showed the other officers."

"What did Narek say when you confronted him?" Angelis asked.

"After we got him held down, we couldn't get him to talk," Richie said.

"Why'd you lie about all of this to the unis?" Escobar asked.

"We gave all the essentials, just left out some backstory," I said.

Angelis looked at Richie. "You see the Armo who stabbed you anytime lately?"

"I haven't," Richie said. "That's got nothing to do with this."

I said, "LAPD must be investigating Armenian Dominance for something major."

Escobar rolled her eyes. Neither of them denied what I was implying.

"Our agenda is to find Shayla," I said. "That's all. We don't want to get in your way. The sooner we finish our job, the sooner we'll be out of your hair."

"You *won't* be in our hair," Escobar said.

I looked at Angelis. "As I understand it, the Armenians are currently deep into kidnapping. Have you heard about them kidnapping women lately?"

Angelis made a thin smile. He liked me. "You're right, we are investigating AD for something. It's bigger than one missing lingerie salesgirl. We aren't letting anyone foul us up, no matter how great one of their sets is at the Comedy Store." Angelis winked at Richie. "Escobar thinks we should go hard on you two. She even suggested filing charges for making a false statement, but I've convinced her otherwise, on one condition."

"I knew we were pals, Ricky Boy," Richie said. "What's the condition?"

"Stay away from New Millennium Honda and the AD in general. If you find any hard evidence connecting your girl with them, bring it to us. We'll take care of it and use police resources to find her and secure her safely."

I looked at Richie. What choice did we have?

"It's hard backing down. But you guys have the shields. I can do that," Richie said.

"You too?" Angelis looked at me.

"Yes."

"Good. We don't know who your girl is, or where she might be. She's not on our radar." Angelis got up to leave. "We're still talking with Narek. Hopefully he gives us some good information, especially about who told him to watch your house. You'll get your gun back in a few days. If and when I can tell you more, I will. For now, assume you're still being watched and take precautions. If you see anyone watching you, call us so we can take care of it."

I GOT TWO cold Harkening Backs from my fridge and handed one to Richie, then put in my old Special Edition DVD of *Martians.* We watched young Joan kick some Martian ass.

Richie was sleeping on my couch that night. It wasn't safe for him at home.

It was hard to focus on the movie because my mind kept replaying what happened earlier. "I chickened out," I said.

"About what?"

"You said to shoot Narek in the leg. I shot into the sky instead. I was too scared."

Richie made a dismissive wave. "If you'd shot him, we'd still be back at the station."

"I'd like to pretend like I was thinking ahead at that moment, but I wasn't."

"If you're telling the story, especially if it's to a girl, make it seem like everything you did was on purpose."

I took a long drink. "Before I biked over to your place, I met Jessica at Dempsey's."

"Oh yeah?"

"Don't get too excited. I fucked it up."

"How? She was clearly down."

"Even though Jessica's not Mormon anymore, she's still pretty sympathetic to her old faith, in a vague sort of way."

Richie shook his head in shame. Usually, he thought my rants against religion were funny. "One of these days you're going to learn how to not run your mouth at all the wrong moments. A piece of ass like her warrants shutting the fuck up. There's no point in taking a stand in a situation like that."

"We covered other subjects," I said. "Jessica overheard Shayla arguing with Arman on the phone, at the store, the day before she disappeared. Shayla had made a hiking date with someone Mormon and Arman was calling to emotionally voice his displeasure."

"Now we're getting somewhere... So, Arman sees his on-again-off-again thing with Shayla as bullshit, and he's had enough... He thinks she's up to something she shouldn't be with this hiking date, and he ambushes her."

If this was right, I hated to think about whatever came after the ambush. "Jessica said it was in Griffith Park. Plenty of space up there to do something shady without anyone seeing."

"You want to go up there and poke around?"

"We told Angelis we'd stay out of it."

"Just going to the park ain't a crime."

"All right," I said. "Let's go early in the morning, before we meet Joan."

TEN

ABOVE US IN the hills, we saw the solid white dome of the Griffith Observatory. We passed the Greek Theatre. Hikers came and went. I knew my way around this park. Before I totaled my Camry on the 101 and had to bike everywhere, I would regularly hike these trails. We arrived up at the Observatory lot. There were the front steps of the big white building, where Sal Mineo got capped at the end of *Rebel Without a Cause*. We looked down at the hiking trails spreading out across the hills. Three Latinas in tight-fitting exercise pants passed us. One smiled our way. Richie gave me a look that said "now I see why you come here."

An old lady was heading back to her car. "Excuse me, miss," Richie said. I was just behind him.

She had two bright-green L.L. Bean trekking poles, a Prada water bottle strapped to her side, and a Dior fanny pack.

"We were hoping to get some advice from a woman who's obviously an experienced hiker," Richie said.

"I've begun my mornings here with Mother Nature for decades," she said. "What did you need to know?"

They began to chat. Richie faked interest in the trails. The old lady's name was Teri-Ann Sage. "We're hoping to find someone who hikes here, Teri-Ann." He showed her a picture of Shayla we'd printed from her Facebook page. "Her name is Shayla Ramsey."

"Why are you looking for her?"

"We're friends of her employer," I said. "Shayla's suddenly gone missing from work and her boss is hoping someone can verify that she's safe."

She examined the picture. "I don't recognize her, but it's a big park. That attendant on duty now is here most weekdays. He's who I'd ask." She pointed. The parking lot guy who we passed by the entrance sat under a small canopy tent with a Dodgers emblem on it.

I felt the heat rising as we walked over to him. He was a short, goateed Latino who must have weighed two seventy-five. He sat under the tent in a blue tailgating chair. Sweat pooled on his chest, forming the pattern of a moist panda bear. He drank from a metal water bottle. His name tag said Juan and he reminded me of a Mexican Sydney Greenstreet, just not as classy.

"Hey, how ya doing?" Richie said.

"*Excellente.* How are you gentlemen doing on this warm but wonderful morning?" Juan had a manic tone and punctuated his words with an awkward, exclamatory laugh. He took a swig from his water bottle.

"We were looking for a woman who goes hiking here." Richie held out the picture again. "You seen her around here?"

"I see hundreds of people around here every day, and my visual's only on this trail." He barely looked. "Folks come and go on the other trails too."

"We're not asking about the other trails," I said. This guy didn't seem right to me. "She might have been on this one with an Armenian guy. Why not take a closer look?"

Richie held the picture closer. "You could see better if you took your shades off." He said this to Juan as an order.

Juan pulled his shades down. "Looks like just another regular lady to me. No bells of recognition." He blurted out another laugh.

Something was off about this guy, but we decided to let him be for now.

"Have a fine morning, gentlemen," he said as we walked away.

BACK BY RICHIE'S Bronco, I stood still. I tried to think like Shayla. The heat pounded down on my face. I walked to the ledge of the Observatory by the row of coin-operated public telescopes. I reached into my pocket. Normally, I didn't carry much change. Today, I had two quarters. I dropped both into the slot of a machine.

"What now?" Richie said.

"Jessica said Shayla likes to come here." I looked through the viewfinder. "I came here to look through these telescopes the first time I ever visited L.A."

I pulled away from the viewfinder. Waves of heat made the city undulate. Low-flying crows called out. I looked down over the ledge. Below us was a long drop to a steep hill, which sloped down to a trail. On the hill there were empty glass bottles of Modelo and a faded, old Chuck Taylor. There was this *gleam* in some chaparral.

I pointed. "What's that?"

"What's what?"

I kept pointing. "That."

"I can't see anything."

I walked back down to the trail with Richie following me.

Sweat dripped into my glasses and I cleaned them with my shirt. At the bottom, I walked around the bend to the area below the ledge of telescopes, then I looked up and tried to estimate where the gleam came from. I crawled up and moved around. My feet slipped.

There it was. The gleam came from a discarded gold necklace. I picked it up. A pendant depicted a tiny gold 747. It looked like it was crafted by hand. Half a wing was broken off.

I turned. Richie was still down below. He wasn't schlepping his Irish ass up this incline. I scaled back down. A teenager jogged by us.

"What is it?" Richie asked, realizing I'd found something.

From my phone, I pulled up the image. I partly covered the screen with my hand. It was hard to make out in the sun, but Shayla was wearing this same necklace. It was in the picture Joan sent us. I showed Richie.

"*Fuck*," he said, zooming in. "It's even broken the same way."

I GENTLY REVEALED the necklace, holding it across the table. Joan looked at the plane with the broken wing.

We were at Café Figaro on Vermont. When we arrived, Joan

was at a booth in the corner drinking a glass of cold white wine. The sunlight came in through the window and made her crystal stud earrings glisten.

I put the necklace down beside her lyonnaise salad and pulled up the picture. Then I took out my phone, zoomed in on Shayla, and showed her.

Joan put on her reading glasses. "Where'd you find this?"

I told her what we'd learned about Arman, the car lot, and Narek. I withheld Richie's history with Armenian Dominance.

Joan took a drink of wine. She looked worried. "One night, Shayla told me why she wore this. Her people never had any money. Most of the Mormons around her in Bear Creek were on welfare, she said. Kids of a certain age were driven by the adults into the cities and would go digging through dumpsters to look for discarded clothes and food. Shayla found that necklace in a dumpster behind a Kmart in Utah. Her childhood was indentured servitude." She took out an envelope and handed it to Richie. "That's a check for this far. Keep going."

OUT IN THE restaurant lot, Richie finished a call. "Angelis wants us to return to Hollywood Station."

"What for?"

"New developments on Narek. He wouldn't say what."

"Developments?"

"After we showed up at New Millennium, Arman must have gotten suspicious we were onto him about Shayla's disappearance, so he sent Narek to watch my house. Sounds to me like Narek talked, and what he's said has something to do with us."

"Maybe. But from whatever's going on at this dealership, we could have stumbled into a lot of different things."

"If they were going to charge us, they would have already."

"Shit, I've really got to call out from work. We've got too much going on." Richie was off today, but I still had to go in for a closing shift.

"Hold on." Richie took out his phone and made a call. "Hello, this is manager?" he said in a Russian accent. "I tell Mr. Adam I must get seedless pomegranates for father. Father say to me, you go to Namaste Mart and get seedless pomegranates, or you don't get birthday bread. So naturally, I go to store. When at store, no one will help me, but Mr. Adam, a very nice man, he say, we sell pomegranate juice. Pomegranate juice has no seeds. This is what he tells me. At first, I am not sure, because it is my birthday and I am very hungry. But I buy and give to father. He even sing to me Happy Birthday as he gives me one loaf of birthday bread. Anyway, I call to say Mr. Adam is great Namaste Mart man and very handsome. Please give him big capitalist raise now."

Richie hung up.

I *howled.*

He said, "Now you can call out."

I took a moment to breathe, then called the store.

Christy answered. "You know, we just got a customer compliment about you."

"From who?" I tried not to laugh.

"I don't know, one of the Russians. Jose took the call. He said you helped him find the pomegranates. I think that's what it was."

"That's nice." Then I called out because I wasn't feeling well.

"I know how it is. Sometimes, you've just got to take a luxury day."

ELEVEN

THE DESK SERGEANT at Hollywood Station had a patrolman lead us past a long metal bench with three suspects cuffed to it, down a hall lined with old Hollywood movie posters like *Sunset Boulevard* and *Singin' in the Rain*. He went through a row of detective's cubicles and into a back conference room. There was a long, boat-shaped cherrywood table surrounded by metal rolling chairs. He said to wait there.

Five minutes later, the door opened and Angelis and Escobar walked in wearing the same clothes as the night before. They looked worn out.

"You know what my favorite bit of yours is, Richie?" Angelis said. "When you do Walken." Angelis turned to Escobar. "Richie's Walken impression's *impeccable*."

"Who's Walken?" Escobar asked. "Wait. You mean the dude from *Balls of Fury*?"

I rolled my eyes. *Balls of Fury?*

"You know I'm a connoisseur of comedy, and I consider you a fucking genius, Richie," Angelis said. "If your record wasn't there, you might have made a good detective."

"I would have definitely been corrupt, though. Let's be real."

Angelis laughed. "Let's get down to business. This Narek isn't validated with Armenian Dominance. On paper, he's been completely clean before last night. His possession charge has scared him and he's talked. He says multiple illegal Armenian Dominance businesses are currently being run through New Millennium Honda. They're sensitive about who comes around. After your visit, Narek was tasked to tail you two."

"Here's someone to explain more." Escobar opened the door.

A middle-aged man in a fancy black suit walked in. He was obviously Armenian.

"I'm Agent Tamiroff, FBI."

Angelis said, "LAPD's been accommodating Agent Tamiroff and the bureau on an operation they've been running through Hollywood Station."

Tamiroff put a mugshot down on the table where Richie could see it. "That's an AD soldier currently operating out of New Millennium Honda. Recognize him?"

"Sure." Richie looked at the face. "He's the pussy who stabbed me."

I'd been drunk, but I recognized him too. It was the guy.

"That's Margos Garabadian, street name Cyclone," Tamiroff said. "Luckily, he wasn't there when you two stopped by New Millennium the other day."

Richie went *phffft*. "Consider that Balkan cocksucker the lucky one."

Tamiroff gave Angelis an amused look, saying "you weren't lying about this guy."

"Easy Dubs," Angelis said. "Agent Tamiroff also comes from the mother country."

"I hate these deranged thugs even more than you," Tamiroff said. "And Armenia isn't part of the Balkans."

"You can hate them all you want, but it's not as much as me." Richie pointed at his side, where Cyclone's blade had dug in.

"Ever hear about the North Hollywood shootout a few years back?" Tamiroff asked.

I had. I knew Tamiroff wasn't referring to the notorious bank robbery from '97, but a lesser-known gun battle between two Armenian gangs that was still shrouded in mystery and occurred much later. "Two factions of Armenian mobsters shot it out in the lot of a private restaurant on Whitsett," I said. "Only one guy was charged. Everyone else escaped."

"It was an internal power struggle," Tamiroff said. "Hollywood Sam was just out of Folsom, after a ten-year stretch for armed robbery. Sam was there, trying to take the gang he co-founded in a different direction than where it went while he was inside, which was under the leadership of an old-school Armenian called the Panther. The Panther doesn't speak a word of English and prefers for his people to do business at a much quieter level than how Sam operates. Sam and his people shot first that day. Nothing was resolved, but the AD attracted the attention of the FBI. My field office opened an investigation."

"So Hollywood Sam's your target, then?" I asked.

"This operation is a task force comprised of the FBI and the LAPD," he said. "We're out to cripple the AD across L.A. County. Believe it or not, this development between the two of you and Narek Yeghoyan has influenced how it might conclude."

"I still haven't heard *why* Narek was watching my house," Richie said.

"Narek's father, Narek Senior, founded New Millennium Honda. Senior sold hot cars on the side, gambled, went into debt with AD loan sharks, and had to give up his business. After years of trying to get his finances in order, Senior had a heart attack and died. Junior was forced to inherit Senior's debts and went to work for the AD under duress. Narek did jobs for Arman. Narek says he and Arman became genuine friends, despite their adversarial situation. This whole time, somehow, Narek managed to stay off our radar, until last night."

"So, why are we here?" I asked. "What's our connection to the 'conclusion' that's coming?"

"Richie, you know the Armenian mob," Angelis said, ignoring me. "The Armenian Mafia knows you've been looking for Cyclone. You've gotten their attention."

I gave Richie a look meaning "you went looking for Cyclone?"

Escobar said, "This is breaking news to the boyfriend."

Richie gave me a look back, saying "what do you want from me?"

"Mr. Funny Man's been seen hunting for the guy who stabbed him around Little Armenia, what, at least half a dozen times?" Escobar said.

Richie made an annoyed moan. "It wasn't half a dozen."

Escobar chuckled. "You were too shit-faced to remember."

Tamiroff said, "We're thinking of folding you into it as one of our cooperators. There's space for us to invent a narrative." Again, Tamiroff said only *you*, referring to Richie, not me. "Instead of causing Sam to get spooked and change up his routines, we think you could go back to them with a story, along with Narek. Beforehand, Narek will report that he made contact with you and that you've changed your mind about the AD. Now, you're Richie Walsh, muscle for hire. You know they make good money and want to work for them. Narek thinks they would find your unique street résumé convincing, if you can sell the performance."

"You can sell it, Dubs," Angelis said. "You're a genius performer. You know I've always thought so."

"Narek will include Richie's previous East Hollywood stabbing incident, creating a seamless verisimilitude," Tamiroff said.

"Creating a *what*?" Richie looked at me for the answer.

"The real stabbing you took and what you make up will both seem real," I said.

"You'll attempt to get yourself recruited for their latest job, a job you're uniquely qualified to help them achieve," Tamiroff said. "You get them planning a major score on tape. Yes, we'll need you wired. But we'll have people watching you every step of the way."

Wearing a wire in a room with the Armenian mob?

Jesus Christ.

"What's the big score they're planning?" Richie asked.

"Hollywood Sam's been using New Millennium as his main office for six months. Arman, after being low-level for years, is now Sam's right hand. Yes, Narek's heard Sam and Arman plan kidnappings, usually of other Armenian wise guys or regular people who owe them money. But Narek says Sam and Arman are currently targeting a significant high-profile individual. Someone with money and power. We've been waiting to arrest him in order to let some other ends of the case be tied up, but because of this kidnapping situation, we'll have to intercede beforehand. We believe you can meaningfully help us with the interdiction."

"What high-profile individual's getting kidnapped?" Richie asked.

"Tamiroff will tell you depending on how the rest of this talk goes," Angelis said.

"So..." I was tired of being ignored. "What if my friend doesn't agree to do your job for you?"

"Angelis is your buddy, but his hands are tied here," Escobar said. "But locking both of you up to stay out of our way would be fine with me."

"Lock us up for what?"

"Interfering with a police investigation and running a PI business without a license, for starters. See if good Agent Tamiroff from the FBI here can't turn that into jail time, plus the maximum fine allowable." She was smiling.

"This may surprise you, dear, but I've actually been to jail before," Richie said.

"Focus on this," Angelis said. "Getting involved could help you locate Shayla Ramsey. Narek confirmed to us that he knows Shayla, but not her current location. He says Arman doesn't know either. We didn't press him on the subject."

"Let me have a crack. I'll press Narek just fine." Richie cracked his knuckles.

"If you walk into this for us, you'll get a pass on all charges and we'll let you question any of these Armenians about Shayla Ramsey, personally, with their lawyers present, and in front of Tamiroff," Escobar said. "I think saying yes is what you want to do. So say yes, Funny Man."

Richie turned, nodding at me. He was sold.

I wanted to say "no way." I wanted to run from this whole situation and go back to just bagging groceries and living a boring, forgetful life.

Instead, I just shrugged.

IT WAS RARE for Richie to lie or withhold anything. Usually, I just got the blunt truth on any subject. We were out in the station parking lot. The heat out there was brutal.

"You've been hunting for Cyclone?"

"One night I was in the Ralph's on Western and I saw the guy, Cyclone or whatever. I thought about rushing him right there in the beer aisle, but again, he had too many of his pals with him. I know they won't fight fair, so I pulled my cap down low and left. That should have been it, but I couldn't let it go. So, I started getting lit and going out into Armenian bars and restaurants, talking shit, and hoping I'd find him under the next rock I turned over. I knew you would tell me not to, so I didn't say anything. I got out of hand and got arrested a couple times."

"For what?"

"Drunk and disorderly. Bullshit. Angelis got it thrown out. He values our friendship. Before now, I didn't know if the real AD guys knew about what I'd been up to or not. A lot of it's hazy from my being so drunk."

"These guys already stabbed you. I don't want them to kill you."

"Remember what I said about roofies?"

"Yeah."

"An Armenian hooker told me that. It happened to a friend of hers. Sam kept her friend cuffed to a bedpost and raped her for a whole weekend. Threatened to kill her if she talked. It's a sick kick of his, one he's done many times. I hope Shayla's not cuffed to a bed in some fucking dungeon right now, but we need to find out if she is. I want to say yes to this."

I thought it over. They weren't asking me to wear a wire in a room with Hollywood Sam. Richie understood the risks. Yes, maybe a personal animus drove him. But someone had to take these guys down, and our random universe was putting the task on Richie.

"You're right. If you're okay with the risk, I say go ahead."

"I'm okay with the risk," he said.

TWELVE

RICHIE FOLLOWED TAMIROFF'S black Lincoln Town Car into Echo Park where we arrived at a Mexican restaurant called El Compadre, a known LAPD hangout. One time, when I'd been here before, I saw Huell Howser, the host of KCET's *California's Gold* at a booth with a bunch of LAPD officers. Huell was buying all the boys drinks.

We followed Tamiroff in through the back entrance. "We're here to meet Jane," he said to the hostess. The Dodgers played on a flat-screen above the bar. A waiter passed, carrying a tray with four flaming margaritas.

Narek sat at a booth, chowing down on chips and guac. Even in the dim light, you could see the bruises Richie gave him.

Beside Narek sat a middle-aged, white Jewish woman in a gray suit, drinking ice water. Her black hair was pulled back into a ponytail and she wore a pair of thick-rimmed black glasses. Tamiroff introduced her as Agent Jane Gould. We sat.

"How you feeling?" Richie asked Narek.

"Fuck you," Narek said.

Richie pointed at the cut above Narek's eye. "Looks like it could scar."

Narek looked at Gould.

"Don't ask her for help," Richie said. "Look at me."

"Enough," Tamiroff said. "Cooperating translates to *cut the shit.*"

"I was just concerned for my friend's well-being," Richie said.

"*Enough.*"

Our waiter arrived. Tamiroff said we could order anything but booze. I got a carne asada quesadilla. Tamiroff and Jane got arroz con pollo. Richie ordered a glass of water.

When the waiter was gone, Tamiroff said, "Clerks at the Federal Court Clerk's Office have been feeding intel to the AD.

Hollywood Sam has well-paid informants all over. As the leader of this operation, I've authorized some unconventional measures in order to stay ahead of our wild target. There's a comedy club called Cackles in Glendale, right? On the roof of the Foxtrot, that re-done hotel on Glenoaks. That venue's become popular lately, right?"

Cackles was where Richie got his first break. He'd since upgraded to the Comedy Store, but he still went to hang out and watch other comedians. I'd been there once, a while back. The Cackles shows were all held up on the roof.

"Sure, I used to perform at that joint. What's that got to do with this?"

"Is it true that Cackles has a special group of comedians in rotation who are able to put guests on their list, gaining access to the VIP area of the audience?"

"Yeah."

"Can you put people on this list?"

"Yeah. Why?"

Tamiroff looked at Narek and made a *go-ahead* nod.

"Ana Safarian goes to these shows lately, yes?" Narek said.

Ana Safarian. The Armenian American TV and social media star. The megahit reality show *The Safarians* chronicled the personal and professional lives of her family. She was in a highly publicized relationship with the rap star Mahad Southern.

A high-profile individual.

"Yeah," Richie said. "I've seen her there."

Tamiroff said, "Recently, Miss Safarian has chosen to speak out against Armenian Dominance. She called the gang 'an organized and insidious plague on her people.' This appears to be one of the reasons why Sam's put a target on her head."

I'd read the comments Tamiroff referred to. Tossed off to a reporter at some elite red-carpet event, they'd been all over the internet a couple weeks back. A family friend of the Safarians had been an innocent bystander in a recent AD shooting. Ana was angry about it and using her enormous media platform to call the gang out. Much of the general public seemed surprised to hear something so substantive come out of her mouth.

"Sam's planning to grab her where?" Richie said. "If Ana Safarian goes anywhere, she rolls with multiple bodyguards. What are you even suggesting?"

Gould touched Narek's shoulder. "Keep talking."

Narek said, "Sam needs a plan to put Ana's bodyguards out of commission. He talk about this two nights ago, with me in the room." Explaining something this complicated was difficult with his limited English, especially under pressure.

"And?" Richie said.

Narek just looked at Gould.

"Narek thinks you, specifically, would be able to present Sam with a plan he'll like," Gould said. She nodded at Narek, telling him to continue.

"Your plan is to attend show at Cackles on night when Ana is in audience. You bring Arman, or one of Arman's guys, someone who has name put on list beforehand, making access to VIP. Then you guys get close enough to needle spike bodyguards."

"To *what* her bodyguards?" Richie asked.

"It's a roofie, but instead you sneak up behind and jab them with a needle," I said.

"When guards are out, Ana will escape club," Narek said. "While you escape in chaos, somewhere outside, while she's still exposed, Sam and others will grab Ana."

The Dodgers scored a run on the TV. People cheered.

Richie looked at Tamiroff. "Angelis come up with this?"

"Yes, and I signed off on it. It's audacious, but correctly plays on Sam's long-established desire to be a part of Hollywood. He won't be able to resist the pitch."

Richie said, "It's the dumbest shit I've ever heard."

"I second that. Her bodyguards would see it coming," I said.

"Not something this crazy. That's how Sam wins. He's *too* crazy," Narek said.

"And it's just a story to get him talking," Tamiroff said. "Richie, you'll pitch it, utilizing your knowledge of Cackles. You'll get Sam to incriminate himself on tape. After a recording's secured, we'll sweep in, and Sam will be charged with conspiracy to kidnap on top of all of the other charges we've gathered against him. After that, a wide array of soldiers underneath Sam will go down too. It'll be a major hit for the AD."

"Why not just arrest him for all of those other charges now?" I asked.

"Like I said, Sam's connections. Leaks have helped this guy skate dozens of times. We're not going into a courtroom until we can play an actual recording for the jury of Sam convicting himself in his own words."

"And if he smells bullshit and tries to whack me right there on the spot?" Richie said.

"Like Angelis has been so fond of reminding me, you're a performer," Tamiroff said. "Sell your performance."

The waiter brought a tray with all our dishes and passed each plate out. He left, and I waited before touching my quesadilla. Our Shayla-related questions to Narek were supposed to come after the bust, but I decided to just go for it.

"Narek, what do you know about Shayla Ramsey?" I asked.

"Arman didn't hurt her."

"How do you know?"

"Arman's not like that. Maybe he was before. No longer."

"Mr. Minor, the reason you're here is because you happened to be with Richie when all this happened," Tamiroff said. "If Arman or any of these AD killers have her, then we've got to stop them. That happens when Richie gets them on tape. Until he does, keep quiet."

"I'm not going to be in a place to ask anyone shit about Shayla when Sam checks to see if I'm wired and then clips me on the fucking spot," Richie said.

"Not how Sam thinks," Tamiroff said. "It took four of his guys to get you down. Sam respects that, even if it's someone he doesn't trust. He wouldn't frisk you. He'd see it as a dishonorable insult."

Richie looked at Narek. "Isn't Arman your buddy? Didn't I hear that?"

"He's also my blackmailer," Narek said.

"Maybe all of this is a line to save your own ass?"

"My family is controlled by these monsters for years. Arman made his choices. I make mine. They can all talk themselves into prison."

"The boys back at New Millennium need to know what happened to Narek," Tamiroff said, digging into his arroz con pollo. "After this meal, he needs to go back and tell them about where he's been. He'll lay the groundwork. Richie, this is your last chance to back out."

Richie said, "I'm not backing out."

RICHIE WAS ASLEEP on my couch again, and probably would be until our Armenian threat passed. Back in my room, I ate an edible bought from a guy I knew in Lincoln Heights and sat down at my desk and read about Ana Safarian.

Like millions of Americans, I knew who she was, but not her proper bio. Ana's father was one of L.A.'s most famous and wealthiest criminal lawyers. She first became a public figure in the early 2000s when she appeared on the reality show of another elite socialite whose star had since faded. But she became a true media sensation and began to properly build her empire after the release of an infamous sex tape made with her then-boyfriend, another rapper. Ana Safarian was the gold standard for how high women on the aesthetics-over-substance path, which Dominique first trailblazed, could now rise in America. Her current worth was 1.2 billion.

The brownie hit and I lay back in bed. Back at Hollywood Station, Richie had signed his agreements. They'd given me forms to sign as well. As soon as Hollywood Sam got arrested, we'd be granted federal immunity from all the charges the LAPD had against us. Tamiroff said I could sit in on one of the listening posts with him. We'd be in the back of a surveillance van, not far from wherever Narek and Richie went tomorrow night.

I couldn't stay on the sidelines. It wouldn't be right. I couldn't let Richie face something this dangerous alone. He had a temper. If he got mad enough, there was no way to calm him down or control him. It could make things go horribly wrong on a job like this. But sometimes, I could walk Richie through his blind rages. I could help. Somehow, I had to come up with a plan to get myself recruited too.

THIRTEEN

I WAS ON the sales floor, filling the eggs.

Richie said, "I asked Jackie what he knew about roofies." Richie was supposed to be up front, working the water. Instead, he was back here with me, riding out the time clock.

"Yeah, but Jackie wouldn't know about needle spiking, would he?"

Our coworker Jackie Mills was a fellow Novice, a really nice guy who seemed to be whacked out on drugs for at least half of his waking hours. Sometimes, he showed up to work high on Special K. If homeless people ever wandered into the store, Jackie would stop them so they could ramble nonsense to each other. One time, at a work party, I watched Jackie roofie his own beer. He used a little dropper he kept in the pocket of his jean shorts.

"I couldn't make sense of anything he said. He kept asking what I knew about the giant frozen chicken who just got hired here. Fuckin' wacko."

"I can't believe you're not freaking out about later on."

"What for?"

"Because you're wearing a wire in a room with Hollywood Sam. That's what for."

He shrugged his shoulders.

A well-groomed man wearing lip gloss reached over me and grabbed a dozen of cage-free organics. "Don't you have anything fresher?"

Richie said, "I'll go ask the chicken we keep in the cooler to pop a few more out."

"Hey! Be nice."

"Those are the freshest we got," I said politely.

The customer put the eggs in his basket and moved on.

"Did you just take my picture?" a familiar voice said behind me.

I turned around. It was Dominique, alone today. She carried a little baby-blue purse, which, of course, matched her miniskirt.

A brunette in jeans and high heels pushed her cart by the fresh salads. She had her phone out and was scrolling. The phone was aimed in Dominque's direction, but I didn't think she'd taken a picture.

"I said, did you just *take my picture*?" Dominique loved her fans, but encounters with other women in the real world got testy. Women were her competition.

The brunette looked up. "Are you talking to me?"

"Not just anyone takes my picture," Dominique said. "This face costs *money*."

"Why would I ever want to take your picture?"

"To study how to apply makeup?"

Richie's eyes lit up. All he needed was popcorn.

"Nobody wants to take your picture. Bitch, you look like the fucking Crypt Keeper!"

Richie walked over to Dominque. "What, you're going to let her get away with talking like that? *You're Dominque*! Who the fuck is she?"

People took out their cell phones and began recording. Dominique stepped over toward a display in the produce section and picked up a long stalk of brussels sprouts, gripping it like a club. She wound up and swung, slapping the brunette in the face. Little green balls flew all over the place, rolling in every direction.

"*Bitch*," the brunette said, removing her high heels. She lunged at Dominque, clenching a fistful of her hair, and dragged her toward the eggs, close to me. I got out of the way just as the brunette shoved Dominique into the egg display, breaking open dozens of cartons. Dominque's hands, chest, and face got covered with yolk and tiny white flecks of broken eggshells. Her face and breasts were coated a translucent yellow.

Jose, the manager running the front end, ran through the tables of produce back toward us. Our store security guard, Ricardo, was working that night, but must have been on lunch or possibly hiding to not have to deal with this bullshit.

Dominique got to her feet and picked up her purse. She pulled out a small can of pepper spray, put it right in the brunette's eyes, and sprayed.

The brunette screamed and fell to her knees, coughing. The crowd dispersed, abandoning their cell phone videos. A pepper spray cloud spread. Everyone coughed. I pulled my purple-and-blue work shirt up over my mouth and nose. Jose, realizing what just occurred, turned back around. Customers abandoned their carts and left the building.

I touched Dominique's elbow. She whirled around, aiming the can at me.

"They'll call the cops for this," I said. "They'll have to."

"She threw me into the eggs. I *charge* for taking my picture."

"Let me get you out of here."

I led her by the elbow through the emergency exit. This set off the alarm. With all the other chaos, I figured it would take any of the managers quite a while to notice. We walked down a red brick hallway to the side of the building and through another door that came out on Gardner.

I got her to her Maserati, parked near the front. Coughing customers and crew members were still rushing out for fresh air. Realizing how much it had gotten to me, too, I took off my glasses and wiped my eyes with the inside of my shirt.

"No one disrespects Dominique."

"They sure don't," I said. "You should probably make your getaway now."

She wiped more egg off her face, put on a pair of blue shades, and got in her car. "Adam, you're such a sweetie." Then she tore off down Santa Monica.

I'd seen Dominique get mad before, but her outbursts were never this extreme. I wondered if she was still upset about an article published in the previous month's *L.A. Weekly*. For all of her decades in Hollywood, no one knew Dominique's real name, age, or history. There was no past, just the voluptuous sex-kitten persona she'd manufactured for herself.

But the truth was now out.

Born in Poland, Dominique is the only daughter of Jewish concentration camp survivors. Her birth name was Dobra Garfinkel and she grew up mainly in Brooklyn. Her father, a man who'd lived through some of Europe's most unspeakable horrors, had been physically and psychologically abusive. In the late '60s, he moved the family across the country to the Fairfax district of L.A. After high school, Dobra cut ties with her people completely and legally changed her name to Dominique. She was now sixty-two years old.

Richie was by the front door, taking a break. I'd lost track of him inside, but the pepper spray didn't seem to have bothered him much.

I walked over as he lit himself a cigarette. He never liked Dominique, but right now he was impressed. "I didn't know the old broad had it in her."

FOURTEEN

BACK AT HOLLYWOOD Station, the conference room blinds were drawn. Tamiroff and Gould were there with three new Feds. A corkboard with pictures of faces and names pinned to it had been rolled in. All the faces were Armenian mobsters. Hollywood Sam was at the top. Beneath him were Arman, Cyclone, and over two dozen others.

Tamiroff looked to Richie. "You and Narek will meet Arman at Verdugo Bar in Glassell Park in just over two hours. Both of you will be wired as we discussed. The tech guys are on their way now."

The conference room door opened. Escobar brought Narek in. He walked over to us, looking nervous. I said hi politely.

"If all goes well," Tamiroff said, "Arman will take you on to Sam, who was spotted by our surveillance teams driving into the lot of New Millennium Honda forty-five minutes ago."

A Fed pulled Tamiroff away. Richie walked over to the window, cracked the blinds, and peeked through.

"Minor-man, come here." He waved me over. "You see that cop standing in the back. The fat one?"

A fat Irish patrolman was in the corner. "What about him?"

"Tubbs busted me for a bar fight six months ago at the Three of Clubs." He put up a middle finger up to the window.

I decided to just come out with it. "I've got to go with you tonight."

He was surprised. "The fuck you do."

"What's the point of me even being here?"

"*Ohh*, you're here because you're my partner. That's the point."

"Still, I'm coming along."

"Shove it up your ass you're coming along."

"So I just sit back like these well-manicured college boys from the FBI while you and this shady Armenian who's been doing errands for the guys he allegedly wants to bust take all the risk? *Fuck that.*"

"You're serious."

"Let's tell Tamiroff I'm going with you. Wire me up too."

"Adam, I respect the sentiment. You're a good friend. But this isn't for you..."

"Like I said, fuck that."

"They don't need you. You're the one who's been smart enough so far to not get himself stabbed by the Armenian Mafia. This is because of my bullshit. What if I don't make it through this? Someone needs to give Joan an answer about Shayla."

"What got us here doesn't matter. We're here, and either I'm your partner or I'm not."

"Tamiroff's talking up his tactical command, but that won't mean shit in the room with Hollywood Sam. Who knows how this could go?"

"My point exactly."

"Stay behind and watch. There's no shame in it."

"Nope."

He looked at me for a long time. "You sure?"

"I'm sure."

Out in the hall, we got Susan on the phone at her home in Studio City. We quickly recapped everything over the line.

"My take?" she said. "The charges they're threatening you with sound like a bluff. But you tell me you want to go. So, I'll say, based on this limited information, and if it really is the only way to find this latest missing girl, go ahead, with the caveat that all of this sounds incredibly dangerous, which is probably already obvious to the both of you, because we've long established that both of you are certifiably insane."

IT TOOK SOME pressing. Richie threatened to pull out of the job, even if it meant them throwing the book at us. Tamiroff said no way. We told Tamiroff that our lawyer already knew everything. We were going together or we weren't going at all.

After more back and forth, he agreed. Time was of the essence. Tamiroff needed Sam's voice on tape.

"All right," he said. "Both of you can go. Just remember, I know all about the Emily Glass case. Armenian Dominance isn't Stan Hammond."

I said, "If Hollywood Sam clips us, then you've got him."

We rehearsed our story. Our wires weren't bulky boxes taped to our chests like in the movies. I'd been picturing technology like what Treat Williams wore in *Prince of the City*, but my recorder was inside a regular office pen. They told me I should keep it in my front pants pocket. In most cases, it recorded through clothing. It felt heavier than a normal pen, but not by much. Richie was given a Zippo lighter. Narek's wire was in his belt buckle. He was the least likely to get frisked. Richie had stopped sniping at Narek. He'd been forced into the situation. We both accepted that.

The technicians told us to walk around and sit down. We got some practice in moving with the equipment on us. A guy in the van outside said we came through fine.

"Really though," I said to Narek, "what if they're looking for wires?"

"I already said, they won't," Narek said.

"But what if they do?"

Narek watched Richie, expecting him to provide an answer.

"Then we bluff," Richie said. "Let me take the lead."

I thought about calling my mother to say goodbye, just in case. But I remembered it was the middle of the night in Ohio and she wouldn't answer this late.

FIFTEEN

NAREK DROVE US in his Monte Carlo. We were in the backseat. A Fed car followed a few car lengths back and another one I couldn't see ran parallel. The van with Tamiroff, Angelis, and Escobar, and all of the surveillance equipment was even further behind.

We hit the freeway. Narek had his AC on but it was still hot, even this late. He looked in his rearview. "What is Shayla connection here? What are you guys up to?"

"Shayla's disappeared. Maybe she was kidnapped, maybe worse," I said. "Her ex-boyfriend is the gangster who sent you after us, so here we are."

"But Arman really loves Shayla."

He sounded sincere. Maybe he was. Maybe he was right. It didn't make any sense to worry about it right now.

"*Oh shit,*" Richie said. "I almost forgot, Minor-man."

"Forgot what?"

"Remember how I recognized Evette, but couldn't remember where from?"

"Yeah?"

He took out his phone, googled a porn site, and pulled up a video. He held it up and pressed play. "This is her!"

Evette was doing a solo webcam performance. She was in high heels and wearing a barely visible red thong. She shook her ass right at the camera to "Baby Got Back" by Sir Mix-a-Lot. It had to be on the wire for Tamiroff and the other Feds to hear.

NAREK PARKED ON Verdugo. This was Glassell Park, up the street from where Arman waited for us at Verdugo Bar. We passed a parked red Firebird, which I assumed had to be his. Arman was by the front door, smoking. He wore a Members Only jacket and still had the same big crucifix around his neck.

"Nice to see you again, sweetie," Richie said in his effeminate voice.

"You want to make it through the night, you better cut that stuff out."

"I told you, Richie's a comedian," Narek said. "You can't take him too seriously."

"There's a great endorsement, considering what we need to talk about tonight." Arman stubbed out his cigarette.

Inside the bar, low-key jazz played. Business was early-evening slow. A group of hard-looking cholos in Dodger blue were at the front bar. Arman led us to a table on the back patio.

"Go get us some beers," Richie said to Narek. "I'll take Bud Light."

Narek looked at Arman.

"*Yes*, do what he says," Arman said.

Narek got up and went to the bar.

"Why don't we start with that scene back at the lot," Arman said. "What was that about?"

"Me and Adam, we find people," Richie said. "Your ex-girlfriend Shayla went missing. We were hired to find her."

"Finding her includes driving around town, pretending to be fags?"

Richie shrugged. "It was pretty funny, you've got to admit."

Narek returned with four glasses of beer. He struggled not to spill them.

As Arman reached for his glass, I saw a pistol in a shoulder holster under his jacket, possibly a Ruger. "What I know about you two is that you have a beef with Cyclone and that I've got no reason to trust either of you."

"It's like this," I said. "If a case leads us someplace where the money's better than what our client pays us, we say fuck the client and chase the bigger bucks. When we saw that Shayla had AD connections, we went to your car lot, fishing. You got suspicious and put Narek on us. We spotted him, and had a talk. Narek said we might be able to help you with something. We're all ears about what that might be."

"But before we even get into that, there's this one thing," Richie said.

"What thing?"

"The guy who stabbed me outside Dartmouth and Flower. Cyclone."

"He remembers you too."

"Whatever type of business agreement we might come to, keep that motherfucker away from me. I don't care if he rolls with Hollywood Sam."

"Be careful, speaking his name."

"Who? Hollywood Sam?"

"I'll run it by the big man if we get that far."

"There's a reason why I'm here specifically, isn't there?" Richie said.

"Narek says you can get anyone you want into Cackles in Glendale. The place on the roof of the Foxtrot?"

"I've got connections there, sure."

"We have our eyes on a target that frequents comedy clubs, especially that one." He waited, leaned in, and whispered, "Someone big. If we can get someone in and help neutralize their security in advance, we can take the target outside the club."

"Neutralize?" Richie said. "In a comedy club? How?"

"Your business will be getting us in and getting us close."

"I can do that. But what's in it for me?"

"*How* can you do that?"

"I can get someone on the list. If you're on the list, you can get into the VIP section. VIP means being close to anyone else in the VIP section. If this high-value target is in the VIP, you'll be able to get close. I'll repeat, what's in it for me?"

"A cut of the ransom, when it comes."

"How much is that?"

"This target? There'll be heat. But she'll go for high six figures, easy."

Richie whistled, then looked at me. I nodded.

Richie said, "We're in."

"Next stop, we continue this conversation with the boss. See what he thinks of you."

SIXTEEN

A SPOTTER WAS out again that night at the New Millennium lot, sitting in a blue Honda NSX parked close to the entrance. Arman stepped out of his Firebird and the three of us got out of the Monte Carlo. He unlocked the showroom door and we walked through rows of empty sales desks and down a linoleum hallway. At an office door, Arman knocked.

A voice came from within. "Yeah?"

So far, Arman hadn't been concerned about wires. If I believed in any sort of God, I'd be praying the man on the other side of this door wasn't concerned about them either.

Arman cracked the door. "Those guys are here."

"Bring them in."

Framed photos of Hondas hung on the wall, all in need of dusting. There was a sleek black lacquer desk with chrome accents and two chairs for visitors. A thin Armenian teenager in a red skirt and a faded *Harry Potter* shirt sat in one. She looked about sixteen and was high on something. Her hair went down to her waist and was jet black.

A man stood in the corner. He wore Italian wool dress pants, a wife beater, and suspenders. A flat-screen TV mounted to the wall played *The Suze Orman Show*. The man I recognized as Hollywood Sam muted the show.

"Who's this?" he said, staring me down. "All I heard about was the comedian."

"He's the comedian's partner," Arman said.

Sam laughed and clapped, suddenly jovial. "Hey, why not? Join the fuckin' party." He looked at Arman. "Jaqueline and I just had a development."

Jaqueline reached slowly over the desk, picking up what looked like a pregnancy test. Sam grabbed it from her hand and showed it to Arman.

"She's not going to have it," Arman said, calm and professional. "We can take care of it. Especially if she knows this soon."

Sam threw the test into the trash beside the desk, hardened his features, and swung his closed fist into Jaqueline's jaw. She made a yelp like a cat whose tail was just stepped on and fell over.

I tried to send Richie a psychic message: *Stay cool.*

I could hear his nostrils flaring.

"If she lives through tonight, Jaqueline's having my baby," Sam said, then helped Jaqueline up to the bathroom. "The only way to live forever is through your children."

The bathroom door stayed open. Jaqueline spit blood into the sink.

"Why wouldn't she live through the night?" Narek asked.

"Because tonight, we'll be discussing some major shit with people I don't know." He raised an incriminating finger at us. "These two here could be colluding with law enforcement. Maybe they've got eyes on me, or even ears. If, for example, anyone would try to arrest me tonight, the first thing I'll do is slit Jackie's throat."

"But why?" Narek asked.

"Because I'm not going to jail tonight. Always have insurance."

"You don't have to hit the girl. Leave her alone," Richie said.

Sam reached into his pocket, drew a Buck knife, and opened the blade. "I hear you're all about defending women, Comedian. How do you feel knowing it gets me hard to hurt them? What you just saw me do, that's my kick."

"I feel it means you're asking for heat. You wanna get busted," Richie said.

Jaqueline was in the doorway, a blooming bruise on her face. Whatever dope she was on seemed to be dulling the pain.

"I've got enemies in my midst," Sam said. "The Feds want me. Some Feds... talk to me. I happen to know the FBI is watching this building right now." Sam grabbed Jaqueline by the hair, pulled her toward him, and put the blade to her jugular.

No one moved.

Sam then smiled, let go of her hair, and closed the blade. He pointed to the couch against the wall. Jaqueline ambled over to sit where he pointed. He walked around the desk and sat in the high-backed leather swivel chair.

"Do you guys know how old I was when I co-founded Armenian Dominance?"

"Pretty young," I said.

"Seventh grade's pretty young. Have a seat."

I sat on the couch beside Jaqueline, who was asleep. Richie took a chair opposite Sam.

"L.A. County was flooded with Armenian immigrants when I first moved here. This organization was created to give my people the chance to grow strong. We take on the dirty work. Most young Armenian Americans have only ever known the privileged atmosphere I fought to give them. Some of these youngsters have the audacity to criticize me. Did you hear what Ana Safarian said?"

"She was talking shit about you and your soldiers," I said.

"Where does that big-assed bitch get off?"

"Ana Safarian goes to Cackles at the Foxtrot Hotel in Glendale," Richie said. "She's a billionaire. A high-value target. She who you want to grab?"

Sam grinned but didn't answer.

Jaqueline slumped over onto me. Her head rested on my shoulder.

"I've got one of Ana's security guards on my payroll," Sam said. "Yes, an ex-college football star named Jamal Barrie took out a loan from my people and couldn't pay it back. His boss is worth over a billion dollars and she can't even adequately pay the people tasked with keeping her safe. Shows how in order her priorities are."

Tamiroff claimed he'd researched every angle of this operation, but he didn't know Sam had a Fed talking to him, he didn't know about the girl who would be here, and he definitely didn't know Ana Safarian's personal security team had been compromised.

"I've agreed to let Jamal get right with favors," Sam said. "He's to give me a heads up about Ana's schedule. Tonight, she's going to Cackles."

Tonight?

"Like I told Arman, I can make a call," Richie said. "Get people on the list. Getting on the list will get you close enough to needle spike them or whatever."

"Not or *whatever*." Sam looked at Arman. "Get him in here now."

Arman sent a text. Thirty seconds later, a knock came at the door. Arman opened it.

Cyclone walked in carrying a small black display case.

Richie got up.

I got in front of Richie, blocking his path to Cyclone.

"It's *him*." Richie's fists were clenched.

Time slowed. I was genuinely afraid about what Richie would do.

"Both of you sit the fuck down," Sam said.

Richie and I sat. Cyclone walked around the desk and stood behind Sam.

"Show them," Sam said.

Cyclone put the case down on the desk, facing us. It was right under the light. He opened it. The material inside was red velvet. It was meant to hold four pens. Instead, it held four disposable syringes, all full of liquid.

"Rohypnol, midazolam, temazepam," Sam said. "My own cocktail. It's going to take anybody out. You'll get us close to Ana's bodyguards while they're at the crowded show, and you're going to stab at least two of them with this."

"Get *who* close?" Richie said.

"You two and Cyclone."

Richie looked at Cyclone, then back at Sam. "This fucking mook ran up on me when I wasn't looking and stabbed me."

"So?"

"So, I don't work with mooks."

"You're working with Cyclone." I don't think Sam knew what mook meant.

"The whole plan is shit," Richie said.

"I've needle spiked plenty of girls," Sam said. "Concerts, music festivals. It's a blast when you get the hang of it. Much easier than it seems."

"A crowded music festival and this venue, which is being attended by a billionaire's muscle, are two distinctly different fucking situations," Richie said.

"Enough of your negativity. Here's what's going to happen. You're going to call this rooftop comedy club. You're going to tell them you'll be coming in tonight with your buddy here and Cyclone, whose real name is Margos Garabadian."

"Be sure to refer to me as your good friend," Cyclone said.

"We'll drive you over," Sam said. "You'll get in with these spikes hidden under your clothes. When Ana comes, you three take out the guards. Once the remaining guards see something is up, they'll make a run for it, and we'll grab her outside the club." Sam made a gun with his finger, pointing it at Richie.

"You said there's law enforcement watching this now," I said.

"And?" Sam said.

"What if they tail you to the club? Why wouldn't they?"

"We've got a way out of here no one outside this room knows about. They won't know where we're going. I can shake tails."

This wasn't ideal, but Tamiroff still knew our final destination was Cackles.

"So you're just going to go full cowboy in the parking lot of a comedy club?" I asked.

"Yes," Sam said. "That's exactly what we're going to do."

"How do we know you'll give us our cut?" Richie asked.

"You don't."

"How do we know you won't just clip us?"

"If you don't call the club right now, I'll clip you here and now."

Richie took out his phone and made the call. He confirmed he was coming that night with two guests to the VIP area. "Their names are Adam Minor and Margos Garabadian," he said, then made chitchat for a few moments and hung up. "All good."

We got ready. Sam changed into dark sweats. Arman checked the ammo on the automatic he carried under his jacket.

Cyclone wrapped the syringes in blue felt towels and gave us two little belts to secure them around our thighs. Richie and I both took off our pants.

My pen fell out and landed on the floor.

I stayed cool and casually picked it up.

Richie and I secured the syringes to the belts and tightened them around our legs. So did Cyclone. Once they were secure, we practiced walking around.

"If it sets off the detector at security, just tell them it's your belt," Cyclone said.

I tried not to look at Narek, whose wire was in his belt.

"They probably won't even run a detector if they see me," Richie said.

"In any case, we won't have to keep them there long. We'll take them off in the john, then stick those motherfuckers in the back when our inside man sets us up."

Sam woke Jaqueline up. "Babe, you're coming with us."

Jaqueline yawned.

Sam stood. "Narek, you stay here."

Narek nodded.

While holding Jaqueline's hand, Sam led us out the back way and across an alley. There, he unlocked another gate and we walked into the lot of a detailing shop for cars. It must have had an entrance on Orange. Sam took out some keys, opened a door, and led us into a garage where two of his guys waited by a long gray Ford cargo van. One handed Sam the keys.

Arman got in first. Two pump-action Mossbergs with ammo slings were propped up against the wall beside him, and a roll of duct tape rested on his seat. Richie and I sat behind him. Jaqueline lumbered all the way to the last seat in the back, leaned her head against the wall, and closed her eyes. Her mouth pooled with blood-tinged saliva.

Sam started the engine. He looked back at us. "Let's teach this reality show bitch a lesson."

SEVENTEEN

THE SHOW AT Cackles had already started. Laughs floated down from the roof. In front, a line of people ran for a block. These were people either waiting for a later show or hoping a spot in the current one would open up. Cyclone, Richie, and I got out of the van and stepped out onto the sidewalk. Sam drove up the block, turned the van around, and idled with the lights off.

Would the Feds appear now? Just swoop out from behind every corner, guns out, and put the cuffs on Sam? They had what they needed on tape.

But Jaqueline was in the van. Sam had clearly threatened her life. He was courting a confrontation and had a documented violent history. Anyone who moved now would get her killed. This meant our saviors weren't coming yet. I didn't know when they would.

We would have to keep walking this tightrope.

"You see that?" Richie said to Cyclone, pointing at the long line. "All Sam wants is Ana Safarian. He doesn't care if you come back. You're in my world now and *you* aren't coming back from it." He let this declaration float around in Cyclone's brain. "Unlike you, I've got respect enough to give a guy a warning."

Richie got the attention of a bouncer. He was a big, muscular black man in a black suit and a red Kangol beret. "Wilson!" They fist-bumped and took a moment to catch up.

Wilson took out a clipboard, checked off our names, and let us in, bypassing the line. He didn't frisk us or run a metal detector, just as Richie had suspected.

It was a quick elevator ride up to the top. The doors opened, and I looked around. There were rows of seats and tables for about fifty or sixty people. This was the general admission area and every seat was full. Waitresses in red tartan skirts took drink orders. The hot, dry wind curled my hair and made me feel even jumpier. A comedian onstage performed under a spotlight.

Richie spoke to the hostess. She led us into the roped-off VIP section, close to the stage. I looked around. No Ana Safarian yet. There were two other empty tables besides ours. One was near the front, close to the emergency exit. I figured that one was hers.

Many people had their phones out and were filming. Richie had already clarified that phones were not confiscated at Cackles.

The comedian onstage had his name on a screen behind his head. It said KENTUCKY WALTON. Kentucky Walton had thick and curly black hair. "No one ever says hello to each other in the streets of L.A. Back in Kentucky, where I'm from, everybody says hi. Don't matter if they're strangers or not. You see a woman on the street, you call her ma'am. If you call someone ma'am in L.A... *shit.* It's no different than calling her an old bag..."

I kept trying to think of ways to signal to Tamiroff. In the van ride over, I had repeatedly clicked the top of the pen in my pocket, hoping to have the people listening realize I was trying to tap out SOS. This didn't work, of course, because I'd never learned Morse code.

Our waitress arrived, and Richie ordered a Bud Light. He seemed relaxed, like this was a normal night for him. I ordered a Negroni.

"Nothing for me," Cyclone said.

When she was gone, Richie said, "Keep acting like such a pussy and see if people don't notice. There's a two-drink minimum here, stupid."

"We're not staying that long." Cyclone huffed, then looked back to the elevators, watching for Ana's arrival.

"Stop being so obvious," I said. "When she gets here, she'll get here."

"Both of you stop riding me."

Our drinks arrived. I drank my entire Negroni in two gulps.

Kentucky Walton noticed a beautiful woman in the front row with an OBAMA 2012 shirt. She was to his far left. "*Hello,*" he said. Obama's face was positioned directly across her noticeably large breasts. "Go Obama!"

The woman went red and she laughed, covering her face.

A commotion broke out behind us. The people who were filming turned their phones away from the stage and toward the elevators. A five-person entourage had just arrived. It was four large black men, obviously bodyguards, and a much smaller person in the middle. The hostess led them across the floor and over toward us in the VIP section.

At their table, Ana Safarian first became visible to me. She wore a black jacket, which she took off to reveal a one-shouldered, leopard-print minidress. She took off her shades.

"Wave to them, Ana," Kentucky Walton said. "Wave like the Queen of England!"

Ana laughed and waved. The crowd gave her a light, reverent applause. The bodyguards eyed the crowd.

Richie leaned toward me. "Why do you suppose she comes here alone?"

"She's with four bodyguards. They're right there," I said. Some liquid courage from my Negroni had arrived.

"I mean without her boyfriend."

"Maybe Mahad isn't a stand-up fan."

"Or maybe they're taking a break."

Kentucky Walton continued with his set. I wished I was drinking my second Negroni.

"It's time," Cyclone said.

As planned, Richie left first for the bathroom. While he was gone, I looked around at the crowd, hoping some savior would emerge. There were a few out-of-place guys in suits near the bar. I hoped they were with Tamiroff, here to intervene soon.

Richie emerged from the bathroom. My turn was next.

In the stall, I took down my pants and removed the syringe from the belt around my thigh. The concoction inside gleamed. I thought about pleading to Tamiroff through the pen wire, but the door to the bathroom opened again, slamming this time. Cyclone already, I figured, and got too nervous about speaking up. When I stepped out of the stall, there he was. Sam must have coached him to not leave us alone for long.

Outside the bathroom, Richie waited for me, his syringe concealed in his hand at his side. I walked up close to him. This was the first time we'd been alone since our trip to the station.

"We can't actually go through with this plan," I said. "It was supposed to just be a talk, not *this*. What the fuck are we going to do?"

Cyclone came out. It took him half the time to get his syringe off than either of us.

"Just follow my lead," Richie said to me.

Beside us, Cyclone took out his phone. "Get ready," he said, and sent a text.

Ana and her bodyguards watched the show. There was a clear path from us to them. One took out his phone and looked at it. Then he scanned the crowd. He locked in on us. He made eye contact with Cyclone and nodded. Jamal, the inside man. *There you are.*

"I remember the first time I ever visited Chinatown in L.A.," Kentucky Walton said. "I looked at my buddy and I said, 'You think this is what the real China is like? Just a bunch of Mexicans everywhere?'"

Jamal laughed convulsively. Until now, he'd been subdued like the other bodyguards. This was a jarring change. Jamal knocked over Ana's drink. It spilled on her dress. Ana slid back in her chair, startled. Ana got to her feet.

On stage, Kentucky Walton noticed the scene.

"*Now*," Cyclone said, and started walking toward Ana.

Richie stepped in front of Cyclone, blocking his way. He pushed Cyclone in the chest. "You didn't think this was actually going to work, did you?" He pushed him again.

Ana began to dab at the spill on her dress with a napkin.

Cyclone looked confused. There wasn't much time, and Richie blocked his way. Over at the table, everyone's attention was still on the drink spill.

Richie held up his syringe, his thumb on the plunger.

"Me, I love Chinese food," Kentucky Walton said. "Except General Tso's Chicken. They could've just stuck with Orange Chicken, but they had to rip off Kentucky's own Colonel Sanders. You ever notice that? There's General Tso's, and then there's *Colonel* Sanders..."

Richie seized Cyclone by the back of his neck, forced the needle into his bicep, and sent the plunger down.

Cyclone broke free from Richie's grasp, removed the empty syringe, and tossed it to the ground. Still holding his own syringe, Cyclone started again toward Ana's table. Before he could get far, Richie knocked him down. He fell face forward and his syringe rolled away, landing by some lady's feet.

The crowd turned our way. The men I thought might be Feds just stared with gaping mouths. Kentucky Walton looked at us, the harsh spotlight in his eyes.

Richie held a knee to Cyclone's chest. The drugs hadn't taken effect yet. "I gave you a warning," Richie said.

"They're after Ana!" I shouted at the table. Ana herself locked eyes with me. "It's the Armenian Mafia! They're ready to grab her downstairs. Jamal's in on it!"

The three other guards turned toward Jamal.

Jamal's face said "you gonna believe this random guy?"

Jamal vibed *guilty*.

Ana took cover behind her other three men.

Kentucky Walton said, "Awww shit!"

Two of the loyal bodyguards rushed Jamal. One of them covered Ana. Jamal was thrown back. His chair flew and his head bounced. The nearby audience jumped out of their seats. They made space between themselves and the struggle. Jamal was overpowered. People filmed it on their phones. The third guy kept Ana covered while the other two kicked his ass.

Cyclone faded from the jab. Richie still had him pinned.

One bodyguard got Jamal's handgun off of him. Another removed his zip ties. They rolled Jamal onto his stomach and secured his hands behind his back.

I took the pen from my pocket. "Cyclone's down," I said, speaking into it. "The inside man on Ana's team is down. Sam and Arman are still in the long Ford van up the street from the hotel. Sam's hostage is in the back. Repeat, Sam's hostage in the back. If you can hear this, proceed with caution. Don't get her killed!"

The other patrons were mesmerized watching me talk to my pen.

On stage, Kentucky Walton hadn't taken cover. "Well, this sort of shit doesn't happen at every show..."

Down below on Glenoaks, overlapping sirens blared. Red and blue lights flickered. I rushed to the ledge. There was Sam's van up the street, still idling in the same spot. Fed cruisers and LAPD squad cars had it surrounded.

I was eight stories up but had a good angle. Tamiroff was in front. The yellow FBI lettering on the back of his jacket was easy to spot. Just behind him were Angelis and Escobar.

It was a standoff. Jaqueline's life was in the balance.

People in the audience followed me to the ledge. They kept filming. They reached their arms over the ledge to get a better angle on the scene below.

I turned back around. Two of the bodyguards had rushed Ana off. I had no visual on her. Another bodyguard stayed with the zip-tied Jamal. Cyclone was out cold. Wilson, the hotel bouncer, took over watching him. Richie pushed through the mass of people and joined me at the ledge.

Below, the standoff continued. Tamiroff took out a loudspeaker. His amplified words were scratchy and hard to make out. The gist was "surrender peacefully."

The passenger side door of the van opened slowly. Arman stepped out with his arms raised. The driver's side door opened. Then Hollywood Sam got out. He was giving up.

"Turn around," Tamiroff said into the microphone. They obeyed. "Interlock your fingers and place your hands behind your head."

Sam and Arman obeyed. Tamiroff and Gould moved forward and cuffed them.

Angelis opened the back door. Slowly, Escobar brought out Jaqueline. Jaqueline moved slowly and needed to be propped up, but she was alive.

EIGHTEEN

TAMIROFF AND GOULD were busy, so some lower-level Feds took our statements. Susan drove from Studio City to Hollywood Station in the middle of the night to sit with us as we kept repeating each detail to them, over and over.

Tamiroff came in, looking relieved of a great burden. "We've begun arresting Armenian Dominance gang members across the city. Over a hundred warrants are currently being served. This operation was never just about Sam. It was about crippling the whole organization."

"Over a hundred," I said. The number seemed *too* big.

"We were timing it this way all along. The bracelets had to go on Sam first."

I wondered if I would be outed as a cooperator and a target for any AD guys still on the street after the bust.

"Jaqueline got taken to Cedars," Tamiroff said. "Her parents were notified. She's a high school sophomore from Burbank who went missing a month ago. We don't know how or why Sam targeted her, but she's safe now and getting the help she needs. I wish we could have stepped in sooner, but I wouldn't authorize risking her safety after Sam made such a direct threat. Thank you for keeping control of the situation after that curveball."

"Was Sam bluffing about hurting her?" Richie asked.

"I can't say. Now that it's over, I do think this whole Safarian kidnapping caper was about wanting to get himself caught. Maybe he feels like he's got more control in jail. He spent a long time there."

"Was New Millennium raided?" I asked.

"Yes."

"Did they find Shayla Ramsey? Sam's got the building across the alley behind New Millennium too. Did they search there?"

"No, they did not find her after searching both locations.

There were a few AD members at New Millennium, all people we ended up having fresh warrants for. But no Shayla, or any other women besides Jaqueline. I'm sorry."

"Ana Safarian?" I asked.

"She got out safely. Her bodyguard Jamal's also talking. Ana's lawyer has told us we can expect her complete cooperation. She's just taking her sweet time getting over here." Tamiroff got up to leave. "At first, I thought you two were bad news. Jokes. Detective Angelis convinced me otherwise. This operation hasn't just been my job, it's been a personal crusade. You helped me cross the finish line. Thank you."

"If you really want to thank us, help us find Shayla Ramsey," I said.

"I'm working on it."

THE CONFERENCE ROOM was packed with Feds. Little Post-it notes saying ARRESTED had been pinned to many faces on the board. Electricity was in the air. At the end of the table, we saw Narek. He walked over and hugged Richie.

"All right, all right." Richie isn't big on hugging.

Next, Narek hugged me. I'm not big on hugging either.

"Many thanks to you, many thanks." Narek shook his head at the wild night we'd just been through. "Good thing Jaqueline is okay."

Agent Gould pinned another ARRESTED note to a fresh Armenian face on the board.

"What's your next move? Witness protection?" I asked.

"No." His voice was firm. "Armenian Dominance acts like they own Glendale, but they don't own Glendale. I go back to my life now."

"People there might think you helped with this," Richie said.

"I won't be hard to find, if they have problem."

"Good for you," Richie said.

RICHIE, SUSAN, AND I were brought into a different

interrogation room. Tamiroff and a Fed lawyer were there waiting. So was Arman, at a table. Sitting beside him was his public defender, a heavyset, middle-aged black woman with thick-lensed glasses and waist-long extensions. Susan stood behind us in the corner, her briefcase at her side.

Tamiroff gestured us forward. "Go ahead," he said when we were seated.

"What happened to Shayla Ramsey?" I asked Arman.

"I don't know."

"We know you were back together," I said.

"Earlier this year, I met with her. I begged for her help in getting myself out of the life. I didn't think she would even speak to me, considering how bad I'd been to her before."

"What would Shayla know about leaving Armenian Dominance?" I asked.

"Shayla escaped the Mormons. They're basically a mob too."

"Who was Shayla going to meet in Griffith Park that day?"

This question surprised him. "Some Mormon."

"What Mormon?"

"Shayla wasn't a regular Mormon like the ones you see in dress clothes, knocking on people's doors, you know. She came from a polygamist compound called Bear Creek."

"We know," I said. "What Mormon was she seeing at Griffith Park?"

"A polygamist, I think. I don't have a name. I don't know why she wanted to meet him, or what was going on. She'd been acting strange. Shayla was running from the marriage her parents forced her into at fifteen. It was to some old man who already had a bunch of other wives. It was the top duty she'd been raised for and she didn't want it. Then, all these years later, she was suddenly planning to go hiking with some Mormon? I said it wasn't a good idea. I don't think she thought it was a good idea either. But she said to mind my own business, so I lost my temper and we fought."

I took the airplane necklace from my pocket and hung it out in front of him.

"Where'd you find that?"

"Griffith Park."

"They got her?" Arman's voice was trembling.

"*Who* got her?"

"I don't know. That's what I'm asking you."

His sincerity rang out. He'd been angry with her on the phone because he was worried, not because he or his boss had targeted her in any way.

"So you really were trying to get out," I said. I believed him and he could tell.

"I was low-level for years, mostly just selling cars. Then Sam just picks me as his top guy... The things he made me do... Yeah, maybe Sam isn't the mastermind he used to be, but he's still insane... I told her I wanted to escape like she had, and I asked for her help in getting there. I'd been going to church again, even to confession. Shalya agreed to let me back into her life, to help me. We started dating again. We weren't perfect, sometimes it was like she was in outer space. But it was better than three years ago. I was different now that I had Jesus back in my life. But there was too much in my way. Sam is paranoid. He gets... possessed. Satanically possessed. I didn't try hard enough to leave."

It was undeniable now. Someone Mormon had taken Shayla, or knew who did. This whole Armenian business was a sideshow. Tomorrow we would have to start back at the beginning.

RICHIE AND I went outside to his Bronco, where Richie got out his cigarettes. I had one with him. Normally I don't smoke, but that night I felt I'd earned one.

Press vans lined Wilcox. Patrolmen watched the perimeter so none snuck in. It was five in the morning and dawn loomed. The Feds and the cops were done questioning us. Susan went home to get some sleep. She had a court appearance at nine. Tamiroff said he had something important to show us. He asked us to stick around.

We got our phones back. I searched for news updates. The

Armenian mob arrests were showing up. Joan had left L.A. on a short business trip. She was opening her first out-of-state store in Atlanta the following year. Our plan was to update her about all this when she got back.

A long white 2013 Navigator turned into the lot. The reporters on the street recognized it and filmed it. The driver cracked the window and talked to one of the patrolmen. The officer let the vehicle pass into the station lot, where it parked in a back corner.

A door opened. One of Ana's bodyguards from earlier stepped out from the driver's seat and walked our way. "She wants to see y'all." He had on dark shades.

"Maybe she should check in with the Feds first," I said. "They're expecting a statement."

He shook his head. "She wants to speak with you before that."

We followed him back, where he opened the back door for us. We climbed in and sat in the plush leather seats. There Ana was, across from us.

She had changed into a black leather jacket and gold-trimmed designer sunglasses. Under the jacket she had on a different dress from the one at Cackles. It was even shorter than before. Her legs were crossed, revealing her thick, perfectly shaped thighs.

Another bodyguard sat beside her, looking protective after the night's close call. The other sat in the passenger seat, looking back. The third guy, the driver, stayed outside.

"My name is Ana Safarian."

A square minibar was between us. It was stocked with top-shelf liquor.

"We know," Richie said.

"I wanted to thank you two."

"We had our own motivations for getting involved. In the first place, I mean," I said.

"You two are detectives, searching for a missing woman."

"We thought Arman or Sam might know what happened. We thought wrong."

"Either way, you helped make many good people happy tonight."

"A lot of Armenian wise guys are going down in this, but not all of them," Richie said. "This Narek guy who helped will be known as a rat on the street. The AD put him through some shit, and he took it like a man, but Narek's no gangster. The Feds are going to cut him loose, free of any charges, and Hollywood Sam's going to jail, but Narek needs to not be looking over his shoulder every time he walks down the street."

Ana said, "I know some people."

The way she said *some people* gave me chills.

"Maybe these people can help Narek," Richie said. "And maybe they can help us too?"

"That's not unreasonable to ask."

Richie smiled, then sat back, relaxed. "I heard you're a big stand-up fan. I'm a comedian, you know. I used to do sets at Cackles all the time, like twice a week."

She smiled. "Are you any good?"

"Darling, I'm an undiscovered star."

TAMIROFF BROUGHT US into a small office. A two-way mirror looked into an interrogation room. "Sam's finally done stalling," he said.

Sam and his lawyer were on the other side of the mirror. The door to the interrogation room opened. Angelis and Escobar walked in. They had an FBI lawyer with them.

Escobar carried a laptop. She put it down on the desk. She opened it and slid it around. An audio file was pulled up. She hit play.

It was a recording from earlier. Sam planned the kidnapping of Ana. It was unmistakably his voice. Escobar hit pause.

"We've been ready to charge your client with racketeering, premeditated murder, intent to distribute, fraud, theft, coercion, and blackmail," Angelis said. "After tonight, we're charging him with conspiracy to kidnap Ana Safarian. The reign of Hollywood Sam is over. Your client is going away. The amount of time is the only choice he has to contribute to the rest of his life. If he wants to make things difficult for the Panther, he should start talking."

Sam and his lawyer whispered back and forth.

His lawyer looked up. "If Sam were to cooperate, and give you information he thinks you might be seeking, what type of arrangement would you offer?"

Tamiroff turned to us and smiled.

NINETEEN

MY HEAD FELT light and woozy, like a champagne hangover. But early that morning had been my first time going to bed sober in months. It was 10 a.m. and I'd slept through the day's first round of parrot squawking. I could tell overflow adrenaline would fuel me for another day, even though I'd only been out about four hours.

I made coffee using the Keurig my old roommate left when he moved out. It was Saturday, and Milo lay on the living room couch. He was on the phone talking about how his favorite Echo Park donut shop had just gone out of business due to gentrification. Milo seemed unable to speak more than a few sentences those days without bringing up gentrification.

My phone buzzed from a text. Richie was heading over.

As I sipped my hot coffee, I sorted through the news articles about the previous night. The first headline said ANA SAFARIAN KIDNAPPING PLOT FOILED. The main points appeared in the story. The actions of Richie, Narek, and I were all attributed to the FBI and the LAPD. The three of us were not mentioned. I scanned other articles and the gist of them was the same. There were six or seven Facebook messages and emails from reporters who had tracked me down and wanted an exclusive. They hadn't written about us yet but were on the scent. I didn't respond to any of them.

The sweeping arrests were getting far less attention than Ana. In the *L.A. Times* it said thirty-nine members of Armenian Dominance had been arrested, but this number was expected to rise significantly over the next few days. The recently apprehended included a wealthy Bel-Air lawyer and a three-year veteran of the L.A. County Sheriff's Department.

On Twitter, I found some uploaded videos of others who had been at Cackles. I found myself and Richie a few times, but we looked like bystanders.

While sorting through all of this online material and considering my direct connection to it, I kept thinking about my friend James LaSalle. James has epilepsy. His seizures first started in high school, and some of the ones he's had over the years have been pretty serious. He's been taking medication to regulate them, which usually works, but not always. Once, I asked James what it felt like when he woke up after a seizure and realized he was going to be okay.

"I feel like taking more risks," James said.

"Why?"

"Because if this didn't kill me, it feels like nothing can."

Right then, I knew how James felt.

Our metal front door clanged open. Then Richie appeared in my bedroom doorway. "Guess where I went last night." He was smiling.

"You didn't go home?" The night before, Richie seemed pretty grateful it was no longer dangerous for him to go back to Lexington. I couldn't imagine not going home and crashing.

He shook his head.

"You went out and picked up a girl?"

"It was a girl... yes."

He was like a kid, expecting me to play a guessing game.

"So it wasn't another hooker?"

He shook his head, still smiling.

"No..." I didn't believe it.

He nodded.

It must be some joke. "*How?*"

"She gave us her number, remember?"

"Yeah, but she wasn't expecting us to call, was she?"

"Why give us her number if she isn't expecting it?" He held up his hand like he was swearing an oath in court. "I officially take back any negative thing I've ever said about Armenians. Consider my outlook to have taken a complete one-eighty, kid!"

"You had sex with Ana Safarian last night? *Really?*"

"What am I going to do now, climb Mount Everest? What's left for me to do?"

"What about Mahad Southern?"

"What about him?"

"He's her boyfriend."

"They're on a break, I think. I don't know. He never came up, except for her to emphasize to me a couple times that he has no sense of humor at all."

"She give you any update about the favor we asked for? The people she knows?"

"Oh yeah. That reminds me, I gotta call Angelis back." He sat on my futon and called Angelis on speakerphone.

"Dubs?"

"Yeah, it's me, Ricky Boy, sorry I was so late returning your call. I was catching up on sleep." Richie smiled. "What have you got?"

"A county jail snitch who reports to Intelligence just said the word was sent down from the new king of the AD, the Panther. The Panther says there's to be no street response for the Hollywood Sam takedown. It's too much heat. He wants everything quiet. You'll probably be asked to testify at Sam's trial, which will be at least a year off. But it looks like you guys are safe from the Armenians for now."

"Music to my ears," Richie said.

RICHIE AND I both had to put in appearances at the store that day. He started at noon and I had a closing shift. I put my work clothes into my backpack as well as the MR73, which Angelis had returned to me the night before. My phone said the current weather was already ninety-six.

We got in the Bronco.

"So Ana actually bailed us out?" I asked. "The AD's backing down because of her?"

Richie drove us past Sunset Junction. We passed the Vista movie theater and went north on Hillhurst. "I saw her make the call. One of her lawyers knows the Panther's lawyer. If they agree to no reprisals on us and Narek, she offered to keep quiet about them. Ana didn't like doing it. She genuinely hates the AD. But she wants us to be safe, and I think she was spooked about how bad it could have gotten last night."

"We just trust Armenian Dominance at their word?"

"Didn't you hear Angelis? The word's already out in the can. The heat from this thing is so bad they just want quiet. Her reaching out worked."

"Unless Cyclone or one of the others going down tries to work out revenge on their own, apart from whatever the current boss wants. They can hire people out from inside."

"Well, we can't help that." He shrugged.

"Thanks for the reassurance... Jesus, I still can't believe you're fucking Ana Safarian."

"All of the shots you don't take are failures."

He parked again in the Observatory lot. Juan the parking lot attendant was out sitting in the same chair and under the same tent.

"That guy's wrong," I said. "We were too easy before."

"Think he saw something?"

"We should have pushed harder. Want to brace him?"

"Yes, Minor-man. Yes, I do."

We got out of the Bronco and walked over to Juan. I was already sweating from the heat by the time we made it to him.

Juan's Oakley shades covered his eyes. "And how are you gentlemen doing on this fine Saturday morning?" He was in the same peculiar and manic mood. His triple XL Dodger-blue shirt was tainted a few shades darker from all the chest and belly sweat covering it. I couldn't tell if he remembered us from before.

"We have questions," I said. "We're expecting answers."

He made a confused face. I removed Shayla's necklace from my pocket. "You recognize this. I know you do." I held it out in front of him. It hung at a tilt.

"What do I recognize?" He looked away from it.

Richie pulled Juan's Oakleys off and tossed them on the grass.

"Don't fuck with us," I said.

Richie grabbed Juan's water bottle. He screwed off the top and smelled it. "He's pounding tequila on the job." Richie poured the booze out on Juan's shoes.

Juan shouted something in Spanish. It was too fast for me to follow.

"We're looking for a woman that went missing at this park. This was her necklace. I know you recognize it," I said.

His lizard brain searched for an answer. "There's a girl who hikes here," he said finally. "She comes by regularly. She has maybe the nicest big nattys I've ever seen."

"Are her tits bigger than yours?" Richie asked.

Juan looked down at his own chest. "Yes," he said, embarrassed about looking. "Sometimes I do photography of the girls here." Now he was reserved and gentle. He wanted sympathy. He nodded at the airplane. "She was a special one of mine. I looked forward to when she would come, so I could take her picture. She really was something."

"Let us see who you're talking about. Show us your photography," Richie said.

He scrolled through photos. A thin cloud had passed over most of the sun. It helped us see his screen in the midday light. There were dozens from the same album. They were all women who went hiking at the park. Most were from his current vantage point. He got to the one he was looking for. There was Shayla. She was in a light-green T-shirt and gray exercise pants. The airplane necklace in my hand rested low around her neck.

"That girl went missing, and the last place she was at before she disappeared was right here at this park," I said. "What happened to her?"

"She came up here two or three times a week. Once, I picked her some flowers. She thought that was nice and always said hello after that. Sometimes, she came through with coworkers and sometimes she was with lames who were just trying to smash. Sometimes she was alone. The last time I saw her was on a night shift. I get scheduled late if there's a nighttime event at the

Observatory. That night she was meeting these two weird dudes."

"Weird how?" I asked.

"Like they were dressed for the Oregon Trail or some shit. One guy was younger, with really long hair. The other guy was much older and had a white beard. They weren't in regular hiking clothes. But both had on heavy-duty boots, like they spent time in the mountains."

"And?"

"And the three of them went inside the Observatory for a little bit, then out on a trail."

"Stop dragging this out. *Talk*," Richie said.

"I thought maybe I heard a woman scream."

"Was she the one screaming?" I asked.

"It's hard to tell, sometimes what I think is a scream is just girls laughing and there's a weird echo sort of like, sort of changing it, you know? But it seemed like her. After a while, her and the two dudes came back together. Now she was like hypnotized or some shit."

"Calling the cops ever cross your mind?" I asked.

"The Oregon Trail dudes rolled in a fresh black Porsche. They were balling-ass mountain men. I was thinking about *feria*. One of them came up to me and said he'd pay me to keep quiet about them ever being here. He pointed at the girl and showed me she didn't have any outside bruises or nothing. He just said his boss valued his privacy."

"Did the younger one pay you?" I asked.

"Yeah."

"Describe him in detail."

"Suit, beard, long hair. Tall-ass white dude. Looked either like he was going to come out in a Western movie, or like he maybe was going to Coachella."

"How much did you get?"

"He offered five hundred, cash. I asked for more. Seemed like they could afford it. The boss said yes. We settled on a g. They told me where I could pick it up."

"Where'd you pick it up?" I asked.

"The Sunset Tower. I waited for him at the bar. He came down and gave me the envelope." Juan waited. "Please don't tell the Oregon Trail dudes I snitched."

TWENTY

OUR NAMASTE MART lot was almost empty. When the heat was this bad, sales were usually slow during the day but tended to pick up fast when the sun went down. Right now, it had passed a hundred. Richie and I sat in his Bronco while he smoked a cigarette. There were nine minutes before he needed to clock in for his shift.

"So either these Mormons have Shayla or they know where she is and are willing to fork over cash for Juan to keep quiet," he said.

"Why do you suppose Shayla screamed?"

"If I were a broad, I'd shriek every time I saw one of these freaks."

"Were they holding something over her head? Something that scared her? I'll bet she never paid back her loan."

"We should poke around the Sunset Tower. Maybe they're still there. Shit, maybe Shayla's just been at a hotel with some Mormons this whole time."

"That wouldn't make sense." I shook my head.

"Anyway, I've got to get inside. You still coming tonight?"

Tonight? We both had to work. "To what?"

"My show."

His show at the Comedy Store. I'd bought a ticket over a month ago but forgotten about it. Richie didn't always invite his friends out to shows. It was only when he had material that he was proud of. All of our drama lately hadn't made him consider backing out.

"Shit. With everything going on, I forgot. Yeah, I'm still coming. Of course."

"I don't go on until eleven. You're off at ten, right?"

"Wouldn't miss it."

He held out his keys. "Since we can't go after work, why don't you take my ride now and go check out the hotel."

THE SUNSET TOWER was an art deco high-rise in the heart of the Strip, just up the block from where Richie's show would be later. At the entrance to the Tower Bar, a pianist in a black suit played Irving Berlin. Pictures of old movie stars hung on the walnut-paneled walls. Funny bubble captions were written on the glass. There was an outdoor terrace where more tables were lined up beside a pool. Tables were filled with the lunchtime crowd. All the clientele seemed like Industry people. I sat at the bar and ordered a Negroni.

I had on New Balance tennis shoes, a pair of faded jeans I'd worn to shifts at the store dozens of times, and a T-shirt for the documentary *Burden of Dreams*, which had a drawing of Werner Herzog pulling a boat up a mountain for *Fitzcarraldo*. I wondered if I violated the dress code, but figured they must have all sorts of tourists who came in dressed like slobs.

Just as my Negroni came, a woman sat on the stool beside me. She was short and had thick, curly black hair. I guessed she was of Indian descent. When she sat, she let out an exhausted sigh. She didn't strike me as a guest at the hotel. The bartender looked at her and she ordered a martini.

"Long day?"

"*Shit.* Long decade. And we're only three years in."

"I've never been in this building. It's nice."

"My boss is a guest in a suite." She pointed to the ceiling.

"You travel with your boss?"

Her martini came. "She lives in a mansion out in Pasadena that's probably fifteen times the size of my apartment. Sometimes she feels like a change of pace so she rents a hotel room here. When she does, I have to make the drive over from Echo Park, where I live." She caught herself, then made an awkward smile. "Why am I telling you all of this?"

"That's all right. People tell me their problems all day."

"Oh yeah? What's your racket?"

"I work at the Namaste Mart at Santa Monica and Gardner." Despite how long I've been doing it, for some reason, I never just announce myself as a PI.

She went through the usual spiel about her favorite products, but this time I didn't just zone out as usual. "Sometimes I wish I just worked at a place like that," she said. "Being the assistant to a famous actress isn't as glamorous as it sounds. But you've got to play the networking game."

"My name is Adam," I said, and offered my hand.

"Amyra," she said.

"Your boss is an actress. Are you one too?" She didn't seem like it.

"No. Believe it or not, I just sort of fell into this gig. What I really want to be is a writer."

I was about to tell Amyra how I was a writer too. I would tell her how I lived in Silver Lake, just one neighborhood away from Echo Park. I would to ask if she wanted to get coffee with me sometime. But in the mirror behind the bar, I saw a long-haired man in a suit cross the room. He was leaving the tables at the terrace and I turned around just as he passed.

I'd seen this man before.

I got up, leaving Amyra and my drink. I moved fast and got in front of him by the entrance to the bar, blocking his way.

"You ever been to a lingerie shop in East Hollywood called Joan's Bras?"

It was the guy who asked me about the figs a couple days ago at the demo station. He carried an old leather briefcase.

"Who are you?"

"A friend of Joan's."

"You never witnessed me at Joan's."

This was true. The man on the grainy black-and-white security footage was far older. "So, you know the place then."

He looked around, like maybe I wasn't alone. His deep-brown tan was the kind it took months to develop.

"I didn't bring any backup."

"Am I to have faith you'd disclose your backup if, in fact, you weren't alone?"

"Why does the mention of Joan's Bras make you nervous?"

"I think I recognize you too." He stroked his beard.

This happened a lot. People recognized me from when they came into the store but couldn't place me out in the world.

"You shop at the Namaste Mart on Santa Monica. I work there."

"That's it." He snapped his fingers. "Normally, I don't shop at that location, but I just came to like it over time because it has a decent parking lot with regular spaces. My home is never as crowded as L.A. I value a decent parking lot while I'm here."

"I wouldn't expect a guy like you to do regular grocery shopping. The Sunset Tower crowd strikes me more as the room service type."

"My employer favors the low-sugar Namaste Mart ube spread your company carries in the summertime. He insists I buy it for him every time we visit Los Angeles. He's a morning person, always has been, and he won't have a California breakfast without it spread upon his first slice of daily rye."

His employer.

"Where do you normally live? Where's home?"

The only noise came from the piano. "The Best Things Happen While You're Dancing."

"Stick to being a grocer," he said.

I decided to needle him more. "Don't you want to know why I'm here?"

He stepped around me and moved on down the hall. I rushed back to the bar to see that Amyra was now gone. The bartender shook his head, disappointed in the speedy screwup. I chugged the rest of the Negroni and paid him.

Outside, I was just in time to see the guy get in a black 2013 Porsche delivered by a valet and drive off down Sunset. I took out my notepad and wrote down the plates.

GLEN, WHO ALSO worked the milk cooler with me and Fabian, was facing all of the many Namaste Mart varieties of coconut milk. I grabbed a smoothie to drink before clocking in.

Glen saw me. "Crazy, huh?"

I assumed he'd heard about some version of our night. Richie was probably in the break room right then, retelling it with comic flourishes.

"So you heard?"

"He was just riding his bike like usual. He was such a nice and positive guy."

"What? Who was riding his bike?"

"Iko..."

Iko was another crew member who moved to L.A. from a small island in the Philippines. The island was controlled by Iko's father, a career politician with his own private military force. Like many Filipinos, Iko moved to the States so he could work and send money home. Once, Iko confided to me his deeper reason for moving, one more important than the favorable exchange rate. Iko's father had been tasked by the national government with ridding their region of the country of Islamic militants, who were attempting to create a stronghold there. He sent his firstborn son to California because it was safer here.

I hadn't heard any news about him, but I had noticed many fresh Novice crew members in the store.

"You didn't hear?"

"Hear what?"

"Iko got hit by a car. Jackie was with him. They were both off and they were riding from Silver Lake all the way to Venice Beach." Jackie Mills was Iko's roommate. "Iko's dead."

IT WAS AN employee meeting in the back room. Richie stood beside me. People cried. The fresh faces were all from other locations called in to cover.

Iko and Jackie lived near me in Silver Lake. Iko rode his bike to work sometimes, like me. If we had similar shifts, we would run into each other on our rides.

Christy said, "So if you need to go home from your shift to grieve, or just take what we'll call a 'mental health day,' that's permitted. Are there any questions?"

Stefan, who was really close with Iko, raised his hand. "Do we know what happened?"

"The way it's looking right now is that the driver just didn't see him," Christy said. I wondered if Iko and Jackie had been high on their bike ride. Jackie almost certainly had to be.

"That's how it was relayed to me. Also, the police have all the information about the driver, so it wasn't a hit and run."

Many crew members walked up to speak with her one-on-one. I was sure it was about going home. Richie and I talked by the wine backstock.

"I think I found the long-haired guy who paid off Juan at the hotel."

"You talk to him?"

"Yeah, I tried to rattle him by bringing up Joan's Bras, and I got these." I showed Richie the plate number. "A 2013 black Porsche. Exactly the kind of car Juan saw at Griffith Park."

"He seem rattled?"

"Hard to say."

"You think he might check out of the hotel?"

"He didn't seem in a rush to."

Richie checked the time. When we'd been deep into cases in the past, having to make our appearances at Namaste Mart was always one of the most difficult parts. Today felt different.

I nodded toward the growing line of crew members who were waiting to speak to Christy about leaving. "Are you going home like everyone else?"

"They all seem pretty broken up," Richie said. "I don't blame them. It's a tragedy. Fucking kid was only twenty-three."

Richie and I looked at all of our good coworkers around us experiencing death with the gentle sensitivities we'd both long shed.

"I figure they need me here," I said.

"Yeah. I'm staying too. I say we go back to the Tower tomorrow. Have a look-see."

"I agree."

TWENTY-ONE

FOR MY LAST break, I stepped outside with Richie. Our lot was filling up with customers, far more than I'd predicted. They didn't care about the heat. A memorial formed on the front wall. People left flowers and wreaths. Many were Filipinos. A manager filling in from another Namaste Mart location brought out a corkboard and different colored stacks of Post-it notes so people could leave messages. Iko was close to so many of them. If any of the boorish behavior they exhibited to us every day got under his skin, he never showed it. Iko always had this zen-like calm.

"I'm getting a lift to the Store," Richie said, meaning the Comedy Store. "Why don't you keep my keys and take the Bronco over when you get off?"

"Who's picking you up?"

"My new broad."

Shit. He'd said it casually, like dating Ana Safarian was the most casual thing in the world. "She's going to the show?"

"As we know, she's a comedy fan. A *connoisseur*." He rolled his eyes in near disgust. "Last night in bed, she actually said Jimmy Fallon was funny. I decided to keep my mouth shut about that one, a skill you desperately need to develop someday." The familiar white Navigator turned off of Gardner and into our lot. "I'll tell her you're coming too." It stopped in front of us. "See you there." The back door opened and he was off.

I watched two regulars walk up to the memorial. It was magic hour. One left a bouquet of magnolias. There was no way I'd get this much love from our customers if I died unexpectedly.

I PARKED IN an underground garage at Crescent Heights under the movie theater and walked down the Strip to the Comedy Store. Andy Dick's name was on the marquee. Richie hadn't mentioned he would be the headliner. I got inside and went to the main room, where the show hadn't begun yet. I passed a sign: No Cell Phone Photography. Policy Enforced. It was quarter to ten and the crowd was quickly filling in.

There was Ana, sitting at a booth. She wore large black Gucci sunglasses. Her same three bodyguards watched her. I approached, slowly. They recognized me and let me continue.

Ana hugged me. "Sit with me?"

I nodded too eagerly. It was thrilling to take a seat beside this lovely billionaire I'd helped save from serious danger, despite the fact I hadn't cared about her at all before a couple of days ago. I tried to place her perfume. I picked up cashmere, wood, and maybe tuberose. "I was going to sit with other people Richie and I work with, but I don't think they're coming. One of our coworkers passed away today in an accident."

"That's tragic." She took my hand. "I'm *so sorry*."

At the booth beside ours, Jeff Garlin sat down with his wife. I saw him look right at me. "I don't mean to be a bummer. Life is just crazy sometimes, you know."

"I do."

From a waitress, I ordered a Negroni. Ana chose a mezcal on the rocks. I told her all about what happened to Iko, everything we knew. Most of it was me repeating stuff I'd told probably two dozen customers during my shift earlier in the day, but with Ana, I was able to be sincere. She listened closely and made me feel like I was the only person in the world. As I spoke, I felt grateful to still be alive.

"Has the press contacted you about last night?" she asked.

I could feel people in the room watching us. Wherever Ana went became a circus and she was clearly gifted with some peculiar psychological ability to not let it bother her. "I've just been ignoring them. The media is full of vultures."

"Of course they are," she said, charmed by my innocence. "The key is to get them working for you, which they are always more than willing to do if you handle them correctly. Publicity can always be spun into a good thing. I'll get you guys in touch with one of my brand managers, pro bono. You'll see."

She gave my hand a gentle pat, then interlocked my fingers with hers. Our drinks arrived, and we sat sipping them and holding hands.

A FILL-IN ANNOUNCER read Richie's name. Andy Dick, who was supposed to go on first, hadn't arrived yet, and the show went on without him.

Richie walked on stage, full of energy and with a big smile. The audience applauded. Ana and I made the most noise.

"*Ohh*, there's more people in here than Andy Dick's last intervention!" Richie said.

This brought *ohhhhs* from the crowd.

"What? He's a fucking drug addict." The audience laughed. Richie walked to the edge of the stage. "You know, I was raised a Catholic, back in Queens. Those nuns supervising me were *sooo* against masturbation. If anybody might be playing with themselves, that set those old broads off like you wouldn't believe. They always told me how important it was to remember that if I ever jerked off, I'd grow hair all over the back of my hands. I thought about this. Pondered it. But after about two fucking seconds I decided that throughout my formative childhood years, I would just wear mittens. Better than letting the back of my hands look like an Armenian's asshole." This got a big laugh and he paused to let it ride out. "I'm Richie Walsh, and I always like to open with Armenian assholes!" The crowd applauded. "You know, I've got some good news tonight. I recently experienced a positive personal breakthrough in my life. A new friend taught me some things and inspired me to change my mind."

I looked over and saw Ana make this sweet smile.

"And by new friend, I mean my new relationship with a *lady*. I know, I know, this is West Hollywood... girls are *soo yucky*." A group of gay men at the table next to us roared. "You see, this brilliant, sexy woman is an *Armenian*." More eyes in the audience turned away from Richie and toward us. They were putting pieces together.

"I admit, I didn't use to like Armenians," Richie said. "You ever notice how being openly racist against Armenian Americans is kind of socially acceptable here in L.A.? Like even a perfect, tolerant liberal who still has their John Kerry bumper sticker and that Coexist one that's made up of all the religious symbols will still just openly denigrate Armenians? This used to be fine with me because during my time living in L.A., I've met some Armenian assholes. L.A. has the biggest population of Armenians in the world, outside of Armenia. I said to myself, '*Who are these people*?' In Ozone Park we didn't have any. I presumed Armenians must be some sort of mountain Mexican... but they're whites." He waited. "Did you guys know Armenians are officially considered whites?" He waited again. There were scattered cackles. "I swear, it's true, I looked it up. They had this whole case up in Fresno and the judge ruled that Armenians are whites, like me. This threw me for a loop which I'd been struggling with for a while. How can I continue to be racist against my own race?" Richie posed like Rodin's *The Thinker*.

Jeff Garlin spit out his drink and leaned forward, coughing and laughing at the same time. There was a sense of danger in the room. How far would Richie take this?

He walked over to the other side of the stage. "For one of my jobs, I encounter a lot of people from eastern Europe. I work in a grocery store called Namaste Mart." Our store name got applause. "I know, I know. Namaste Mart. It's the happiest place on earth. Me and my coworkers are walking orgasms dressed in hippie shirts. At my store, we don't just have Armenians that come in. There's Hungarians, Ukrainians. But most of them are Russians. At first, I didn't understand Russian behavior. Their attitudes were a mystery to me. What made them tick? Now, I'm not talking about somebody with some 23andMe speck of Russian DNA or whatever, I'm talking about old, vodka-pounding Russians who lived through the Soviet era, who've shrunk down to midget size at this point, and the only thing really keeping them alive is goat milk, rage, and anti-state paranoia. I would try, at my job, to tell jokes. I like making people laugh, but I could never get *them* to laugh. Usually, I couldn't even get a smile. But one day, this old Russian man walked up to me. This is a true story. He says this..." Richie changed to one of his Russian accents. "I will tell joke to you now, Mr. Funny Man. Man walks into grocer. Man says 'Do you have goat milk?' Grocer says 'No, but we have... *goat sausage*.'" Richie held a pause, then returned to his regular voice. "*End of joke.*" He waited again. "You see, it's funny because in Russia, they have a *lot* of famine. I'm telling someone else's joke here, but funny's funny. Plus, that joke is telling."

The laughs grew. I'd never heard Richie mention any of this material before. I was pretty sure he'd abandoned the ten minutes he'd been preparing for months and was just riffing.

The red light began to flash. "I told all of this to the new Armenian lady I've been seeing. She explained to me that most eastern Europeans and Russians do not waste a smile, basically because they've been through so much shit. The Armenians had a genocide and a genocide can have a cultural effect. Smiles are valuable to these people. You need a *good reason*... This whole time, I thought they were just assholes. I didn't understand. Now that I've got this new perspective, I wanted all of you to know that I've completely changed my opinion about the Armenian population of Los Angeles. Yeah, I'll still joke around, like I do with everybody, but I think they're all right now." Ana and I both stood and cheered. Everyone was applauding. Richie waved goodbye. "My name is Richie Walsh. Thank you for coming along with me on this heartwarming journey of self-improvement."

I TOLD RICHIE I would drop the Bronco off at his place.

"Keep it if you want," he said. "I'm spending the night with Ana."

I was still feeling high off the show. It had been a great night. Richie's set had killed and I was happy for him. "That's all right. I'll drop it off and take the 704 back home. It'll be fine." My plan was to take it slow and meditate about the next day's search. I would get a good night's sleep and be prepared to get some real answers in the morning.

Richie shrugged. "Leave the keys on my counter, then lock the door behind you."

Back on the road, I took my time crossing the neon-lit surface streets. 113.FM The Eagle was on the radio. Classic Rock. "Sway" by the Stones.

At Richie's, I found a space right on Lexington, walked through the gate, unlocked the door, and went in. Just as I switched on the lights, someone hit me in the back of the head.

The floor came at me fast and blackness washed me away.

TWENTY-TWO

THE BLINDS WERE drawn. My vision blurred and coppery blood pooled in my mouth. A sharp pain ran through the bone in my nose. I straightened my glasses, which were tilted on my face. Both my hands were free.

I squinted. The long-haired man from the Sunset Tower held an old stainless-steel revolver, a .357 Magnum, I thought. It looked like a model from the '80s, or maybe even earlier.

"You like hitting people in the back of the head? It must be easy, sneaking around like a bitch..." Sometimes, if I'm alone and find myself in a potentially dangerous situation, I get aggressive and go on the offensive, hoping Richie will be proud of me later on when I tell him the story.

"Neither of your hands are bound," he said.

I hoisted myself upright, enraged. Bad idea. I couldn't balance yet, and my vision was still rough. I became afraid I would pass out, so I sat back down and tried to get my bearings.

Heavy boots crossed the tile floor of the kitchen. An old man stepped into the light. He was tall and wiry, with short white hair and a trim beard. On top of his head was an aged bowler hat with a curled brim and a feather plume. He wore an open and light sheepskin duster the same color as the hat. The duster was too heavy for this heat, but it didn't seem to bother him. Underneath, he wore an ivory-white suit. Its color was so vibrant it strained my weakened eyes, and I felt like I was being visited by some demented angel. From his breast pocket, he removed a white silk pocket square, unfolded it, and laid it on the edge of the futon.

"In my community, *Uncle* is a term of respect." He sat. "My name is Orson." Mr. Long Hair holstered his revolver and stood just behind him. "Uncle Orson Reed."

I felt a little bit like Lopez, Joan's character in *Martians.* I was facing a dangerous, unpredictable enemy who might as well have been from Mars.

"You've met P.Y., who isn't just the senior deacon of my church. He carries my proxy. I've chosen to come here for this visit because P.Y. said you have some important questions to ask me."

My revolver was in my backpack when I came in. Trying to be subtle, I scanned the room. There it was by the front door, on the floor near where I'd fallen, still closed. It didn't look like they'd searched it.

I tried to focus. There was no reason for me to expect Richie. He would be with Ana all night. These Mormons had me, and I was all alone.

"P.Y.," I said.

"An abbreviation."

"Of what?"

"P.Y.'s baptized name in the false church of the supposed Latter-day Saints is Jacob Barnabas Cannon, but his name in the true Mormon church is Porter the Younger."

"So I'm dealing with the *true* church here. Who is Porter the Elder?"

He laughed, loud and bellowing. It made a dog outside howl. "Even still, I underestimate the ignorance of the gentiles. Orrin Porter Rockwell was the fearsome protector of our Joseph. He was the *Mormon Samson.*"

Summoning all the Mormon religious history I'd hate read in order to prevail in possible situations like this was hard after the blow I'd just taken. "You're talking about... Joseph Smith's bodyguard?"

"Correct."

"And P.Y. here is Porter Rockwell's reincarnation?"

"Yes, Mr. Walsh. He is."

Mr. Walsh.

"My name isn't Walsh."

He made a dismissive wave. "Need we play games, Mr. Walsh?"

After leaving the Sunset Tower, P.Y. must have circled back behind me. He'd gotten Richie's plates and from there, somehow obtained this address.

"You've broken into Richie Walsh's house. Earlier, I drove Richie Walsh's car. But I'm not Richie Walsh. When you looked up his info, you obviously didn't get a picture. Otherwise, you'd know my name is Adam Minor, cocksucker."

P.Y. stepped forward and slapped me. I fell out of the chair, my ears ringing. I spaced out, gazing at the old man's white loafers.

"Put him upright, P.Y.," Orson said.

My lip felt split in multiple spots. P.Y.'s hands went under my arms and he lifted me back into the chair. The ringing intensified. P.Y. reached into my pocket and removed my wallet.

Orson held my California driver's license out under the light to look at it clearly. "You were being honest with your uncle. Good." He tossed it on the floor. "Why are you looking for me? Who hired you?"

"We're looking for a woman."

"What woman?"

"You know what woman."

"My property is my property. My will is my will. All attempting to inhibit my will shall, eventually, bend or *break*. Oppose my will and you will receive a meddler's punishment. I have important business pending and I've come to determine if you're a threat to it."

It came to me then why he hadn't bothered to tie me down. Binding my arms would have been an insult to his self-image. This asshole didn't believe anyone would dare strike him. "Shayla Ramsey isn't your property."

He bizarrely blurted out the sound of a wrong answer horn, like on a game show. "Incorrect."

"By what Goddamn right do you call another human your property?"

"If you still haven't learned how to speak respectfully to the Prophet, I'll be happy to give you another lesson," P.Y. said, wagging his finger. "*No blasphemy.*"

"Were you hired by Shayla's boss at the undergarment store?" Uncle Orson said. "Joan?"

I spit blood onto Richie's floor. "In the contacts section of my phone, I've got numbers saved for the LAPD and the FBI. You can kill me now and risk the heat that will bring or you can tell me where Shalya is and let me speak to her. Pick one door or the other."

"The worldly arrogance and presumption of a man in your position presuming to speak about options. Maybe Shayla doesn't want you to find her."

"Are you saying that? If you are, then you're lying."

P.Y. hit me with a hard right hook to the jaw, fast. I saw stars.

"You must appreciate how protective P.Y. is of his prophet. If you keep acting disrespectful, he's going to keep reprimanding you. If I speak it, then it is not a lie."

I became fueled by a strength I didn't know I had. I felt ready to take whatever pain either of them dished out. "He can hit me all he wants," I said. "I'll ask you again, Uncle Orson. By what right do you claim someone as your property?"

"The right bestowed from God Almighty."

"There's a lot of gods out there. A lot of churches."

"A lot of false gods and false churches. I'm a Mormon, a true Mormon. Not of the worldly abomination which went astray a century ago, nor of the other frauds who purport to have gotten back to the fundamentals. Joseph was given the truth by the angel Moroni. My rights come from the wisdom laid down directly by heaven to Joseph alone."

Warm blood seeped down the back of my neck. "You've got courage," I said. "You don't backpedal, rationalize, and make half-assed excuses like almost all the other modern churches do when confronted by the evil and lunacy in their own pasts. You embrace the evil. I respect that."

"It's pitiful, the way the leaders of these lost organizations can disingenuously rationalize. If you are not a Mormon, Mr. Minor, to what church do you belong?"

"None."

"The pomposity of youth... I'm so grateful I was raised by a man who never let the evil of the world take control of me."

"My father tried to hide the world from me. He never understood what a weak method that was. Being free is the only way to live. Or trying to be free, at least."

This seemed to interest him. "Only while in a direct relationship with God can we ever be free. Shayla is a wonderful woman born into a God-fearing Mormon home that practiced celestial marriage within the borders of the continental United States. Even I wasn't that lucky. My father was forced to leave America and establish his own kingdom in another nation. Yes, Shayla had everything, but her mind still became poisoned by the outside world. Shayla ran into the darkness. This was a mistake."

"Until you brought her back to her original state of freedom?"

"Shayla tried to run. Heavenly Father caught up. You understand."

"Where is she now?"

He smiled.

"I promise my partner and I will just keep coming for you. We won't stop."

P.Y. cracked me with another right hook to the jaw.

"I'm enjoying this talk, Mr. Minor," Uncle Orson said. "My rare trips to L.A. are always filled with business, never religion. But you will stop looking for Shayla. Return to Mrs. Goldman and tell her Shayla has reconnected with her faith and is willingly turning her back on her life here. Forget you ever heard her name or saw either of our faces."

In the fullness of time, one side was really going to win the argument we were having and another would lose. "Joseph Smith was a lying criminal," I said. "The encounter he described with the angel Moroni never occurred. Your whole religion is a con and you're an evil, misogynist degenerate, like Joseph."

P.Y. hit me again in the jaw and I felt myself rush out of my body while I still sat upright. I floated off somewhere. My own body slamming into the floor brought me back. I stared at my own hands on the floor, and I sucked in air. I was trapped inside myself, unable to retake control.

Then a figure raced in from the kitchen, slamming into P.Y. He fell back onto the floor and his revolver flew across the room.

It was Richie. He jumped on P.Y., pressed his neck down, and began to hail hard rights down on his face. Richie's fists went slick with streaks of blood.

Uncle Orson looked at me. My senses returned. I suppressed my torment and stood. Orson was an old man. I could take the bastard.

In one quick move, he unsheathed a blade from inside his duster and swiped it at me. I raised my left arm and the blade opened up the skin on my forearm. Blood poured out. I hobbled backward, trying to contain the leakage by squeezing the gash back shut.

Uncle Orson went for Richie.

"Richie!"

Richie looked up at the knife. P.Y. threw Richie off of him. Uncle Orson slashed the blood-smeared knife at Richie. Richie dodged it. I moved on Orson from behind. Orson turned back around and slashed at me again. He missed.

P.Y. scrambled for his revolver.

"Duck!" I shouted.

Two of P.Y.'s shots plugged into the wall, over our heads. I pulled Richie to the far side of the futon and shoved it in front of us. P.Y. fired again. Yellow stuffing launched into the air as the shot went through the futon.

I pointed at my backpack by the door. "The gun's in there."

Richie unzipped it. P.Y. and Uncle Orson moved to the kitchen. Richie gripped the MR73. He stood and raised the gun. The kitchen side door opened. Richie followed, into the kitchen. Tire rubber screeched outside, then everything got quiet.

Richie came back. "Jesus, Minor-man. Those wack-a-doos really fucked you up." He put the pistol down and got me a towel to wrap up my bleeding arm.

The floor was smeared red beneath me. I was lightheaded and felt like falling asleep. I poked around my mouth with my tongue and a loose molar came out completely. I spit it onto the floor. "I thought you were staying with Ana tonight."

"Mahad made a surprise appearance. He knows I'm fucking his lady and was being a big crybaby about it. She said it was best I just go home. So I took a cab."

"Shit, man. I'm glad you did."

TWENTY-THREE

AT HOLLYWOOD PRESBYTERIAN, I learned I had a concussion. Eight stitches were put in my left forearm and I'd lost the molar. I was told to see a dentist after my release because of the other teeth that had come loose.

Two LAPD patrolmen stopped by my bed. Richie had filed a report back at his pad. I gave them all the major points about the attack but left out anything incriminating. The concussion made it hard to be precise. I gave them the plates of the black Mercedes.

I fell in and out of sleep. Richie kept sending me texts. He was back at Hollywood Station with Angelis. Angelis was still deep in the aftermath of the Armenian operation, but he'd spoken to Richie and said he would try to help us locate Uncle Orson and P.Y.

An APB was out on the Mercedes. Richie would be at the hospital to pick me up when I checked out. I texted: *Not sure if I'll be able to walk out of here, but I'm leaving in the morning.*

His text back said: *Strike Team, baby.*

I Googled Uncle Orson on my phone, and couldn't find a word. The concussion made it hard to focus. Eventually, my attention zeroed in on an article about Mitt Romney and the new, more progressive direction the LDS church was heading in the aftermath of his failed presidential campaign. It was cynical political pragmatism disguised as religious revelation and did nothing to explain the pure faith I'd seen in the eyes of the men who almost killed me.

After a while, all my focus dissolved and I fell into a deep sleep.

IT WAS CHECK-OUT time, the next morning. I left the kindhearted nurse who urged me to quit detective work and just focus on a Namaste Mart career full-time and made my way slowly through the hospital doors and out into the street and the hot sun.

Richie was waiting for me on Vermont. Inside his Bronco, empty Marlboro packs littered the floor and the soundtrack to *A Bronx Tale* played. "I called the store," he said as we got on the road. "Both of us were taken off tonight's schedule."

His eyes were bloodshot, like he hadn't slept. I looked at the cuts and bruises on the knuckles of his hands. He'd given P.Y. a hell of a beating. Some of the damage looked even fresher than from the night before, but I wasn't sure.

We'd had a call with Joan an hour earlier, while I was still in my hospital bed. She was back in L.A. and ready for an update. She also had something important for us. Our next stop was her house.

"Fill me in about what I missed," I said.

We hit a red light on Sunset. At the corner by the Metro station, Beyonders dressed in purple flight-attendant uniforms handed out pamphlets to pedestrians. They were always out at this intersection.

"Angelis let me ride along with the LAPD guys who were sent to the Sunset Tower. Orson and P.Y. checked out yesterday while we were still at work. The cops showed a clerk at the hotel a picture of Shayla and he said he'd seen her there. If we hadn't rode out our shifts last night, we probably could have found her there, and ended it then."

"We couldn't have known." I checked our rearview for tails. P.Y. got the drop on me once. It wasn't happening again. "We were focused on Iko."

"They must have taken Shayla with them when they skipped. That's what the cops figured. But get this"—he lit a fresh cigarette with the butt of the last one—"Angelis came through on a lead, just for us. There's a snitch he deals with who's plugged into the finance world. Guy's a Mormon stockbroker who claims to have valuable knowledge on a wealthy Mormon with criminal dealings."

"Is it our Uncle Orson?"

Richie turned left on Franklin. There was Dominique, out on the road. We saw her blue Maserati pass us, going the opposite direction. "Yep. Angelis 'unofficially' gave me a name. Scotty Black. Angelis 'unofficially' told me Scotty's staying at the Langham hotel out in Pasadena and would talk to me in the hotel bar. He's still bogged down in Armenian business, but said it was okay for me to drive over there as long as I promised to not start any drama."

"You? Richie Walsh? *Drama*?"

Richie chuckled. "I wish you'd been there. I'm clueless with this Mormon shit. But this place, the Langham, is a nice hotel. Scotty was there at the hotel bar, waiting. Real fancy dude. Had a gold belt buckle and drank some pretty cocktail. I asked him where I could find Uncle Orson. He said he knew exactly where we could find him, but wouldn't give it up until he got paid. I asked him how I could trust what he said was true."

"What'd he tell you?"

From Franklin, Richie took North Beachwood. "That he's a mainstream Mormon who got busted for drugs years back. He started snitching out white-collar crooks to save his ass. He's proven himself to be a valuable asset to the LAPD, the sheriff, and the FBI for years. Snitching became a second career and a lot of the shady deals he knows about involve polygamist Mormon businessmen. He said the Feds were paying for his current stay at that joint, and until I ponied up five grand in cash, I wouldn't get any of the info I wanted. He acted like he was clean now but you could tell the guy's still some sort of a junkie."

At Scenic, Richie climbed the hills on the final stretch to Joan's. I checked the rearview again. Our coast looked clear. If it wasn't, it would be hard for anybody behind us to stay hidden on these narrow and twisting roads.

"Even if I had the dough, I'm not getting squeezed by some rat. I said no deal. Then I pretended to leave, but waited down the hall. Fifteen minutes later, a classy working girl sits down with

Scotty. I mean this girl's clearly expensive, far above my price range. She and Scotty have one drink, then leave for one of the hotel cottages. Once they're inside, I knocked on the door saying I was room service delivering champagne. Scotty opens it for me like a dummy and I slammed the door into his cheese-eating face. After the girl was gone, I slapped the shit out of him until he talked."

I was right. Some of the damage on Richie's hands was fresh. "Let no one say your methods aren't effective."

"The lowdown is this: Uncle Orson's owed a big bag of cash from a crooked Pasadena lawyer named Shem Jensen. I actually wrote that name down. Shem Jensen. This money is a big reason why Orson's in L.A. and we got lucky with the timeline. Orson's supposed to pick it up from Shem at midnight tonight at Washington Park in Northwest Pasadena."

"How much cash?"

"A quarter mil, according to Scotty."

"Why does some Pasadena lawyer owe Uncle Orson so much?"

"Scotty said Orson's a Mormon loan shark, giving out major loans all over the place. If they don't pay him back, he sends P.Y. Shayla got out through a loan shark, remember?"

"The timing feels too convenient," I said. "The handoff just happens to be tonight?"

"Us poking around must have spooked Orson. He wants to get his business over with and go back to wherever he came from."

"So you think Scotty's story's legit?"

"Yeah, I do. He was *way* too scared to be lying."

I thought about it. "Sounds like a good break."

We arrived at Joan's. "I threw him twenty bucks and left. Sounds like there's no way Orson leaves L.A. before he gets this money. If we jump his ass cowboy-style during the pickup and brace him, we can make him give us Shayla."

"On something like this, P.Y.'ll be there and he'll be armed."

"We could use backup. Go in heavy."

"After last night, I'm good with that."

"Why not call Felix? He'll give us some hitters. We'll need to pay them, but those guys won't be afraid to get their hands dirty."

"Yeah, I like that idea."

TWENTY-FOUR

JOAN STOOD BAREFOOT, looking out the back window at her view of the city. Her curly hair was pulled back tight. She'd left the front door unlocked, expecting us. When we came in, the first thing she noticed was my face and my arm.

"Oh my God."

"It looks worse than it is." This wasn't true, but I didn't want to worry her.

I sat on the couch. My head throbbed and my vision blurred around the edges, but I seemed to be past the worst of the concussion. Joan got two glasses, poured both full of sparkling water, and handed them to Richie and me. After hearing his voice, Cassie the dog raced in and flopped down at Richie's feet. "*Who's my best friend? Who's my best friend?*" Cassie squealed and kicked her legs as he petted her.

I filled Joan in. I told her about how Shayla and Arman were reunited, but mostly keeping this quiet. Yes, we confirmed Arman was a gangster, but he wasn't connected to Shayla's disappearance. "He says he doesn't know where Shayla is and he isn't lying."

"It's so sad to know they reconciled," she said. "I don't get what she was thinking."

"She was helping Arman get out of the life. He wanted to change."

"Evette was watching internet footage from the comedy show in Glendale. She spotted you two there. I couldn't believe what I saw. Was all of that connected to Shayla?"

"Richie and I do things the hard way sometimes."

Joan looked me over again. My arm seemed to worry her the most. "Did Arman's friends do this to you? The Armenian mob?"

"No, but before we get to that, you have something for us?"

Joan picked up her phone from beside a gardening book on the coffee table. "This came from an unknown number late last night." She handed the phone to me.

It was a text message. Richie and I both read it.

This is Shayla. I'm safe. I appreciate all you've done for me. Please don't worry and tell everyone at the store to forget about me.

"She obviously had someone watching over her shoulder while she wrote this," I said, thinking about the scream Juan reported hearing at Griffith Park. I decided against telling Joan about it. "And that's if she actually wrote it at all."

Richie was nodding. "Yep."

"Nothing in it sounds like her," Joan said. "Getting a random message like this in the middle of the night just worries me more. Shayla would understand that."

"Did you try calling the number?" I asked.

"At first it went straight to voicemail. I kept trying and now it's out of service."

"If the police see that she's contacting you saying that everything's okay, they might not put finding her as too high a priority," Richie said.

"I called the Missing Persons detective again. He says Shayla called him and left a similar message. He seemed to regard it as authentic, which I couldn't believe. It's like he was just blowing it off, like she wasn't really missing... Who do you think was watching over her shoulder while she wrote this?"

Cassie jumped up beside Richie on the couch.

"We think it's the old man in the footage you showed us," I said. "He's a secretive, rich fundamentalist Mormon with a crazy, violent bodyguard and he'd been keeping Shayla at the Sunset Tower. After we found out about it, the bodyguard and the old man snuck into Richie's house while I was there and did this to me. We reported my assault to the LAPD, who apparently aren't sharing the different pieces of information we're giving them."

"Once, not long after I first hired her, Shayla told me her father, a church elder, a bishop I think, took part in an old Mormon ritual called Blood Atonement. It was a top reason why she had to leave, knowing that practice was in her family."

"What's Blood Atonement?" Richie asked, looking at me.

"It's when Mormons say God gave them permission to kill someone for being against the church, or not being a good enough Mormon."

Richie looked at Joan. "Who'd her father want to kill?"

"The leader of some other sect he thought was stealing his followers. Does this old man want to force Shayla into marriage? Does he want to kill her for leaving? I'm imagining so many horrific scenarios." Joan looked at my arm again. "I'll call Missing Persons again and keep bugging the detective for answers. But I'm glad you two already take this seriously."

"I don't think he'll keep Shayla in town for long," I said.

"I hope you can find her while she's still here."

Richie gave Cassie a goodbye head rub.

"I wouldn't worry, but the Mormons know you hired us." I got up on my feet. "Until this thing is settled, I wouldn't leave any doors unlocked."

Joan got her checkbook out of her purse on the kitchen table and began to write out another one for us. "To prepare for *Martians*, the director had the whole cast go through a month-long boot camp run by a famous former Marine and Vietnam vet. You don't forget an experience like that. I've got guns here and know how to use them."

"Understood," I said.

JESSICA LIVED ON the second level of a lime-green building on Melbourne in Los Feliz. I found her apartment all the way at the end and knocked. When she answered the door, her red hair was down and tousled. She wore tight-fitting jeans and a low-cut V-neck T-shirt. It was far more revealing than anything I'd seen her wear before.

After asking if I was okay, she invited me in. "I heard you and Richie have been busy." She closed the door. My earlier comments about her former religion seemed forgotten.

I told her how we ruled out Arman's involvement in Shayla's disappearance.

"What can I do for you?" There was no aggression in her tone. It was even a little inviting and she maintained this thin, Mona Lisa–like smile.

I looked around her apartment. A dream catcher dangled from her ceiling. A beanbag chair was in the corner next to a rolled-up yoga mat. Posters from hipster Echo Park bands were taped to the walls. A copy of Bukowski's *Hollywood* was on a shelf, next to a small statue of a sitting Buddha, which she'd probably bought from a Goalmart. The book didn't look like she'd ever opened it. Down her hallway, the doorway to her bedroom was open.

I said, "I need to learn more about polygamist Mormons."

"Why ask me?"

"Jessica, you shouldn't have withheld what you knew when we first met."

"I told you. I didn't trust your friend. I thought you were different."

Richie was outside in the Bronco, taking a much-needed nap. "He saved my life last night. Richie's more trustworthy than anybody I know. He's just got some rough edges."

"Is it true he's dating Ana Safarian?"

"If you'd talked sooner, we would have gotten to the truth sooner."

Her face got solemn. "Do you know something about Shayla?"

"A dangerous and wealthy Mormon polygamist kidnapped her."

She closed her eyes. "Oh my God."

"I need someone who knows this world. I've got a bad feeling about what I'm dealing with and I need to learn more. To prepare."

"I don't know polygamists."

"Who would? I need you to think."

"I know people who've come to my ex-Mormon meetings that had polygamy in their family. But I don't know any of those people well and it would be a betrayal of their confidence to just tell someone else about them."

"If they knew what Richie and I are trying to do, you don't

think they would understand? Shayla is in danger."

"The people I know who have polygamy in their family history... it was over a century ago... It's got nothing to do with how any modern-day polygamists behave. The FLDS survives by being secretive."

I thought about Orson's words. *Nor of the other frauds who purport to have gotten back to the fundamentals.* "I don't think this guy is FLDS. I'm pretty sure he's some sort of independent, doing his own thing."

"That's even rarer. Adam, I don't know what to tell you."

"I need you to *think*. For Shayla."

She paced, then turned back my way. "Maybe there is somebody."

"Who?

"This guy Jake Beckstead. Big Jake, people call him."

"Who's he?"

"He's an old ex-Mormon and cowboy actor. You still see him on TV shows every once in a while." She walked back toward me, animated about the idea. "He left the church a decade ago but has become a sort of father figure to a lot of ex-Mormons in L.A. He was even *born* in Bear Creek, like Shayla."

"How do you know this guy?"

"He would come speak to the ex-Mormon group. Even though he's been out of the religion for years, Jake knows everything. He's a history buff."

"And he would talk to us?"

"He knows Shayla, from the meetings, so I think so. Let me see if I can track him down."

RICHIE TOOK A call as we rode down Sunset.

"Ricky Boy!" It was Angelis, on speakerphone. "Did you beat the shit out of that CI I turned you on to?" he asked.

"That's an excessive interpretation." Richie looked at me and made this mischievous smile. "But tell me, how much money does that guy make snitching that he gets put up by the Feds in that luxurious hotel?"

"I gave you him as a favor, for how you helped us this week. I assumed, foolishly I see, that you wouldn't act like a fucking moron with such a sensitive, multi-department asset. But you seem intent on testing me."

I'd never heard Angelis angry with Richie before.

"I'm sorry, Ricky Boy. Sincerely. I was thinking about how bad things could have gone last night when those guys had Adam, and I saw red. By no means was I trying to disrespect you or make your life more difficult. My apologies."

"Don't let it happen again."

"It won't." Looking at me, Richie shook his head no.

"What'd Scotty give you?"

If Richie talked, Angelis would order us to avoid the meet that night. We could lose our last chance to find Shayla. This was our job, not theirs. "It was just background info on Uncle Orson, which was helpful. That old timer's a piece of work. Scotty didn't know where to find him."

"So it was all for nothing." Angelis huffed. "The goodwill you earned the other night has officially been used up, Dubs. You're on thin ice with the LAPD for the foreseeable future. Consider this your only warning. I can't help you anymore, or your partner."

Angelis hung up.

Richie made a dismissive wave. "He just needs time to stew."

TWENTY-FIVE

BIG JAKE BECKSTEAD lived in a white, single-level Craftsman bungalow in Angeleno Heights. This was just a few streets away from where I'd lived with the witch during my first months in L.A. When he opened the door, we saw he was well over six feet tall and lean. He wore a gray-and-black flannel shirt neatly tucked into his blue jeans.

"Jessica said you were coming." Jake looked at my injuries and yawned. I think we'd woken him from an afternoon nap. "Come on in, so my cats don't get loose."

Inside, he steered us down a hall. Posters for old Westerns hung on the walls. Bits of cat litter were strewn on the floor. A beige cat who must have weighed fifteen pounds stepped in front of me and rubbed against my leg.

"That's John Wayne, officially. But he answers to Duke."

"Good name for a cat," I said.

"I got five. There's Duke, Calamity Jane, Coop, Wyatt, and Doc. They're around here somewhere. Can't let 'em outside 'cause of the coyotes."

In the living room, Jake sat back in a recliner and Richie sat on the couch covered in cat hair. I looked around. A framed black-and-white picture on the wall showed a young Jake with a full head of blond hair at a Mexican cantina with the actors Strother Martin and L.Q. Jones. Jake smiled earnestly and appeared sober. Strother and L.Q. did not.

Jake's TV was set to Turner Classic Movies. It played *Picnic* with William Holden and Kim Novak. Jake muted it but left the screen on. "I hardly watch anything anymore but old movies. Can't stand the news." One of Jake's cats, a calico, hopped into his lap. "Jessica says you boys are detectives and you've got some LDS questions."

"We've been hired to find Shayla Ramsey, who's gone missing,"

I said, sitting down. "It looks connected with her Mormon background. We heard you were born in the same town she was. We hoped you could help us understand her situation."

"Yes, I was born in Bear Creek, same year as the raids. 1953. But I got expelled at fourteen. The Prophet Uncle Randolph Meacham ordered my parents to cast me out for my imperfections, so I was driven to the side of a desert highway and abandoned."

"What do you mean, imperfections?" Richie asked.

"The official charge? Disobedience. I got caught playing football at a time the Prophet outlawed it. But the real reason was that Uncle Randolph had to reduce competition for wives at Bear Creek. His most devoted followers were to be rewarded with the widest selection of females possible."

I said, "So you turned ex-Mormon young..."

"I was on the street at fourteen. But I needed food, water, and shelter. I got adopted by a mainstream LDS family in Salt Lake City. For my remaining teenage years, I gave belief in Joseph Smith a sincere try, and the results weren't horrible. By and large, most Mormons are nice people. They're like Canadians. Either of you ever meet a mean Canadian?"

Richie and I both said we hadn't.

"My point exactly. But, coming from Bear Creek, I was privy to things my adopted family wasn't. I tried to believe, really give it a go. But I couldn't get there. There was a huge world outside Utah and I had dreams about it. I was tall and knew how to ride a horse. The ladies called me handsome. So, at eighteen, I left for Hollywood to have a go as an actor. It's been a wild time ever since. Gradually, folks learned I'd left the church. They saw I was doing fine as an ex-Mormon, so they started coming to me for helpful advice. I developed a sort of reputation for getting others out."

"I can't imagine the church appreciates you depleting their ranks," I said.

"Oh, over the years I've had a few heavies follow me around, revving their tires in the mud. Been served with lawsuits, all of which got thrown out. Every few years or so someone from the church tries to bring me back into the fold. 'You want a dozen pretty young girls in your bed, they're all yours, just bend the knee.' That sort of thing. I could tell you about some of those rich, crazy types on those compounds. If Jessica's got it right, it sounds like Shayla might be jungled up with that sort?"

"Guy's name is Uncle Orson Reed. His bodyguard did this to me."

"This bodyguard wear his hair long?"

"Yes."

"And you're still here to tell the tale. That's impressive. Supposedly, Orson told P.Y. to grow his hair long, just as Joseph told the original Rockwell. As long as he never cuts it, he can't be hurt. Just like Samson."

"Who are these guys?" I asked. "What's their history?"

"Orson's father Hiram was an employee of Howard Hughes, who developed a strong affinity for Mormons late in life. Mormons were the only people Mr. Hughes kept close, and Hiram was with the Hughes Las Vegas operations in the '70s at a time when the old man got determined to buy every gold and silver mine in Nevada that he could. Hiram was ambitious. He was also a devout polygamist with at least two dozen wives he was responsible for financially."

"Two dozen!" Richie said. "I thought it was mostly just ten or eleven at most."

"When Wade Meacham of Bear Creek was arrested seven years back, he had over seventy. Claimed in revelations God told him he was meant to have a hundred."

"Imagine all the nagging," Richie said.

Jake laughed heartily, and gave me a look that said "this guy." "Well, old Hiram went on an acquisition spree with Hughes's reserves, purchasing mines all over Nevada. Spent twenty million in two years. Later it came out that almost all of the deeds turned out to be worthless. Some of what Hiram bought weren't even mines at all."

"Hiram just pocketed twenty million?" I asked.

"That's the consensus. At the time the truth behind this acquisition project was coming to light, Hiram was seen at the Beverly Hills Hotel, having dinner at the Polo Lounge with a real-estate associate who'd probably learned about his Hughes scheme. The next morning, the associate's body was discovered in one of the suites, sliced up dead by a straight razor. The police never found who did it and that case is still open, far as I know. Hiram escaped to Mexico, and with his money formed a polygamist compound for his wives and kids, his followers, and all their wives and kids near the resorts of Cancún. He gained converts and added wives. He preached of the need to bring polygamy back to the world, by any means necessary." Jake took a moment to look down lovingly at the cat in his lap. "Hiram passed in '83, leaving control of his whole empire to Orson. He's run the Mexican compound for thirty years now."

Duke the cat jumped onto the couch beside me and sniffed my hand. "Orson told me his man P.Y. was the literal reincarnation of Porter Rockwell. The pictures I looked up of Rockwell looked almost exactly the same as the man I saw."

"Porter Rockwell was Joseph Smith's protector and probably the fiercest of all the early Saints. Near the end of the Missouri Mormon wars in the 1830s, he shot but failed to kill Governor Lilburn Boggs on behalf of Joseph, as revenge for the extermination order Boggs issued. After Joseph's murder in the Carthage Jail, Porter left for Utah with Brigham Young and became one of the West's earliest gunslingers."

"How does a conman like this Smith guy get so many followers?" Richie asked. "I understand he invented a religion where you get a lot of tail, but still..."

Jake laughed again. "When Wade Meacham was arrested, he was wearing baggy Bermuda shorts. At the time, he was number two on the FBI's most wanted list, just after Osama Bin Laden. One of Wade's most devoted followers quit the FLDS the moment she saw the arrest photo. She'd seen Wade kick so many people out of their homes just for showing unapproved parts of their skin. That was the final straw for her. Before that, when Meacham told her he wanted to marry and bed her twelve-year-old daughter, she went along willingly. In this woman's book, letting the Prophet marry and rape her preteen daughter was forgivable. Bermuda shorts were not."

Duke the cat lay down beside me. "Why do you think Orson picked Shayla?" I asked.

"Picked her?"

"Shayla had Bear Creek in her rearview. Suddenly, this mysterious character appears in L.A. at her work and follows her around. There's no trace of what happened, except a fake text from an unknown number, saying she's fine. What happened?"

Jake scratched his chin. "You want me to guess?"

"Whatever you think."

"Far as Bear Creek goes, the only places someone like Shayla can go to fund their escape are these Mormon loan sharks, controlled by Orson. You find them at Bear Creek gas stations or general stores. Shayla probably borrowed money from him and didn't pay it back."

"We know for a fact she borrowed money to escape Bear Creek," I said.

"Guys like Orson have a long memory. I'll bet he'd say she's repaying her debt by becoming his latest wife." Jake lowered his head. "I don't like to think about what that fanatic's been actually doing to her since he found her."

"'SUP, FOOLS!" FELIX, wearing a Dodgers jersey, let us in through the back door of his house. We did our fist bumps. The TV in the living room was on and we could hear his gang in there watching a ball game.

"Yo, you really fucking Ana Safarian?" Felix asked Richie.

Richie huffed air on his fingernails and wiped them on his shoulder.

"My man." They high-fived.

"Seriously though, we got something heavy going on," I said.

"This about the Armenians? They're the ones who fucked you up? 'Cause those fools claim trece, which presents complications in my world."

"No. This is about the Mormons now."

"The *who*?"

"Mormons. Guys from the religion where you get multiple wives."

"Those fools with the long beards? You mean Jews?"

I remembered Felix, despite being a lifelong gangster, was also a devout Catholic who didn't appreciate my anti-theism.

"Not Jews," I said. "It's fanatic Mormons who kidnapped this girl who works for Damien's mom. Tonight they'll be at a park in Pasadena. One definitely has bodies on him. They probably don't have backup, but we can't be sure. We need them to talk and give up a location on the girl. We'll go hard if necessary."

Felix looked me over, appreciating this fresh violent side he was seeing in me. "How much y'all down to pay?"

Richie and I had figured this out on the drive over.

"Three grand," I said. "For you to split up amongst you however you want."

Felix shook our hands, then led us into the living room, where four more Kingsley gang OGs watched a Dodgers away game on TV.

Felix said, "This is Chuy, Wino, Nino, and Loco Mike."

I'd met Loco Mike once before at Felix's birthday party, but I don't think he remembered me. Richie seemed to know all of them quite well. He sat down on the couch between Nino and Wino. All four of them asked Richie about Ana Safarian. Apparently, the whole world knew.

I explained the job again.

"These Mormons... they're packing cuetes?" Chuy said.

"Expect them to be," I said.

"Those fools probably fuck with some rusted-ass old prairie scattergun. Fuck," Loco Mike said, "their heat's probably even older than that, like from the Revolutionary War or whatever."

"We need them to hand over the girl."

"Old Mormon dude's going to talk," Felix said. "Don't even trip."

We got ready. Felix had an extra Glock .380 with the serial number filed off and gave it to Richie, knowing I would carry the MR73.

Richie and I started out for the park with two cars full of cholo gangsters trailing us. On the road, I accepted this wasn't just about finding Shayla, not for me, not right now. On the inside, I'd lost control of my rage. It was luck these Mormons didn't kill me the night before, and this was my chance to send serious pain back their way.

TWENTY-SIX

AN L-SHAPED STRETCH of Chinese elms ran the length and width of Washington Park. Richie and I stood among them in the dark, watching the lit-up parking lot. It was a quarter after midnight and neither side had shown yet. People came and went from the Washington Boulevard Banquet Hall next door where a wedding ran late. There was music, dancing, and drunken laughing, but here the park was still. Richie had parked the Bronco two blocks up on El Molino and we'd quietly arrived unseen from an alley behind some houses.

Felix and Loco Mike waited in Felix's Chevy Impala lowrider, the single car in the lot. Chuy, Wino, and Nino hung over by the basketball court at the far corner of the park, ready to move on our word. Time stretched on.

At 12:20, the spectral figure of a single man slowly came in from the north. He wore a tan-striped dress shirt with a band collar, had a long dark beard hanging down to his chest, and carried a big black gym bag that hung from a strap on his shoulder. It sagged low, full of something. He stopped under a light pole to wait.

"Is that him?" Richie asked.

I'd looked Jensen's face up online. "That's a Mormon, but it's not Jensen." I texted Felix to wait.

Then we heard overlapping thumps coming from the short wooden bridge that crossed between the row of elms separating the parking lot and the basketball court. Chuy, Wino, and Nino appeared, running straight for the Mormon bagman.

"What the fuck are those guys doing?"

They'd been given instructions to wait for our word. The bagman saw them coming for him and just stood there. Chuy collided with him first, hard, like a linebacker. The bagman got knocked down. Wino kicked him hard in the jaw. Nino elbow dropped him in the gut, WWF-style. Wino ripped the gym bag from the guy's grip, unzipped it, and pulled out the contents. It was all old magazines.

Richie stepped out from among the elms with his .380 at his side. I followed just behind him, clutching my MR73, rushing toward the parking lot. Both of us stepped into the light. Felix and Loco Mike bailed from the Impala with both of their pieces drawn.

Then shots went off. Rifle fire.

I ducked and searched for their source.

There was a gasp. Loco Mike fell back, clutching his leg. Nino and Wino ran for cover behind the Impala. Felix took cover with them. I ducked low behind a nearby park table. The bagman ran back toward Washington, the way he'd come. All of us looked for the shooter as people inside the banquet hall screamed. There was a break in the shooting.

Richie pointed. "There!"

I saw a shooter situated over the roof of a Silverado pickup parked among the wedding guests. He stood in the cab, directly facing us in a sniper position. Gun smoke hovered around his head like a halo as he reloaded.

Richie raised his Glock, tightened his arms, and squeezed the trigger three times.

The shooter's shoulders pitched back and his rifle fell, hitting the ground beside the truck. His body landed back in the cab.

More overlapping shots went off. They hit the elms behind me. They were coming from another source, someplace farther off. Staying low behind the table, I located the moonlit outline of two more shooters crouched low near the trees by the playground.

"It's a setup!" I shouted. "They knew we were coming!"

A black Mercedes tore into the lot. It headed our way.

Richie spotted the fresh Mormons. "Over there!" he shouted to the cholos, pointing. The Mercedes kept tearing straight at us.

Felix and the others raised up toward the trees, zeroed in on the two fresh targets, and opened fire. They lit up the park but hit nothing. I aimed. But I knew there was no chance I'd hit anything and didn't squeeze the trigger.

The Mercedes screeched to a stop near the empty lowrider. Its back door opened. Porter the Younger, clad in an all-white suit, stepped out. His hair hung down to his waist. He held a pump-action Remington, raised it, and let off a series of shots at the cholos who once again took cover behind the Impala. Loco Mike left a trail of blood as he sought cover. He made it behind the lowrider just as the back windshield took a hit and glass shards scattered the pavement.

Over by the playground, the two other gunmen dashed toward their getaway car. P.Y. was providing suppressive fire for their retreat.

Richie, who still hadn't taken cover, aimed a single, focused shot at P.Y.

It connected. P.Y. clutched his arm. Blood seeped through his fingers, staining his white sleeve. His face said "this isn't supposed to happen to the Mormon Samson."

P.Y. and Richie locked eyes. P.Y.'s eyebrows narrowed and his mouth tightened. He racked the slide on his Remington and aimed. He shouted, "Die, Gentile! Die!"

Richie ducked just in time. More elm splinters flew behind us. P.Y. fired at me. He hit the bench of the table. Concrete shards pelted my face. They scratched the lenses of my glasses. P.Y.'s third shot went high into the trees again.

My ears rang. Cordite stink was everywhere. My blurry concussion vision was back. I tried to focus. Over the gate by the banquet hall, the Silverado with the dead Mormon in the back peeled away. There was Richie ahead of me, still standing.

The two other Mormons made it safely inside the Mercedes. P.Y. was alone now, facing us with his empty Remington. His arm bled heavily. It was soaked dark red. The Mercedes pulled up close, its door open.

Richie fired one more shot. It made P.Y.'s hair waft as it passed. P.Y. finally ducked into the Mercedes and it was off.

STILL IN A haze, I cracked open a fresh Modelo from the fridge in Felix's kitchen and tried to stay cool. As I drank, I watched through the kitchen window as Felix backed his shot-up Impala into his garage and covered it with a black tarp.

Loco Mike was awake and coherent, but the bullet was in his thigh, under the Dodgers jersey Nino had used as a makeshift tourniquet. Felix told Wino to get him dropped off safely at an emergency room. Loco Mike seemed cool about it and kept telling us how he'd already been shot twice before. This one, to him, was no big deal.

"What are you going to tell the hospital when they ask who shot you?" I asked him.

"That some random-ass fools was blasting and I got hit."

After they left for the hospital, Felix saw my nerves were shot. He offered me some Vicodin and I washed two down with a second Modelo.

A Kingsley gang mini-soldier came by. His name was Ulisses and he looked about thirteen. Ulisses dutifully collected all the guns everyone had used and took them to be destroyed. Since I'd never fired it at the park, I kept the MR73. I hoped Ulisses knew how to properly get rid of weapons. Richie would be majorly fucked if the .380 ever appeared again.

Felix must have caught the concern on my face. "Don't trip. Ulisses is one of my sons. He's dependable at melting them shits down."

More Kingsley gang homies showed up. The Vicodin got my heartbeat mellowed out and I retold the story. It got them majorly heated. They'd wounded one of ours. Richie probably killed one of theirs. They still demanded more blood. I must have heard "Let's ride on those Mormon vatos" a dozen times.

I ran through the night in my head, all the details that could bury us. Just before Richie and I had gotten on the 134 Freeway to escape, two Pasadena PD squad cars with red Rose Bowl roses in the center of the P's passed us in the opposite direction with their sirens blaring. They hadn't noticed us. Pasadena had its own police department, but killings there fell under the jurisdiction of Sheriff's Homicide. I didn't want to think about them hunting us.

Richie and I might be on street surveillance cameras. There had to be wedding-goer witnesses at the banquet hall who'd seen something. What physical evidence had we left behind? Would Angelis learn about the Mormon Richie had almost certainly killed and connect it to Uncle Orson, the Mormon he knew assaulted me?

I pulled Richie out to the back porch.

"All that story time with Big Jake and we still walked right into a trap," I said.

"Luckily none of those Mormon tough guys can shoot." Richie lit a cigarette. "You thinking what I'm thinking?"

"Scotty Black the snitch."

"That's what I'm thinking."

Since Felix and his homies might raise eyebrows among Pasadena's wealthiest, Richie argued the two of us should go to the hotel alone.

"Nope," Felix said. "Loco Mike's with me and his ass took a hot one. Could be limping forever. Plus those fools shot up my whip! I'm *going*."

We at least convinced him to change into the suit jacket and dress pants he wore for his court appearances.

TWENTY-SEVEN

WE RODE ONTO the hotel grounds. The Langham was in Oak Knoll, on the opposite side of Pasadena from Washington Park. Since Felix's car was out of commission and we didn't want to risk Richie's Bronco being seen in the area, we had called a Hollywood taxi and overpaid with cash. The driver agreed to wait and keep the meter running.

Inside, the front lobby had marble floors, a crystal chandelier, and Victorian-era tables and chairs. It was quiet and empty, except for a lady behind the front desk. Richie led us down a hall and through another set of doors. Outside, we crossed over a bridge lined with overhead wooden slats that had hand-painted scenes from different parts of California on them. We came to stairs leading down to a sidewalk that ran along the edge of a pond. We ended up at Scotty's cottage, which was covered in stands of purple wisteria.

Richie covered the peephole with one hand and knocked with the other. After a wait, the lights flipped on, and the door opened. Richie kicked it hard, slamming it into the guy's face. Inside, I switched on the light.

Scotty was on the floor, on his back, holding his bleeding nose. He had bruises on his face, a black eye, and a big cut on his lip, all from Richie's earlier visit. His hair was blond and he wore an open bathrobe and green silk boxers.

"Remember me?" Richie said.

Scotty got to his feet and retreated to the other side of the room.

Richie followed him, and as soon as Scotty had backed himself into the far wall, Richie kicked him hard in the balls. "As you can see, that trap you set for us didn't work out." Scotty clutched his balls with both hands and struggled for breath. He kept making little *ah, ah, ah* sounds and I thought he might vomit.

I checked the bathroom and the bedroom. "He's alone."

Scotty looked up at Felix, obviously wanting to know who he was but probably too terrified of what the answer might be. "I can explain," Scotty said, looking at me, the one he found the most sympathetic. While this man must have caused untold damage to people's lives during his time as an informant, I doubted he'd ever been physically hurt before his first encounter with Richie the previous night.

"Explain it then," I said.

Scotty got up, closed his robe, and moved to one of the fuchsia-colored couches. "I was mad that he beat me up," he said, nodding at Richie, but not looking at him. "And I needed more money." He gestured his hand around the room.

"You call that shit an explanation?" Felix said.

"P.Y. picked up the money Shem Jensen owed him someplace else and planned to ambush you at the park. He paid me ten grand for the tip. They just didn't want you messing around in their business. I had no idea they would try and kill you."

"Bitch, yes you fucking did!" Felix said.

"How did you get in contact with Orson and P.Y.?" I asked.

"Through a number."

Scotty's phone was on the cherry coffee table between a coke-frosted mirror and two empty bottles of Schramsberg rosé. I tossed it to him. "Show me."

He scrolled through his contacts. "Here."

He pointed at one labeled *Prophet.* I took a photo of it with my phone. "You leave a message," he said. "If his people want to call back, they do."

"Why do you have this?"

Scotty wiped blood from his nose onto his sleeve. "I run hedge funds for Mormon businessmen. Give them calls about what stocks are going to get shorted, that sort of thing. I hear things. People talk to me. I was given the number. It changes a lot and a new one comes every few months."

"Who gives you the number?"

"Some devoted follower of Uncle Orson's brand of Mormonism. A jerk who thinks being a nineteenth-century polygamist is the only correct way to be LDS. He probably has at least one teenage wife, a beard, and wears prairie garb. All of his friends probably fit the same description. I don't have a name and never asked for one."

"Orson's just okay with you ratting on Mormons?" Richie asked.

Scotty looked up, finally able to make eye contact with Richie. "Most of the people I rat on are FLDS. High-level Bear Creek types. Financial crimes, welfare fraud, human trafficking. Orson's at odds with those guys and willing to pay good money to find out what they're up to."

"And what specific crimes is Uncle Orson committing?" I asked.

"There's the loan-sharking. Lately, he's into energy fraud. Orson collects subsidies from U.S. government programs for collecting clean energy and ships the same barrels of biodiesel back and forth around the country. You can make billions doing that if you're set up right. Supposedly, Orson's in bed with the cartel that controls the region of Quintana Roo where his compound's located. He's isolated down there. Most of the other Mexican plyg compounds are up north. He's got so many wives and who knows how many kids. Plus his followers and all of their wives and kids. He has to have a fortune coming in."

"Besides Shem Jensen, why's Orson in L.A. now?" I asked.

"My guess? Something cartel related. The don of Quintana Roo actually lives in East L.A. now. He calls all the shots from up here."

"Tell us what you know about Orson's compound," I said.

"It's called Ciudad Reed and it's somewhere in Cancún, by the beach. He's got an army down there. It's mostly white, English-speaking Mexican citizens."

Richie leaned forward. "Where is the ten grand you got for setting us up to be killed tonight?"

"They wired it to one of my accounts."

I turned to Felix. "You want to get even for Loco Mike, now's the time."

Felix stepped forward and hit Scotty with a hard right. Blood flecked the couch and the coffee table. Scotty yelped. Felix grabbed Scotty by his shoulders, pulled him to his feet, and pummeled his face with closed-fist punches. I let Felix get it all out. After hearing a blow that probably broke Scotty's jaw, I pulled Felix away. Scotty flopped over, crying.

"That was for Loco Mike, fool," Felix said.

Richie kneeled down. "So what do we do with you now, Scotty?"

Scotty kept his face flat on the carpet. "Now?"

"How do I know you won't rat us out again to someone else as soon as we leave?" Richie asked. "Your word doesn't exactly come with credibility."

"I won't. This... hurts too bad."

"Scotty, you might think we've been hard on you, but that's because the three of us are men and you're just a dirty snitch." Richie spoke to the back of Scotty's head. "This doesn't mean you can't turn things around and become a man yourself someday. In the meantime, the important thing to remember for your continued safety is that we were never here. Say it, and say it in a way that makes me believe you."

"You were never here."

Scotty would be quiet this time. We could tell.

"Time to get going," I said.

Felix picked up a whiskey-brown-colored leather belt with a gold, circular belt buckle from the dining room table. "Looks expensive."

Scotty raised his head, eager about how close we were to leaving. "The buckle's old Mormon money." Seeing him speak, I was sure his jaw was broken.

Felix touched the buckle. It was a large coin. "Is this real gold?"

Scotty didn't answer.

"It's real," Richie said. "He was bragging about it earlier."

I took a look. The coin was dated 1848 and around the edges of the circle were the words *To. The. Lord. Holiness.* In the center was an image of two hands shaking.

"Oh, I'm definitely taking this shit." Felix rolled the belt up and put it inside his suit jacket. Then we left.

On our way out, we cut through a courtyard with a fountain right in the center. In the front lobby, just before the exit, the front desk lady blocked our way. She stared at Felix with open suspicion. "Can I help you?"

"We're on an architectural tour," Felix said.

"At three thirty in the morning?"

"For night tours our guide charges a reduced price. Pasadena's beautiful on a starry night. Our guide's in the restroom right now and we were just having a look around the grounds."

The lady smiled, immediately charmed. "Well, let me know if I can be of any assistance," she said, and returned to her post behind the front desk.

Felix said, when she was out of earshot, "My baby mama and I went on one of those tours around here with her parents. You gotta love those Pasadena Craftsmans."

TWENTY-EIGHT

FOR A SPAN of about three seconds, I had no customers at my register.

Then a woman said, "You look *bored*."

It was a blonde in a black pork pie hat and her long-haired Indian boyfriend. They struck me as most likely an Indie folk duo visiting West Hollywood from somewhere in Echo Park. The cart her boyfriend pushed behind her was mostly full of greens.

"Find everything okay?"

"Of course. But you should never shop hungry. Oh, I almost forgot." She reached into her basket and pulled out a bag of frozen cauliflower gnocchi. "I don't want this."

I was amazed she had no comments about my injuries. Almost every other customer did. I looked pretty crazy today. "Then what did you bring it here for?" I asked. I turned my eyes toward the boyfriend, who took out his phone and began scrolling through Instagram.

"Because I thought I was going to buy it."

"But you're not?"

"No."

"You know, Namaste Mart is an environmentally conscious company. We believe in giving back to Mother Earth."

"I *heard* that."

"It's important for us to not waste food unnecessarily. I'd be happy to make sure this gets back to its home in the frozen section for you."

I accepted the gnocchi from her and returned it to its proper place in the frozen aisle by myself. When I got back, the boyfriend was still on his phone. He hadn't noticed my lengthy absence and the woman was now on Instagram too. As I began to ring up their groceries, a line formed behind them. Their groceries piled up quickly.

At Namaste Mart, we don't have baggers. Unlike most of Europe, where customers must bag for themselves, at Namaste Mart, the cashier currently operating the register is obligated to do the bagging if the customer opts to not contribute.

I don't mind bagging. It's easy. I regularly have to break down pallets full of milk when working the cooler in the back. Compared to that, bagging is a breeze. What bothers me is when able-bodied people refuse to bag, especially when there's a line behind them.

Five people now waited behind these two in line. The stack of their items was so high that some began falling to the sides of the register.

"I would help, but I don't want to mess up your flow."

This shift was going to last forever. "My flow?"

"You know, the way you bag the groceries. You guys are great at it. Bagging was never my calling."

I was about three-fourths of the way through bagging their stuff. "You think when I get up in the morning, I look at myself in the mirror and say, 'Damn, I'm going to bag those groceries so perfectly and so fast, I hope no one gets in the way of me and my calling'?"

She pretended not to hear me and swiped her credit card in the machine three times. "It's not letting me pay."

Last year, L.A. County passed a law that any customer who needed paper bags at a grocery store would have to pay ten cents a bag. "I can't total it until I know how many bags to add. Almost there."

She furrowed her eyebrows. "Can't you just guess?"

"Miss, please stop messing with my flow."

She looked at her boyfriend, seeking support, or at least involvement. He finally put his phone down at his side. "I thought all the peeps at Namaste Mart were like, tuned into their spirituality. Are you always this sarcastic, man?"

"Just on Mondays." I finished bagging, added the bags to her total, read it to her, and smiled. When she was done paying, I handed her the receipt.

"Have a great day," I said, smiling.

"I hope yours gets better."

"How could that be possible, now that you're leaving?"

THE NIGHT BEFORE, at home, I'd called the *Prophet* number, which rang and then went to voicemail. I called three more times and no one picked up. On the fourth try, I left a message. "It's the guy looking for your supposed property. Call me back at this number." I paced in my room for over an hour. No one called back. I crashed, still in my clothes.

Shrieks from the parrot woke me. I tried the number again. Nothing. This number was my last connection to Shayla before they shipped her down to Ciudad Reed, if she wasn't already on her way. I got online and looked up the numbers of upscale hotels across L.A., thinking maybe Uncle Orson might be staying in one. I called them all, and got nowhere.

There'd still been time before I had to go in to work, so I scrutinized articles about the previous night's shootout. If they were accurate, the sheriff's investigators didn't have much. The body of the Mormon Richie probably killed wasn't mentioned. P.Y. must have gotten rid of it on his own. Maybe P.Y. wanted to settle his beef with us, but he wasn't involving the cops if he did. Most of the banquet hall wedding-goers had taken cover quickly when the shooting started and hadn't seen much. There were no descriptions of me, Richie, or any of Felix and his crew.

I'd called Felix on a burner. He was working a morning shift and was on his lunch break, eating pupusas from Zermeños on Santa Monica. He'd been in touch with Loco Mike, who'd had the bullet removed and was doing good. No one at the hospital seemed too interested in scrutinizing his story. We looked clear there.

We were lucky, but I didn't feel lucky. I felt like a giant anvil was teetering above my head and about to crash down hard.

MY COWORKER TEDDY Adler walked into the break room.

Teddy, who was in his sixties, had worked for years at a famous Silver Lake video store that recently shut down after being crushed by internet streaming. Before the video store, Teddy spent decades as a Buddhist monk. He'd known guys like Allen Ginsberg, George Harrison, and still hung out with Richard Gere. Teddy was bald but wore a thick gray beard that made him look like a Buddhist Santa Claus. He took a seat beside me.

"Dude, you seem like you could use a day off."

"I wouldn't be here if I didn't need the money. The PI work's paying well these days, but it's never been reliable. Before this job, work was dry for months."

"These wounds, they're from your case?"

"Juggling it and this job is too much right now."

"Maybe the answer's easy? Talk to Christy and ask to be put on a leave of absence."

I hadn't thought about this. Our other cases had all been solved so fast.

"All we have is the present moment and there's no reason to spend it someplace you shouldn't be. You can be gone up to three and a half weeks and come back refreshed. Last Christmas I took a full three weeks off to visit my mother down in Boca Raton. She made me hot cocoa every morning. Ask Christy. I think she'll be cool about it. And of course, don't forget, grocery slinging has been recession-proof since time immemorial. We'll still be slinging them like any other day when you return."

RICHIE AND I stood under the *Eat, Love, Namaste* sign. It was my last break of the night. Richie had snuck in over an hour late to his shift, but so far none of the managers had mentioned his tardiness. He smoked a cigarette, looking out at the boulevard with bloodshot eyes. I presumed he'd been late because he was spending time with Ana.

I said, "I haven't called Joan."

"Me neither."

"Shayla's probably in Cancún by now, on that compound."

"If she is, it's not because we didn't try."

The only direction to go was forward. "We need to keep trying." I waited a moment, not sure how he would take this. "We need to go to Mexico."

"Might be the only way." So he'd been thinking about it too. "You think Orson brainwashed Shayla? That must be the explanation, right?"

"All the LDS ever did was brainwash her. Her parents married her off at fifteen. Shayla just needs someone who actually gives a shit about her well-being to intervene. We're the guys who took down Hollywood Sam. What's to stop us?" I told Richie about Teddy's suggestion, and how I figured we both might as well give this a try before our benefits got re-structured and it was no longer an option. "We spent three grand paying Felix and the homies. A trip to Mexico will cost a lot. Even then, if we manage to get down there, I've got no idea how to find the place. This could take time."

"*Ohh,* you just reminded me of something." He took out his phone and showed me a picture of a bathroom mirror selfie of Mike Leroux, the actor from the '90s sitcom *Roomies.* Leroux's hair was gray now and he was shirtless, wrapped in a towel, and still wet. He had a stupid grin on his face and his pubic hair was visible.

"What the hell is this?"

"Ana's sister's fucking Mike Leroux. From *Roomies.*"

"I recognize him."

"Last night she showed me this, just to clown on the guy. He took it himself. I told her to text it to me. She made me promise to not show anybody. Soon as she did, I was like 'Why in the fuck would you do that? Of course I'm going to show people.'"

"Okay, but what's this have to do with Mexico?"

Richie hit me in the arm, like I was missing the most of obvious point in the world. "We'll sell it to TMZ. People make fortunes on this shit all the time. Mike Leroux isn't worth a fortune, but it's got to be worth two plane tickets to Cancún. And we're still getting the grand a day from Joan. The trip's practically paid for, Minor-man."

"If you say so."

"Plus, it's not a bad idea for us to be out of the country until the heat dies down regarding our..." He cleared his throat. "... recent escapades. Jesus, last night was a wild one, kid."

Fifteen minutes later, we sat down with Christy and she signed off on our leave of absence, no questions asked. After finishing our shifts that night, we were free from Namaste Mart for up to three and a half weeks.

THE TMZ OFFICES were located on the second level of the plaza at Sunset and Crescent Heights, above another Namaste Mart location. I waited in the courtyard while Richie went in. After forty-five minutes passed, he came out with a white envelope.

"Five grand in cash is what a Mike Leroux shower selfie goes for in today's America. The TMZ guy said Leroux would be happy to see this out there. Guy hasn't had a decent part in years, and he's looking for whatever attention he can get." Richie opened the envelope so I could take a look at all the fresh bills. "I love this country."

At Richie's, we got online and quickly purchased two tickets for Cancún. Our flight would leave from LAX the next morning.

I returned to La Fayette and packed my luggage. I was lying back on my futon, looking up at the ceiling and thinking about all the unknowns ahead when Richie called.

"Remember the number Scotty gave us. You know, Prophet?"

"I tried it. No one answers."

"I tried too. They called me back."

"Who called you back?"

"P.Y."

"Really? What'd he say?"

"That asshole wanted to talk shit. I mean, the connection wasn't good, and I didn't understand his Mormon words. I told him to put Shayla on the line. He wouldn't, but he did say he wants to have a showdown with me. I understood that."

"He does believe he's the reincarnation of an old cowboy."

"That reincarnated fuck doesn't realize we'll be seeing him soon."

WE BOARDED OUR Alaska Air flight drunk on early morning airport Bloody Marys. Our fellow passengers were rich L.A. tourists heading down to party at the resorts. I sat by a pot-bellied guy named Gino who took his shoes off, exposing his dirty socks.

Richie had his phone on airplane mode. The Mike Leroux pube selfie had hit TMZ. He showed me and we laughed.

"There goes Jimmy from *Roomies*," Gino said, mumbling over my shoulder.

Somewhere over the Southwest desert, I fell into a deep sleep.

TWENTY-NINE

AFTER CUSTOMS, WE retrieved our luggage and walked out to the arrivals area. It was a humid day at the Cancún airport and we easily managed to hail a cab. The driver was a young guy named Rafael who spoke perfect English.

"The Blue Coconut, please," I said. It was a two-star hotel I'd looked up, not too far from the Hotel Zone, the area where all the resorts were and, possibly, Ciudad Reed.

While we were still stuck in gridlocked traffic at the airport, Rafael said, "Please, feel free to have a drink from the cooler at your feet."

We both opened Coronas. At the Blue Coconut, there were no vacancies, so we asked Rafael to recommend a similar place. He drove us a little farther north to El Centro, the downtown section, and we arrived at the Hotel Tequila. It was three floors and painted in Mexican pastels. "They have a nice pool here," Rafael said.

A guy out front said yes, there were vacancies. We paid Rafael and unloaded our luggage. Before he drove off, Rafael gave us his card.

Behind the desk of the Tequila, there was a heavyset clerk named Francisco, who was blind. Beside him was a little boy. We paid with Francisco, and the little boy gave us our sets of keys.

Our rooms were on opposite ends of the second floor. Mine had a bed, a TV, and a table with a broken Keurig coffee maker. The walls were thin, and I heard people speaking Spanish in the next room over. I stepped out to the small balcony and in the distance saw the bright blue water of the Caribbean Sea.

OUT IN THE streets, the sun began to set, and the air turned cool. Buses full of tourists passed us, heading north toward the Hotel Zone. Someone out there in the real Cancún had to know about the Ciudad Reed compound, we just needed to find them.

State police pickup trucks made patrols. Some Jehovah's Witness missionaries handed out pamphlets on a corner. We came upon an Afro-Brazilian dance club. Its name, Bahia, was written in neon lettering over the front door. Samba music blasted. Six black girls in short skirts got out of a limo, led by a tiny Mexican in a cowboy hat with a holstered automatic. He slipped cash to the bouncer, who let them in.

Richie said, "Want to just go for it?"

I didn't have a better idea. "Yeah."

The bouncer got up off his stool when he saw us coming. In broken, accented English said, "Sure you guys are at the right place?"

Inside, there was a dance floor full of Mexican and Caribbean-looking girls. Not a single one was a skinny L.A. actress. There were long rows of banquet tables off to the sides for people to sit at. Richie and I found ourselves a space.

Bahia wasn't a tourist joint. The two of us were the only white people in the building. Figuring we should stand out less, Richie went to the bar and ordered a large bucket of Corona bottles on ice. Back at our table, we each opened one and began freely passing the others out to people around us. Everybody accepted one.

After starting my third, I got up and started approaching groups of people, asking "Donde esta Mormons?" or "Donde esta Ciudad Reed?" Most pretended like they couldn't hear me, and no one said anything helpful.

A commotion broke out. Voices shouted in Spanish. Someone yelled. I moved across the floor, pushing through a crowd. I slipped on someone's spilled margarita and fell on my ass. When I got there, Richie was fighting with a tiny but vicious-looking Mexican guy in a concrete-stained T-shirt that said *Little Girl, Big Attitude*. Richie had been chatting up a sexy Mexican girl and the little guy wasn't happy about it. I arrived just in time to see Richie pick the guy off his feet and body slam him into a nearby table.

People scattered. Chairs tipped over. The music stopped. Two bouncers rushed in fast and pulled them apart. They let the Mexican guy go but held onto Richie, zip-tying his hands behind his back. They led him out to the street where a patrol car had already arrived.

"Come on guys," I said to their backs. People from the club had spilled out to the street to watch. "Just leave him with me and I'll get him out of here."

One of the cops said something aggressive to me in Spanish. It came out so fast I didn't pick up any of the words.

"Don't worry, Minor-man," Richie said. They shoved him into the backseat. "Just go back to the hotel to get some bribe money, then show up to the jail with it!"

THE CANCÚN POLICE department was a single-story white building with POLICE STATION, POLICÍA TURÍSTICA MINISTERIO PÚBLICO written across the top in black lettering. Rafael, who'd picked me up at the Tequila, said he'd wait for us out front with the meter running.

The middle-aged desk sergeant was clean-cut and polite. He dealt with a lot of entitled tourists on a daily basis and didn't want any drama.

"My friend Richie Walsh was brought here an hour ago. Can I see him?"

He led me down a hall to the three cops currently running the jail. These three were drunk, and they didn't bother to hide the big bottle of tequila they were passing around while on the job, in uniform. *Fuck it,* I thought, and took out three hundred in cash I'd gotten from my room at the Tequila. If necessary, I could go up to five.

"Can my friend leave with me?"

One took the money. "Make sure your amigo is more responsible next time."

They divvied up the money three ways. Then another one of

them walked back to the cell, unlocked the door, and waved at Richie, who stepped away from his many cellmates. The cop let us exit out a side door.

Back on the road with Rafael, Richie cracked open a Corona from the cooler on the floor. "Tonight wasn't a total bust," he said.

"How so?"

"I got that girl's number at the club, the one I was talking to before the fight started. Plus, I made friends. One of my cellmates, this guy from Texas, got busted with cocaine. He swore him and his buddy bought it from two Mormon girls in prairie dresses."

In the rearview, I caught the distinct look of fear in Rafael's eyes.

"Hey Rafael, do you know a place called Ciudad Reed?" I asked.

"I hear stories, but I don't know..."

"What type of stories?"

"Those are Mormons, no?"

"Any idea where we could find them?"

"No, I don't know." He was scared. I saw we could get something good out of him sometime later, when the time was right.

Back at the hotel, I paid Rafael for the ride and we stepped out of his taxi. Rafael rolled down his window and looked at us. "I've got a bad feeling about the two of you. Do not call me for a ride again. If you try it, I'll block your numbers." Then he rolled his window back up and drove off quickly.

THIRTY

THE TAXI DROPPED me off and I stepped onto the street. There was a hand-painted wooden sign hanging from a curved pole. The words *The Bountiful* were painted on it in gold Palatino font over a dark-blue background. The décor resembled an old-fashioned general store. There were rocking chairs and a decorative fireplace on the front porch. It was a big building, probably three times the size of an average restaurant. The parking lot was about a quarter full, and all the vehicles seemed to be beaten-down old vans or luxury SUVs, just one type or the other. People appeared to only come to this place in big groups.

The story the Texan told Richie was this: He'd been getting lunch here with his friends from college. They were all on vacation. The Texan had no idea why they were at this family restaurant until they got called into the back by the dumpsters where his buddy bought an eight ball from two young Mormon women in prairie dresses.

A blue minivan pulled up. The driver got out. He was a middle-aged white man. Out came his wife, who corralled their five kids out of the back. She had feathery '80s hair, thick-lensed glasses, and wore an ankle-length floral dress. All seven of them went in.

The Bountiful was Uncle Orson's joint. I could feel it. It catered to all the white Mormons and conservative religious types in the area. Standing there, I felt a strong urge to go inside and look around. But I remembered drugs were dealt here. Someone had to be watching. They could be watching me right now. I walked up the road and called another taxi to leave, thinking this was a stranger operation than anything I might have imagined.

ON THE ROAD back, I received a text from Richie saying to meet him a few blocks from our hotel at a bar. The Yucatan Cantina was on the ground floor of a two-story brick building painted orange and yellow. When I walked in, Richie was at the bar, drinking salt-rimmed margaritas with three rowdy-looking and large Americans. Each of them wore cargo shorts, sandals, and tropical shirts of just slightly different patterns.

"Minor-man." Richie waved me over. "Adam, this is Todd Frankart."

"Good to meet you," I said. We shook hands.

Todd walked on a prosthetic leg that began just below his left knee. He nodded at Richie. "Any friend of this crazy son-of-a-bitch is a friend of mine."

"And this here's Ronnie and Lucas," Richie said, slurring a little.

Since I was already two rounds behind, Richie ordered a margarita for me. The old, mustached bartender nodded and began to prepare mine. Then Richie pulled me away from the others. "Where you been?"

"Scoping out The Bountiful. It's a Mormon Cracker Barrel, basically. We know drugs are there. We know they've got buyers who show with money. If we just sit on the place, watch for a deal, someone has to lead us to Ciudad Reed." I nodded toward the bar. "Who are they?"

"Friends of the Texan. It was Todd who showed those Texas guys how to score the Mormon dope. All three of these guys here served together in the Navy and they come down here to party at least twice a year. They're all right." Richie laughed. "They don't know where Ciudad Reed is, but they've told me how *we* can score from the Mormons, who apparently sell good shit, usually in small doses. There's a routine to follow, but it's not hard. *That's* what we should do. One of us says we want to buy a decent-sized package of coke, more than what they'll keep at The Bountiful. The other will follow them while they get it from Ciudad Reed."

I thought it over. "You're right."

"Adam." Todd pointed at my margarita on the bar. "Catch up with us."

IT WAS A coin-operated laundromat in a strip mall. Whirring box fans were plugged into wall outlets. A few old Mexican ladies sat, waiting for their tumbling laundry to dry. A TV was mounted up in the corner, playing a telenovela. The noise was turned up loud so the ladies could hear it over the fans. At the end of a row of machines, there was a thin white woman in an Easter-egg-pink prairie dress. She leaned against a laundry basket on wheels, looking up at the TV.

She smiled at me when she saw me. "Can I help you, sir?"

"Are you Fannie or Lucinda?"

Todd gave us those names.

She went *all business*. "How do you know Fannie and Lucinda?"

"My friend Todd Frankart referred me."

"Are you alone?"

"Yes."

"One moment, please." She walked into a back room. She came back and slipped a piece of paper into my hand. "Meet them there and bring money."

It was the address of The Bountiful and it told me what table to sit at when I got there an hour from now.

I WAITED AT the booth I'd been assigned. Every wall of The Bountiful was decorated with Frontier-era Mormon memorabilia. There were old pitchforks, axes, and top hats. My booth had a framed painting of a honeybee. The buffet was a series of extra-long rows of giant metal tins holding mounds of food that baked under hot lamps. The booths against the wall where I sat were all regular sizes, but almost every stand-alone dining table was extremely long. They seemed to begin at thirty feet.

A large family arrived. It was a husband, nine women, and a swarm of too many kids for me to count. I realized all the long tables were meant for parties this large. This was a polygamist family. After settling in, they got their meals from the buffet. One wife got all the food for the husband, who sat at the end of the table in a chair bigger than all the others. His seat was the throne.

When everyone had their food and was ready to begin eating, the husband said a prayer. There was no way the kids down on the other end could have heard him.

Richie texted me: *Two incoming Mormon broads in a fresh SUV.*

The front door opened and the two women walked in. One wore a pastel-yellow prairie dress. The other's was pastel blue. Both wore long, braided hair that went down to their lower backs and was perfectly raised in a wave at the top. They dressed themselves as if it were still the nineteenth century and no one else in the restaurant seemed to care or notice. They stopped at my booth and sat across from me.

"I'm Adam," I said. "Fannie and Lucinda?"

"I'm Fannie. She's Lucinda," the one in yellow said.

"Just tell us what you want." Lucinda had the inside seat, against the wall.

"Well... I was hoping to buy some cocaine." I tried to make myself sound like the sort of partying vacationer they must be used to dealing with. "I've got *quite a week* planned down here. Cancún is like... a total paradise."

Lucinda asked, "How much?"

"Well, my friends I'm vacationing with and I pooled some cash, and we'll take whatever two thousand dollars can get us."

"That's more than usual," Fannie said.

I feigned disappointment. "I was told you could accommodate."

"We can get it. We'll just need to make an extra trip to secure that much from our Priesthood Holder," Lucinda said.

"Right now just give us two hundred," Fannie said.

"And what, I leave empty-handed?"

"You won't leave empty-handed."

I counted out two hundred in cash and passed the bills under the table to Fannie, who counted them, then pointed to a far hallway beyond the buffet stations. "There's an exit down there. Wait outside by the dumpsters."

Out back, a Mexican truck driver unloaded crates of seafood.

A Mormon woman signed his clipboard and other Mormon women wheeled the crates into the back door of the kitchen on hand trucks. The driver closed up his truck and drove off.

A teenage Mormon girl appeared from the kitchen, walking toward me. When she got close, she looked around to see if anyone was watching and handed me something wrapped up with a blue table napkin from inside and held together by a safety pin. I undid it. Inside there was a small plastic bag full of coke. I gave her a satisfied nod, then put the bag in my pocket.

"Meet us back here tonight at ten o'clock with your eighteen hundred," the girl said. Then she went inside.

I walked around the side of the building and managed to get to the front parking lot fast enough to see Richie tailing Fannie and Lucinda's SUV in the maroon '93 Dodge Dynasty he'd rented earlier.

I DID LAPS for hours at the hotel pool while I waited for word from Richie. By nightfall, there'd been nothing, so I began to call and text him. No response. Ten o'clock came and went. By now, Fannie and Lucinda knew I wasn't going to show with the rest of the money. Richie could take care of himself. I knew this by now. But when midnight passed and I still had no word, I began to worry. Maybe they'd spotted him.

At twelve thirty a text finally came, telling me to meet him at the Yucatan. I was out the door running. When I got there, I saw the Dodge parked on the street. Inside the bar, it was crowded. Richie was at a table drinking a margarita and charging his phone from a wall outlet. I sat down across from him. He'd gotten a tan since the afternoon, and he smelled like the ocean.

"You all right?"

"My battery died."

"Well?"

"That first night, you said not to underestimate these Mormons." He took a long drink. "The dope is stored in a house a few miles from the restaurant. It's heavily secured."

"All right." I waited. "But Shayla won't be there."

"I know. I kept following the two broads. They went back to The Bountiful, to sell you the dope at ten. When you never showed, I tailed them out to the Hotel Zone. They turned in toward someplace you can't see from the main road. It was too much jungle. I parked a long way back and went in on foot. After poking around in the dark for forever, I came to this ledge with a steep drop to the ground below. There were more trees down there, but beyond it, even in the dark, I made out the walls of a gated compound."

THIRTY-ONE

BIRDS CALLED OUT from the treetops above. After a long hike through the Mayan jungle, we came to the ledge where we took out binoculars and looked down through the trees.

Ciudad Reed covered at least twenty acres of oceanfront land, maybe more. Down where the ground leveled out, there was a chain-link fence and about a half mile beyond it a much larger stone wall. Watch towers were manned with armed Mormons. From our vantage point, we saw the upper parts of the larger buildings. One was a three-story mansion painted a vibrant white. It had a towering brick chimney with the words *Pray and Obey* printed horizontally on the bricks.

"Jesus," Richie said. "How can this still exist?"

"There's quite a few of them in Mexico."

"I guess now we have to confirm that she's actually in there."

"She's in there."

Ciudad Reed came alive. The automatic brass gate at the stone wall opened, letting vehicles in and out. An armed guard was posted at a booth beside it. Everyone drove high-end SUVs like at The Bountiful. We saw different Mormons in glimpses. Over at the mansion, there was a third-floor bedroom with a large balcony that kept drawing my attention.

"How do we find *where* Shalya is in there?" Richie said. "This joint's a fucking fortress and if Scotty Black was telling the truth, Orson's got cartel protection to boot. When we get in, we can't just take our sweet time poking around."

I didn't have an answer for him, not yet.

Back at the Yucatan, we spent the evening spitballing solutions over margaritas. Neither of us came up with anything, just a vague intention to update Joan soon. We'd been keeping her in the dark since Pasadena, and I didn't feel good about it.

IN THE MORNING, we hiked back out again.

"Everyone I can see looks Mormon," I said. "If there's a cartel connection to this place, it isn't an obvious one."

The automatic gate opened. A black Navigator drove out. It stopped and the back window rolled down. I focused in. P.Y. was in the backseat. Only his face was visible.

"You see what I'm seeing?"

Richie said, "Is he an ugly son-of-a-bitch or what?"

The guard at the booth walked over to speak with P.Y. Then the Navigator moved on to the outer chain-link fence where it was let through by another guard, and drove down one of the roads that snaked through the jungle toward Boulevard Kukulcán.

Later, I looked back at the third-floor balcony of the mansion. I tapped Richie's shoulder. "See that open balcony door? Third floor of the mansion?"

Richie swept over to the balcony with his glasses. "I'm looking..."

"See what's on it there?"

It was a telescope.

"Oh shit. Shayla *loves* telescopes."

"Like I said, she's here. He's probably making her search for Kolob."

"For *what*?"

"Kolob. It's this planet Joseph Smith just made up. Mormons have a thing about outer space. If you're a good enough Mormon and do everything right, you get your own planet when you die. All your wives come with you and you get to keep banging them in outer space."

Richie laughed, then covered his mouth. "So Shayla's in that room then."

"If she is, it's probably not every night."

"How come?"

I pointed toward the north section of the compound, where none of the buildings were high enough to rise above the stone wall. "I suspect the wives get their own houses, over there." Then

I pointed back to the balcony. "That must be Orson's bedroom. It's a guess, but I think he told Shayla she could leave a telescope out there just for the nights that she's... picked."

I DROVE THE Dodge across El Centro to an auto body shop called Reuben's. A Cancún PD radio car was out front. I parked behind it and double-checked the address. Yes, this was where Richie said to meet.

I hadn't seen him since the night before. We'd been drinking at the Yucatan when he stepped out to make a call. He came back with some big, secret idea. He just left the keys to the rental with me, called himself a cab, and said to keep my phone close. I didn't hear anything all night, or all of that day. Then, an hour earlier, he'd sent a text for me to meet him here and to empty out my big suitcase and bring it along.

I got it from the backseat and walked into the shop. Behind the front desk, a guy in an oil-stained blue jumpsuit saw me and stood. Before he spoke, Richie appeared through a doorway behind him. "This way, Minor-man."

Wheeling the case behind me, I followed Richie out to a small backyard behind the shop. Here, I saw the same two Cancún cops who'd arrested him at Bahia, both in uniform. Standing beside them was the beautiful Mexican girl he'd gotten in the fight over. Her long black hair went down below her waist, and she wore tight cutoff jean shorts.

Everyone stood around a fold-up table covered with serious weapons. I didn't recognize any of the guns on sight. Later, I learned they were an H&K MP5 submachine gun, a Beretta 93R, and two .45 Kimber Raptor automatics. There were also six Chinese-made hand grenades.

"Denise here speaks English. She's been translating," Richie said. "Don't worry, I already paid for all this stuff out of my end, we just need to haul it off. Hence the luggage."

I walked with Richie across the yard. "What the hell's going on?"

"We know where Shayla is, we just don't know how we're going to get on the compound and get her out, right? Well, an idea came to me. Remember that shooting you told me about?"

IT HAD HAPPENED the afternoon before at a resort just up the coast from us, in Isla Mujeres. I'd read all about it online and later told Richie all the details.

Six cartel soldiers on Jet Skis, all in military camouflage, rode up to the beach in front of a resort while an American wedding was in progress. They parked in the sand, dismounted, and in front of dozens of witnesses, drew AR-15s. The Americans, by all accounts, assumed these Mexicans were putting on some sort of play for their benefit and just watched as they fired up into the sky. Finally, the wedding-goers scattered. The Mexicans dropped their guns, removed their military clothes, and just walked away.

Serious cartel drama had brewed in Quintana Roo for the past year. The cartels owned and controlled every resort in Mexico. Because of this, conflict was rare. The cartel who'd long been in control of this region was the Castillo group.

Castillo must be, I told Richie, the cartel protecting Uncle Orson and his compound. From Scotty Black, we knew Castillo was being run by the boss calling the shots from East L.A. Castillo was being challenged by the El Rey cartel, who'd just brazenly escalated the feud. El Rey had used the gunmen on Jet Skis to scare Americans, willingly courting international notoriety and spreading hysteria about what their next move would be.

"ANOTHER GUY IN the can with me that night, a Mexican, mentioned how Carlos and Fausto, Mexico's finest here"—Richie nodded at the two cops behind him—"are on El Rey's payroll. Denise, who's a hooker, struck me that night at Bahia as quite the player. She knows people. So, last night I called her and asked if she could get me a sit down with these two. She made it happen. First, I told Carlos and Fausto I had no hard feelings. Then, I explained how I'm here in Mexico to take an important woman away from Ciudad Reed and I was willing to pay if they could help us with our mission in any way..."

"If they work for El Rey, then what's bad for Uncle Orson is good for them..."

"They *wanted* to help us. First things first. Since we can't bust into Ciudad Reed unarmed, I asked if they knew of any connection where we could buy some guns."

I nodded at the table. "I've never touched stuff like that. You can handle those?"

"I've used similar stuff on the range. We'll figure it out."

"What type of a sentence is getting caught with machine guns in Mexico?"

"We aren't getting caught, so it won't be an issue. But these guns aren't the only thing. Carlos and Fausto passed our mission up the food chain and received a message. El Rey's on board with our Shayla grab, it's just not stirring enough shit for them. So, they're giving us a guy whose job is to punch Orson's ticket."

"What guy?"

"One of their people. His name is Emilio and he knows the compound. He's an intense cat and he doesn't cost us anything extra." Richie lowered his voice. "I knew we had to figure something out, so I went for this. It all came together fast, but this is the cartel. Wherever this leads, expect it to be heavy."

Getting closer to Shayla was all I cared about. "I'm good with this."

Richie turned to Denise. "Where'd Emilio go?"

I could tell from Richie's tone that they'd slept together.

Denise turned toward Carlos and Fausto. She translated Richie's question. One of them whistled toward the house on the other side of the yard. The screen door squeaked open and a thin, balding Mexican stepped out. He was in his forties and dressed head to toe in desert camouflage and combat boots.

"My name is Emilio." He spoke good English. "Are you the brains of this operation?"

"I wouldn't go that far," I said.

"You and your partner here are searching for a woman. The Prophet has her."

"We just want to find her and get her back to L.A."

"The Prophet gets married a lot. Even more than his father would."

"This isn't about Orson's marriages. This woman's a captive."

"I know Ciudad Reed. I've studied its layout. I can sneak us in, but we might be seen. If so, there will be a fight, so I'll need some time to prepare you two. Once inside, we'll separate. You'll go for your woman, and I'll go for the Prophet. All of his people will seek to protect him, so you two will have your chance once I've drawn them away."

"Are you sure you can get to him?" I asked.

"That's my business. If I can help you get this woman out of there while I'm on my mission, I will do what I can."

I turned to Richie. "You want me to put the guns in the suitcase now?"

EMILIO DROVE AN old red Ford F-150 pickup. The next morning he drove us out to a firing range about a half hour outside Cancún to test-fire all the guns and see which ones we liked the most. Emilio taught us how to handle them well. He had experience.

We planned the mission in my room. Emilio spread out detailed maps of Ciudad Reed on my bed. He called the high-end Mormon SUVs "plyg rigs." He said my guess about the wives' houses was right. They were all situated in long rows of houses north of the mansion.

Emilio spoke in enigmas. You couldn't tell where he was coming from. A pent-up rage seethed in his eyes, and it amplified whenever Orson's name came up.

We determined who would carry what. My main weapon would be the Beretta 93R. It was a semiautomatic pistol that fired in three-round bursts with each trigger pull. It wasn't great for firing across long distances, but its power was serious. Whatever

I hit would stay down. I also would have one of the Raptors. Riche got the MP5 and the other Raptor. Emilio would take another MP5, one he already owned, a Ruger .380, a karambit knife, and a machete. Each of us would have two hand grenades.

The next day, Emilio drove us to stake out Ciudad Reed again from the same ledge in the jungle. While we watched, he drilled us on all the stages of our plan.

"I've heard Orson is protected by the Castillo group," I said to him. "But every face I see here looks like Mormons."

"The Prophet's able to call Castillo in if he needs to. When we cross those gates, it has to be at a time when Castillo won't be near."

Through our glasses, I saw one of Orson's many other wives appear on the balcony of his bedroom. I pointed this out to Emilio. "Then Shayla isn't in the main house now, right?"

"Correct. Shayla, the Prophet's newest wife, must be out of rotation, over in her personal house in the wives' section of the compound."

I almost corrected Emilio when he called Shayla one of Orson's wives, but kept quiet. Shayla was a captive. She'd let out a scream that day she'd been taken at Griffith Park. "Since Shayla won't be close to Orson, we should go in soon then, right? What else are we waiting for?"

"Our time is getting near."

Later, I saw a long line of kids being led by an old man toward what looked like a school. Each child was female and dressed like a sister-wife. It looked like some sort of school for all the children Orson was married to. When I saw this, Richie had his glasses on some other part of the compound. I didn't point it out to him. I was too scared he'd run down the ledge and try to scale the compound walls all by himself.

I SAT BY the open window of my room in the evening, looking to the street below. A midsummer storm off the coast had shifted the weather. Richie was across the hall with Denise, probably snorting up the last of the eight ball I'd bought from The Bountiful.

I knew this case would end badly for me. The risks ahead were too great and I must have used up my luck with the Armenians. I wouldn't return from Mexico. My family in Ohio would get no answers and I would be forgotten. *So be it*, I told myself, as long as I removed Shayla from the sickness around her.

I saw Emilio pull into the Tequila lot. We had no plans to see him again that night, but there he was. I knocked on Richie's door, giving him a moment to sober up. When Emilio showed in the hallway carrying a dark-green duffel bag, we brought him into my room. He put it on the bed and got out two Kevlar vests. Richie and I tried ours on.

"El Rey's just made an offensive against Castillo. There's a major conflict further down the coast," he said. "All of the Prophet's cartel backup is down there. Now is our best bet. We'll go in the morning, before dawn."

"Tomorrow morning then," I said.

Richie nodded. "Tomorrow morning."

From his bag, Emilio removed a crystal decanter of golden-brown tequila. He gestured at my window, where an empty glass sat on the ledge. I rinsed it out along with another glass by the bathroom sink. Emilio drank straight from the decanter.

"I know the two of you wonder about what's been driving me." He poured our cups full.

"I figured if you wanted to tell us you would," I said.

We toasted. Richie and I waited for Emilio to drink first, then we tasted ours. It was the finest tequila I'd ever drunk.

"My great-aunt Martha was married to Hiram, the Prophet's father."

"Mormons marry Mexicans?" Richie said. "I had no idea."

"Martha was American and half-white. Most people didn't realize she had any Mexican blood in her at all. We were close growing up here in Cancún. She was like my big sister. Her family, like mine, was in the fishing business. Her father was the main fish supplier to the Reed compound. This relationship, over time, brought Martha's father under the spell of Mormonism. He made the whole family convert. My family followed suit and everything changed. The church became the only thing that mattered. When Hiram declared his wish to marry Martha, her parents saw it as God's will to agree. She was sent away to become Hiram Reed's thirty-eighth wife. I wanted to save her, but I was just a boy. On the day of her marriage, Martha was only fourteen."

"Is she still there, married to him now?" I asked.

"No." Emilio took another drink. "I only know what I was able to piece together over the years, but Martha wouldn't display the proper obedience and commitment to her role. Rebellion in a sister-wife is dangerous. It upsets the balance of the compound. So Hiram had her killed. It came to him in a prophecy. Her throat was cut open with the same razor blade he used for his morning shave. They have a ceremony for this."

I said, "Blood Atonement."

"Yes. Hiram ordered the sacrifice of this child so the others would not misbehave. But he did not wield the blade himself. That job went to young Orson."

Richie and I looked at each other.

"When I learned this was how Martha died, I swore revenge. I had no idea how I would get it. At eighteen I moved to the north and applied to the police department in Tijuana. At first, I was proud of being a cop. But Mexico is a corrupt country. Too corrupt, I saw, for any one man to make a real difference. I did terrible things which made me no better than the Reeds. I realized I was corrupt, too, corrupt in my soul.

"I quit the force and moved to the States, hoping to start over. I lived in New Orleans, San Diego, San Francisco. Anywhere I could fish. But running from my past was useless. Getting justice for this act of pure evil became the only way I could redeem myself, the only sense I could impose upon my life. So I returned to Cancún.

"I knew I couldn't kill the Prophet alone. He was too protected.

So I considered aligning myself with his enemies. This meant the El Rey, the Aztec cartel. They were growing strong. They challenged Castillo. If I made myself useful to them, they might turn me loose on the Prophet. So, I joined them." He refilled our glasses. "The Mormons of Ciudad Reed will be alone tomorrow. They will find themselves tested."

Richie held up his glass. "To Martha."

"To Martha," I said.

Emilio said, "To Martha."

THIRTY-TWO

EMILIO DROVE US up Boulevard Kukulcán while the moon was still out, giving everything a lunar gloss. He took a right turn on a dirt road and drove along a twisting path through the trees. We hit a dead end. Each of us got out of the truck and got our weapons ready. Emilio unsheathed his machete. It gleamed in the darkness.

"This way." He hacked away at foliage. It took only a few minutes for us to arrive at our first barrier, the chain-link fence. Emilio took out a pair of bolt cutters and made us a hole. We followed him through.

There was thicker foliage on the other side. We'd made it about thirty yards when a flashlight shone through the trees.

"Who's there?" one voice said.

"Identify yourself," another voice said.

I squinted, making them out in the dark. They were Mormons with collared shirts and beards carrying twelve-gauge shotguns. They were on edge. Their cartel backup was nowhere close. In all the times we'd come out to watch, we'd never seen guys on foot patrolling this area.

"What's your business here?" one said, speaking to Emilio.

"Who are you?" the other said.

Emilio raised his Ruger and shot the first Mormon in the forehead. Moonlit blood sprayed out behind his head. The second Mormon half-turned to watch his partner fall. Emilio fired at him, opening up a small hole in his throat. His shotgun fell and he clutched at himself, sucking for air. Emilio fired again and the second Mormon was dead.

"What's about to happen will be ugly, uglier than this," Emilio said. "If either of you want to give up, here's your chance. I won't tell El Rey."

I looked at Richie. His eyes said the decision was mine.

I said, "Let's keep going."

Moving forward, we came upon the main gate. On the other side, people shouted. Lights turned on. They'd heard the shots.

We arrived at the booth by the entrance. Its window was open. There was a small, bearded Mormon inside, talking fast on the radio. Emilio rushed him. At a full sprint, he removed a grenade from his belt, pulled the pin, and tossed it in. The Mormon tried to run. It went off at his feet. The front wall of the booth blew away and smoke bellowed out. Richie and I coughed at the smell of burnt flesh. Emilio waved us his way. We followed him through the blood-splattered booth. We stepped over the eviscerated corpse of the security guard and through the door on the other side.

Ciudad Reed.

Shots flew. Fast rifle fire. I heard a bullet whiz by my head and keep going behind me. Richie and I found cover behind some thick-trunked palm trees. Emilio stayed out in the open. He located the shooters' position behind a garage in the distance. He raised his MP5, focused in, and let go a series of bursts. Both bodies fell. Emilio tossed away his empty magazine and reloaded a fresh one.

We ran across a freshly mowed lawn. The mansion was close, to our left, about a football field off. I made out the big brick chimney. To our right were the long rows of wives' houses. They went on and on and on.

More shots came our way. Richie and I raced for better cover. We ducked behind a black Subaru plyg rig. Shots pierced the plyg rig body.

"The Prophet will be in there." Emilio pointed at the mansion.

The first light of dawn began to rise in the sky.

"Go that way now and you don't have a chance," Richie said.

A shot hit the plyg rig window, just above Richie's head. Flying glass cut my forehead. The Mormons out there in the last cover of dark got closer.

"Don't forget the exit route," Emilio said to us.

Another shot hit the plyg rig. Emilio rose with his MP5 and returned fired. Richie and I rose up, following his lead. The three of us sprayed the area, firing on top of one another. The bursts from my 93R came out fast and hard. Three more Mormons fell. We ducked back down low. *You might have just killed someone,* I thought as I reloaded a fresh magazine.

"Don't worry about me." Emilio unbuttoned the front of his desert camo shirt. He wanted us to see something. Five blocks of C-4 were carefully secured to the outside of his Kevlar vest, covering his abdomen. A yellow wire ran from the explosives inside the right sleeve of his shirt. There was a slight bulge on his right wrist I hadn't noticed before. The detonator. He just needed to roll his sleeve down to set it off. I didn't know much about plastic explosives but the amount he had on him seemed like a lot. "El Rey has expectations I must fulfill."

"You can't. He'll have civilians around," I said. Warm blood trickled down my face.

"I've measured the radius while training. I'll clear them first."

I touched Emilio's shoulder. "No more women like your great-aunt can die in this place."

"They won't."

We weren't going to change his mind.

"Good luck to you," Richie said.

"Yeah, good luck."

Emilio stood and dashed toward the mansion.

"Protect the Prophet!" a voice yelled in the dark.

I looked up. They were all chasing Emilio.

WE RAN. THE sister-wives' small single-story houses were on both sides of us. Each design was identical, their only differences were the colors of the paint. We looked in windows. We entered porches and opened front doors. We saw no one.

The sun was all the way up now. Gunfire kept popping off behind us.

I stopped and wiped sweat from my eyes. A woman peeked

out of a window from behind a curtain. It wasn't Shayla.

We picked another house. I opened the front door and we rushed in. A girl was in the kitchen. I lowered my 93R and stepped forward. It was one of the wives. She wore a long purple dress and looked about fifteen.

"Are you okay?"

I realized what a stupid question this was.

"Do you know what house Shayla is in?"

She made a slight glance west, in the direction of the next row of houses. Then she picked up an old-fashioned leather journal and a quill pen from the kitchen table.

"What are your names?" Her voice was gentle.

"He's Richie Walsh. I'm Adam Minor."

She wrote something down. Then she pointed the feather on her pen at us. Her eyes became full of hate. "In three years' time your flesh will mortify and the both of you will die!" Now she was a screaming witch. "Three years is all you have left, Richie Walsh and Adam Minor. Three years before an eternity of torture in the fires of Hell!"

She put down the journal, then grabbed a huge cast iron skillet that hung on the wall of her kitchen and hurled it our way. It fell short and skidded across the floor. She was still screaming her prophecy at the back of our heads and tossing other items from the kitchen at us as we made our way back out the door.

We ran over to the next row of houses. The girl had looked this way when we mentioned Shayla's name. The construction on these ones looked newer. They were more recently built.

Someone stood on a front porch. We ducked down. It was a scrawny, suspendered teenage boy carrying an old hunting rifle. He didn't see us. It was the only house we saw with someone guarding it. Orson and P.Y. knew Shayla was a target. Maybe they'd posted the kid there, thinking we might be the intruders.

I stayed low. Richie ran around so we could advance from opposite sides. Richie showed himself first. He shoved his MP5 in the kid's face.

"Who's in there?" Richie said.

I stepped out with my gun raised. "Is it Shayla?"

He just stared at me.

"Is it *her*?"

His face showed signs of inbreeding. He wouldn't respond.

"Take the rifle by the barrel," Richie said. "Lay it down, slowly."

The kid obeyed and ran off.

I turned the gold door knob and pushed in. With my 93R out, I went in.

The interior was just like the last house. The living room was empty. A handmade quilt with scenes from Joseph Smith's life stitched into it hung over the couch. The kitchen was empty. We walked past a basement door. At the end of a short hallway, there was a bedroom.

She was in a long pink prairie dress, sitting on the edge of the bed. Her blonde hair was pulled back into a braid that went down her back.

"Shayla, my name is Adam Minor," I said. "This is my partner, Richie Walsh. We're private detectives, hired by Joan Goldman. We've come to rescue you."

Shayla stood. She wanted to speak, but I don't think she could.

"It's okay." I took her hand. "We have to move fast."

Just as we stepped outside to the front porch, there was the loud crack of an explosion from the north. A massive cloud of brown smoke rose into the skyline of the coast. Debris soared. Bits of it reached us, over a half mile away. From the edge of the porch, I craned my neck and saw some of the smoke rising, revealing that a big chunk of the third floor of the mansion was missing.

Richie said, "We've got to keep moving."

We ran through a long alley between the houses and made it to the beach where we ran across the white sand. Shayla made good time in her constricting getup. I held her hand tightly. "Can we stop?" she said. "I need to stop."

"We can't. Not yet."

The sound of an engine emerged behind us. Some type of off-road vehicle tore through the sand. I didn't look back to see what it was. It got louder. It was after us. There was a large rock formation ahead. It was almost as big as a house. A half mile beyond it was an unmanned guard tower at the gate marking the end of Ciudad Reed.

"Let her go," a voice said.

Finally, we stopped and turned around. It was P.Y., on a dune buggy. He wore dress pants and the top half of his white temple garments. He slowed down. A layer of gauze was wrapped around his left arm. The same Magnum he carried in L.A. was holstered at his side. He stepped into the sand. His hair blew in the wind.

Beside me, Richie kept his eyes on P.Y. "Don't worry, Minorman. I got this." He placed his MP5 at his feet and unbuttoned the holster on his Raptor. "I'll catch up with you."

I pulled Shayla to cover behind the rocks and turned around to watch.

Richie walked toward P.Y. He stopped ten feet from him.

"Many are dead back there, but the Prophet lives." Smoke wafted into the sky behind P.Y.'s head. "Your terrorist attack failed."

"I don't do terrorist attacks. Emilio back there did his own thing."

P.Y. looked out at the ocean, then back at Richie. "I've lived through many duels in my previous body. The Prophet Orson Reed saw long ago that I would be here, in a moment like this, facing a villain like you, as during my time with Joseph and Brigham."

"Brother, you are one Looney Tunes Mormon."

They drew.

Both fired, right on top of each other. I couldn't tell who was first.

P.Y. fell to his knees. His temple garment turned dark red, right around the heart. Richie fired three more shots into his chest. P.Y. let go of the Magnum. He fell back onto the sand. Richie walked forward, his Raptor still out, and kicked the Magnum away. P.Y. took slow, labored breaths. It was the end of his life, there in that place. P.Y. left his body.

Richie reunited with us, and we resumed our escape. Shayla was really lagging now. We got to the gate. It ran down the sand and into the water. A resort started on the other side. We just had to cross and we would all be free together.

"That's enough," Shayla said. "I'm not going any further than this."

THIRTY-THREE

SHE LED US inland to some Mayan ruins out in the jungle. We were still inside the compound gates. Richie closely watched the trees beyond. His MP5 was out and ready. A lizard slithered around a Mayan column close to his head. The chaos from the bomb bought us time, but I knew I had to talk Shayla out of whatever this was.

"Since time began, a hundred billion human beings have lived on this earth. Did you know there's the same number of stars in the Milky Way? I used to imagine this airplane necklace I wore was actually a spaceship that I would just fly away in someday."

The necklace. I got it out of my pocket and showed her.

"Wow," Shayla said. "I never thought I'd see this again." She took it from me. "For all of my childhood, the only thing I cared about was leaving Bear Creek. Every adult in my life pushed me to grow into a dutiful Mormon wife. I was married at fifteen. I was expected to stop being myself and become a wife and mother, as Heavenly Father wanted. I gave birth to my first son just a few weeks before my sixteenth birthday. But the hardening loss of youth I saw in all the kids around me didn't occur in my case, because I rejected all of my roles. All I cared about was scaling the Bear Creek walls and running as fast as possible toward the world beyond. So, I found someone who would loan me cash for my escape."

"Where is your son now?" Richie asked.

"Back at Bear Creek, as far as I know. He would be eight now."

"Shayla, I was raised in a church too," I said. "My story's nothing like yours, but I can relate. I escaped and now I'm free, just living my life. On bad days, I think about going back. But there's nothing to go back to. These Saints you've been around have gotten in your head." I pointed toward the mansion. "There's nothing for you back there."

She seemed to not hear me. "I didn't know then that the cash I'd borrowed came from my husband-to-be. But I made it to L.A. and found my own 'freedom.' For me, this meant becoming a drug addict, a stripper, and a shameless whore. The only authentic, remotely decent relationship I had was with a cold-blooded gangster."

"We know, Arman," I said.

She looked up, surprised. "How is he?"

"On his way to federal prison. He didn't make good decisions after you were gone."

This didn't surprise her.

Fire truck sirens blared through the trees from Kukulcán, racing toward the blast. "At first, Arman and I were passionate for each other. We had fire. But our relationship didn't work. He hit me. I lost weeks to alcoholic blackouts. One night, I ran my car engine in the garage and breathed in the fumes. My roommate barely found me in time. After that, I got sober. Then I left him. For the next two years, I lived a quiet but worldly life. I was free of the church, God, and all of my addictions. And none of this brought me happiness. But I still lied, telling everyone around me I was doing great living as a free thinker. I figured if I pretended to be an idealist for long enough, the happiness would just arrive. I went on this way, living a lie. Later, Arman returned to my life, hoping to make amends. By that point, I'd realized my childhood obsession with rebellion had been a tragic mistake, one I might not be able to fix.

"One night, out at the Observatory, I had a vision. I didn't believe in visions, but one came anyway, with my eyes wide open. I was living on another planet and preparing a vast dinner with my many sister-wives. You could see *this* earth out our dining room window, and every bit of drama upon it was insignificant from our elevated perspective. I saw that Heavenly Father really had made multiple earths and heavens to bring humans closer to eternal life. Somehow, in one form or another, I knew that my lifelong curiosity with outer space had been with me for a reason, because one day I would abandon this earth. Filled with the spirit, I threw this necklace into those bushes in Griffith Park. I knew how I would get to the cosmos, so I didn't need it anymore."

I looked around us. These Mayan ruins were a stage, maybe even the pulpit of some ancient church. "But Joseph Smith made all that outer space stuff up. He made it all up. I'll admit, he was clever for his time. He gave his people exactly what they wanted to hear. You used to understand this."

"I thought I was smart, but my smarts never did me any good. Now I know, Joseph was telling the truth. My running from his truth only brought me misery. The Latter-day Saints have been in a sad state for over a century. Only a true Mormon warrior willing to make sacrifices can right our course. A man fitting this description was the man I would marry. The day after I got this vision, Uncle Orson Reed himself just walked into Joan's Bras looking for me. Should I consider that a coincidence?"

This wasn't the woman we'd been searching for at all. This was someone else entirely. "Not paying back Orson's loan from years ago doesn't obligate you to marry him. Orson's not just a fanatic. He's a gangster, just like Arman and all of his friends."

"*Heavenly Father was at work all along.* I invited the Prophet to meet me at the Observatory. He arrived with P.Y. We walked to a secluded area up on the trails, a place I knew we could look up to the sky and not be bothered. There, the Prophet got on one knee and proposed." She held up her wedding ring. "P.Y. used his authority to perform the sealing. I knew we could go back to his hotel, but the starlit setting was clearly preordained. We didn't wait. And that was that."

I waited. "But why the scream?"

"The scream..." There was a faint recognition in her tone.

"If a wedding night in the bushes was what you wanted, why did you scream?"

She'd forgotten about her scream. Her young life had been full of so much terrible pain. "The scream was an exorcism of the worldly demons inside me," she said, finally. "I wanted to be free of any Satanic influence the first time my husband and I were together. The scream was a purification. After my scream, I was clean again."

I'd gone through this scene so many times in my head. Now, with it actually unfolding, I couldn't think of a thing to say that might change her mind.

Richie lowered his MP5 and turned around. Except for the far-off sirens, the jungle was quiet. "Do you understand what Adam and I have been through to get here? How many times we've risked our lives to save yours? What's happening to you right now *is a gift*."

"I didn't ask for any gifts."

"You've still got a chance." I'd never heard Richie's voice sound so sad. "*Take it*."

"No. You heard P.Y. before you killed him for trying to protect me. The Prophet lives. My place is with him."

"Joan's worried about you," I said.

"Tell her I'm grateful for all the kindness she showed me."

"So you just stay married to this old man, then get married off to some other old man as soon as he dies?"

"And that's if El Rey doesn't kill everyone on this whole compound soon," Richie said.

"If that's my purpose, so be it." She threw her necklace into the trees.

"You can't really want this," I said.

"Returning to L.A. would be to deny myself eternal life."

"Shayla, come with us. *Please*."

She reached out and touched my cheek. "You think you can be free, but God catches up. You've got to serve someone."

"Minor-man, Joan wanted to know she was okay," Richie said. "She's not coming. We can't force her. And we've got to move. Now."

I turned, looking at him. "We just leave?"

"What else is there to do?"

THIRTY-FOUR

BEHIND OUR HOTEL, in a back alley, Richie and I made sure the coast was clear and tossed all our guns down a sewer drain. By now, Orson must have called Castillo for help at the compound. They would have our descriptions from Shayla.

We had to leave Mexico fast.

We booked our return flight home. It was scheduled to leave in three hours. Cancún PD cruisers and state military vehicles kept passing by outside. I was paranoid. Richie was too. Every time I looked through the window, I saw potential agents of the Castillo group.

I was packing in my room when my phone buzzed. It was an unknown number and I didn't answer. When the same number called back right away, I picked up.

"Tell me why I should let you two leave Mexico alive," Orson said.

His voice was hoarse and labored. He tried to sound powerful. He must have gotten my number from back when I'd called the line Scotty Black gave us.

"You've barely survived, and you've lost your Mormon Samson. You're bluffing."

"I told you the truth about everything in L.A. You ignored me."

"You might still be with us, old man, but look around you. The era of your kind is fading fast, and I'm glad to help accelerate the decay. El Rey will finish you off soon."

"Son, in some form, I will always continue."

WE GOT ON the road. The rental agency had an office close to the airport and Richie drove us there to drop off the Dodge.

My call with Orson had been, in a way, reassuring. His talk of letting us leave was obvious bullshit. The blast took a big piece of him, too big of a piece. He wasn't after us and neither was

Castillo. We'd sown too much chaos for them to play offense this fast. My paranoia about them faded. My devastation about Shayla felt like it was just starting.

I called Joan. "We found her."

The connection was patchy. "She's with you?"

"No. She left with the old man willingly. She's staying down here."

"She's what?"

"She wanted to be one of this guy's wives. No one forced her. We tried to bring her back, but we couldn't do it."

The static got bad. I think she was crying. Then the call dropped.

We weren't far from the rental office. "How could I have not seen it?" I said to myself. Beside me, Richie drove in silence. "How could I have been so fucking stupid?"

At the airport we went through security. There was a restaurant. We took a booth and ordered our last Mexican margaritas. Richie tried to cheer me up. He told jokes. He reminisced about the old Russians in our store he played pranks on.

"You know, we've actually achieved a lot on this case," he said.

"Besides our actual goal."

"Minor-man, you can't turn people into something they're not. What I'm talking about is the other stuff. Since Joan hired us, we've been cleaning the world up a bit. You can't deny that. This whole case wasn't some big letdown. We helped put away the top guys in the Armenian Mafia. Plus there's, what, at least a dozen pedophile Mormons who are dead? Maybe more? As crazy as he was, Emilio seemed like he was trying to do the right thing. You and I try to do the right thing. Who cares if we're not perfect? Really, even if we didn't bring Shayla back with us, in this crazy world, managing to kill a dozen pedophile Mormons is pretty fucking impressive."

THE LIGHTS OF Beachwood Canyon shimmered below Joan's. We took seats on her couch. At the sound of Richie's voice, Cassie woke up and jumped into his lap, content to be back with her good buddy. Joan uncorked a bottle of white Bordeaux and poured out three glasses. Her husband was in the bedroom sleeping, so we were quiet.

By now, international media reports had come out about the bombing at the Mormon compound in Cancún. The final count of the dead wasn't specified by any outlet I came across, but all of them were adult men. This was clarified. A woman, one of Uncle Orson's wives, managed to escape Ciudad Reed in the chaos and later gave an interview with a popular Mexican news show. It got a lot of play in the States. Her name was Annie. Annie was seventeen and originally from El Paso. She said the suicide bomber who'd infiltrated her Prophet's home insisted on clearing it of all women and children. Emilio took only bad guys with him.

Orson, however, was still with us.

We weren't worried about what Joan would do with the information we were about to give her. We trusted her. We agreed to accept however she chose to react.

I did most of the talking.

I told her all about Emilio, attributing all of the dead to him, even P.Y. We weren't out to evade responsibility in her eyes. We respected Joan and wanted to be straight with her. But if Richie and I were being honest with ourselves, we both yearned to confess about every morally questionable thing we'd done on this job. Maybe we'd pay a price for our bad deeds someday, down the line. We'd probably deserve it. For now, our job was to make a final report to our client, and it just seemed like Joan would sleep better thinking no blood was on the hands of the men she'd hired in good faith.

When I got to Shayla speaking with us at those Mayan ruins, it became hard to continue. "Never underestimate the power of denial," I said. "Especially with yourself."

"Some people don't want to be saved," Joan said.

I started crying.

"At least now I know." She took my hand. "Thank you for that."

THIRTY-FIVE

AS SOON AS I clocked in for my shift back at the store, I was told Christy had news from corporate. The crew gathered to hear it in the back room.

"Back from Mexico, I see," Felix said. "I've been waiting to tell you that the coin from that fool's belt was worth a hundred and twenty-five k."

"It was *what*?"

"Yup. I had that shit appraised, homie. I guess those Mormons didn't make much of that special Mormon money, so when somebody finds some, it's worth mad feria. We found this dude who got it appraised for us and Nino went with him to an auction in Utah where some other dude paid one twenty-five. We had to pay the auction guy and all the taxes, but the four of us split up the rest. I got right with all my baby mamas and even fixed up the whip from all them hot ones. If you guys ever need some backup again, let me know. Shit worked out."

Christy stepped forward, holding her info sheet. "So, we've gotten some clarification about an earlier notice. Due to the rising costs imposed on the healthcare industry from the Affordable Health Care legislation, going forward, in order to maintain our company benefit plan, every Namaste Mart Novice crew member must work an average of five days a week instead of the previous three. So... you have to spend more time here than before, yeah, but remember, that's still a hell of a lot better than other grocery stores who don't offer any insurance at all, so the signal I'm getting from the higher-ups is that, going forward, we should be grateful about where we're all heading..."

I WALKED THROUGH the door of Beauty Bar, a martini lounge on Wilcox, wearing my baby-blue Dominique T-shirt. A section was annexed off for her newly unveiled paintings, now on display. There was Dominique, surrounded by her fans.

I ordered a Negroni and began to look at the collection. Dominique's first painting showed her with a Star of David painted right in the middle of her gigantic boobs. In another, she was naked except for the yarmulke on her head, and she ate a bagel covered in cream cheese and lox. This one and many others were pretty stupid, but overall, I found her theme strangely intriguing. Through her art, Dominique was finally embracing her Jewish heritage. In another painting she was wrapped up in the flag of Israel. This one was beautiful. It just worked.

"What do you think, Mr. Namaste Mart?"

I turned. There she was, the lady of the night.

"Pretty good, but too steep for me." The listed price was four grand. "Did you know that Mormons think Native Americans are Jews?"

"What?"

"Never mind. You're including your past in your image. You're telling the world it doesn't control you anymore. I dig it."

A crowd formed behind us, wanting her attention. "I knew you'd understand."

"Can we take a picture together?"

I took out my phone for a selfie. Her mouth-breathing assistant said I couldn't just take her picture with a camera phone. He then took out a disposable camera and took a picture of us himself. He said he would develop it personally, following Dominique's approved protocol.

I STEPPED OUTSIDE. My plan was to walk down to Santa Monica and take the bus home from there. A large goateed man in a leather jacket got in my way.

"Bro, are you Adam Minor?"

An Armenian accent. *Shit.* He must have been six foot three and weighed two-twenty. I looked around for help. The closest people were all drunks up the block or across the street. I tried to act cool. "Who wants to know?"

The big guy waved to someone in the distance. A silver Lexus pulled up. He opened the back door for me. "The Panther is asking. Get in."

Jesus. Were they watching me all night? They must have been following me as I left the store. "This is risky with all the heat you guys have seen lately. What if I say no?"

"Not an option, bro."

I got in the Lexus and slid over. He got in behind me.

We were off, heading east. I watched the streets out the window. Maybe tonight, after surviving everything else, my time had finally come. We hit Glendale and I sobered up. The Lexus slowed down on Verdugo and we arrived at a restaurant called Verdugo Italian. The big guy took me in through the back door and through the kitchen. A single cook was on duty, also Armenian. I got the picture. This place was bootleg Italian, Armenian-run and currently closed.

The big guy took me to a booth where an old man sat.

He looked about sixty-five and fit. He wore a black Versace suit and drank from a straw-covered bottle of Chianti. The big guy pulled up a chair and pointed for me to sit.

The Panther stared for a long time at my ridiculous Dominique T-shirt. "You took actions against my organization."

"Your competition's gone now, because of us."

"You crossed Armenian Dominance. I have to account for that to my people."

"We aren't your enemy, we just thought Hollywood Sam had the girl. We were wrong."

The Panther refilled his Chianti. "The FBI watches this restaurant now."

I attempted to stay cool and conceal my relief. They weren't going to kill me, not under federal surveillance. "They were never targeting you, just Sam. Now they're waiting to see if you'll slip up with him gone."

"What you say is true. I've taken into consideration how much you helped me. So my proposition is this: Tell the FBI

I won't run this organization anything like Sam. I will move it toward legitimate enterprises. Convince them of this, and your transgressions will be forgiven. I'll guarantee your safety against any of my people still loyal to Sam. You will come under my protection because you and your partner, we will tell my people, were my agents all along."

"I can't guarantee they'll believe me, but yes. I'll do it."

He leaned back. "Is your partner really involved with Ana Safarian?"

"He is."

He made an impressed whistle. "Now there's an Armenian who's done well in this country. I tell all my people that America is the land of opportunity. Any of us can be as successful as her someday. These are the facts of the situation."

"America withstands all honest scrutiny. I believe it always will."

He liked this. "If I ever need a private investigator, can I call you?"

"My partner and I try to stay aboveboard."

"I have many operations. Do you have a card?"

"We still need to get some printed. For now, most people can find us at the Namaste Mart over on Santa Monica and Gardner. But you already know that." I smiled to show I wasn't offended.

He raised the bottle and offered to pour me some. "I love the organic Guru Garlic Spread they carry in the fresh section of Namaste Mart. I would be heartbroken if it ever got discontinued. Man, that stuff's even better than what they serve at Zankou Chicken!"

THIRTY-SIX

RICHIE PULLED UP to the store just as I arrived on my bike. It was a clear day on the boulevard, great biking weather. I rolled his way.

"Ana threw me out." Up close, I saw he was looking rough. "It's over between us."

"What happened?"

"She got into my phone. A billionaire needs to snoop through my phone."

"What'd she find?"

"Pictures of me and Denise in Mexico. I forgot they were there. But still, it's pretty rich, her getting on her high horse. She fucks around on her boyfriend all the time. Women are nuts."

I'd called Tamiroff and relayed the Panther's message. He said he'd play like he believed it. He told me Jaqueline was doing well. She was in rehab and if she stayed clean, her baby was on track to be born healthy. We'd heard nothing about the Pasadena shooting. As far as Mexico went, it was as if we'd never been there. Joan paid us in full. The Shayla Ramsey case was over.

After expenses, I ended up a few grand ahead. I had spent the morning making calls about a car I wanted to make a down payment on later that week.

As I stocked eggs and filled the milk, Dominique came in to buy her two beefsteak tomatoes and leave me our now-developed photo from the night before. I saw she must have had her film-only rule because film made her look at least a decade younger. Digital was less forgiving. Someday, I would show the world how my past hadn't defined me either.

Later, when I was on register, a group of angry Hindu protestors came in. They were dressed in tunics and saris and held signs saying things like SHUT DOWN NAMASTE MART and RESPECT MY RELIGION. A cameraman filmed their outrage.

"*Ohh*, it's a light-hearted attempt at multiculturalism!" Richie shouted.

He and one of the managers corralled the whole group and slowly edged them out the front door. Most of them remained in the parking lot, displaying their signs and yelling at approaching customers, telling them not to shop there.

After my lunch break, I was on register again when a malnourished crackhead wandered into the store and began pelting organic bananas at the other customers, an act she swore she'd been ordered to perform by George W. Bush, who she'd seen this past weekend in an underground bunker. Our security guard Ricardo advanced on her. When he was close, the lady reached into the frayed potato-sack-like accessory she used as a purse, drew out a pair of rusted scissors, and pointed them right at Ricardo, ready to stab.

Richie materialized, dashing behind the lady. He grabbed her by her bony elbows, raised her off her feet, and shook her until the scissors hit the floor. She ran out the front door, cut through some lingering Hindus, and vanished.

A woman said, "I was hoping I'd see you tonight."

I turned toward her. She was a beautiful blonde and I was ringing up her cartful of groceries, which she bagged herself.

I'd seen her before. She wore a T-shirt from the musical *Wicked*. Then I remembered, she was an actress and had actually appeared in a musical at the Pantages a few years back. The twilight thickened through the store window, outlining her face in a luminous orange.

"Aren't you the detective who works here?"

"One of them."

On the next register over, John the Juggler juggled an old Russian lady's oranges. When he finished, the entire front end gave him a round of applause.

"I've gotten kind of obsessed with your story." She was blushing. "It must have been so scary when you and your friend saved that missing woman last year. My roommates say I should quit talking about you, but then you just now popped up in the news again."

I finished ringing her up. "I haven't been keeping track of all the media coverage."

"Did you two really stop the Armenian Mafia from kidnapping Ana Safarian?"

"It's a complicated story. I shouldn't talk about it." We bagged the last of her groceries together. She swiped her card. "But... yes."

RICHIE HAD BEEN right. He often was. Our pursuits during that long-ago summer, all our reckless stumbling, hadn't been in vain. The world was less evil because of our actions. I realized that I didn't need to insult every believer I met point-blank. People are free to tell themselves whatever stories they choose. You can save someone from a dangerous situation, but you can't save them from who they are as a person. Shayla was lost and had been before we ever heard her name, but the devastation I felt eventually faded. An immense gratitude replaced it. This was Shayla's gift to me.

I HANDED THE woman her receipt. It was time for her to go, so I could start ringing up the next customer, but she hung around.

"I was wondering, are you free tonight?"

ACKNOWLEDGMENTS

Most importantly, thank you to Genevieve, my love.

Thank you to my friend Mike Whelan for allowing so much of your life and comedy to be a part of this story.

ABOUT THE AUTHOR

Andrew Miller is an author, screenwriter and essayist. "Samurai '81," his contribution to the *Jacked* anthology from Run Amok Crime, made the honor roll for the Best Mystery Stories of the Year from Mysterious Press in 2023. His novella *Lady Tomahawk* appeared in the anthology *L.A. Stories* from Uncle B. Publications.

Andrew's stories have appeared in *Apocalypse Confidential, Close to The Bone, Pulp Modern, Switchblade,* and *Broadswords and Blasters.* His film work includes the music documentary *Soul of Lincoln Heights.*

He is a member of the Independent Fiction Alliance, a network of authors, publishers and editors committed to combating censorship and promoting freedom of expression.

Andrew was born in Ohio. He lives in Pasadena, California with his girlfriend Genevieve and their two cats, John Wayne and Calamity Jane.

Printed in the USA
CPSIA information can be obtained
at www.ICGtesting.com
CBHW021541030424
6320CB00005B/75